P9-DIB-692

"CAPTAIN, I'M AFRAID I HAVE GRAVE NEWS . . ."

McCoy moved up quietly behind Kirk, not liking this particular lack of expression in Spock's voice.

"We have just been informed that the shuttle bearing the remainder of the *Enterprise* landing party exploded while in transit."

Kirk's jaw hardened, his eyes very bright. "Exploded." It wasn't even a question. "Have you attempted to raise Chekov or Uhura?"

"I have. No contact has been made."

McCoy watched Kirk close his eyes, hands wound into fists of frustration. He thought the captain would say something, or do something, to shatter the illusion and make it all not so real. Instead, the silence around them only grew, until it finally made a sound all its own.

Look for STAR TREK Fiction from Pocket Books

Star Trek: The Original Series

Star Trek: The Next Generation

STAR TREK®

ICE TRAP

L. A. GRAF

POCKET BOOKS

New York   London   Toronto   Sydney   Tokyo   Singapore

*To Julia, Karen Rose, and Melissa,
without whose inspiration and cooperation
this book would never have been possible*

ICE TRAP

Chapter One

LEONARD MCCOY GLARED at the transporter from which he, Kirk, and Spock had just disembarked. The small of his back felt sticky with nerve sweat, as it always did when he was forced by circumstance to use a transporter rather than a more conventional, *safer* method of travel—like his feet. He snaked an index finger inside the pale green collar of his uniform and tugged gently. If man were meant to fly . . . he thought sourly. "I hate those damned things."

"I know you do, Bones." Jim Kirk paused beside him, his voice tuned sympathetically and, to McCoy's ears, a trifle resignedly to an old and oft-aired complaint. "Just think of it as one of those wonders of the modern space age."

The doctor snorted, glancing up at the tall Vulcan beside his captain. "I consider Spock one of the wonders of the blasted *galaxy,* but I don't like him, either."

1

"Thank you, Doctor," Spock replied. "I shall take that as a compliment."

Kirk's hazel eyes danced with barely contained humor. "As I'm sure he intended it."

McCoy snarled and let it ride. Shifting his medikit from one hand to the other, he looked around.

The transporter room aboard the Nordstral Pharmaceuticals orbital station *Curie* was spare and utilitarian. A flat-finished hue known back in McCoy's school days as "institutional pond-scum gray" colored the unadorned walls. McCoy assumed the only door afforded access to the rest of the station. Behind a glass-fronted area to the right, a lone technician with the bright-hued logo of Nordstral Pharmaceuticals splashed across the front of his coveralls worked diligently at a console, ignorant or uncaring of their presence. McCoy couldn't decide which rankled him more.

"You two didn't have to come with me, you know. I'm a big boy—I can handle a simple medical consultation on my own. You have a rescue team to lead."

"Spock doesn't," Kirk said, avoiding discussion on McCoy's first comment. "This stop won't take long, and I want to find out as much as possible about this medical crisis Nordstral's having before I go down to look for their lost shuttle. After all, Nordstral Pharmaceuticals asked us to help with both problems."

"And they may prove to be related," Spock pointed out.

McCoy grunted reluctant agreement. "Wasn't someone supposed to meet us?"

"That's what I was told." Kirk stepped off the final riser, obviously bent on hailing the preoccupied technician. At that moment the door at the other end of the room slid open to admit a short, dark-haired woman of middle years. She hurried toward them, her pale blue lab smock rustling faintly against her trousers. Her eyes flicked over their rank insignia and she extended her hand.

"Captain Kirk? I'm Maxine Kane, station physician for Nordstral Pharmaceuticals. Welcome aboard *Curie*."

Kirk's hand met hers. "Thank you, Dr. Kane. This is my first officer, Mr. Spock, and my chief surgeon, Dr. Leonard McCoy."

"Mr. Spock." Kane nodded politely to the Vulcan, then offered her hand to the doctor. "Dr. McCoy."

Her handshake was firm, but her palm was damp. She attempted a genuine smile at McCoy, but it faltered at the edges. The skin around her green eyes was pinched tight with fatigue and worry, giving her face a harsh cast. McCoy would have laid odds she was nursing a massive headache. He smiled. "My pleasure, Dr. Kane."

As though unsure what to do with her hand once McCoy released it, Kane shoved it into her pocket. The pull of the smock's loose material showed the fingers curled into a fist.

"I apologize for not being here when you arrived. Things have been . . . hectic lately. Between the shuttle crash and the problems in my own division, I'm usually needed in about fifteen places at once." She chuckled, a decidedly sad sound, and ran a hand through her gray-shot hair. "Too bad our cloning facilities only work for the local plankton."

Spock cleared his throat. McCoy rolled his eyes; he could guess what was coming.

"Unless I am mistaken, Dr. Kane, 'plankton' is not a technically correct term for Nordstral's indigenous marine protists. Plankton, such as found on Earth, are

3

photosynthetic, using sunlight to convert carbon dioxide and water into carbohydrates and oxygen. Nordstral's marine biota, however, use energy from the planet's strong magnetic field to perform the same function."

"I really wouldn't know about that, Mr. Spock," Kane said with a sigh that McCoy thought sounded suspiciously like his own. "I'm a medical doctor—all I know is that Earth plankton and Nordstral biota both float around in the oceans and churn out the planet's oxygen. That's enough for me."

"But since these plankton"—McCoy threw a defiant scowl in Spock's direction—"are the main reason Nordstral Pharmaceuticals is here, it seems to me they can call them whatever they want."

Spock lifted an eyebrow. "The company did not invent the biota, Doctor."

"Yes. Well." Kane stared at the floor when they all turned back to her, then looked up with a faintly embarrassed grin. "I'm sorry Dr. Stehle isn't here to discuss this with you, Mr. Spock. Vernon . . ." She paused. Emotion washed her features, changing them like the permutations of warm wax. "Vernon Stehle headed the planetary research team that vanished. He's the one who could have explained the plankton's pharmaceutical uses—I just do first aid." She breathed deeply and expelled it in a huge, gusting sigh. "Why don't I take you someplace more comfortable to talk?" She left the room without waiting for a reply, trailing the *Enterprise* officers behind her.

Kirk caught McCoy's eye as they followed Dr. Kane down a well-lit corridor. Eyebrows sought hairline as he mouthed, What do you think?

McCoy shook his head and shrugged fractionally, his eyes reading the slump of Kane's shoulders. She was an obvious victim of stress, fatigue, and, if her comments were any indication, overwork.

She led them to a small laboratory. McCoy couldn't help but think that only a scientist would find a lab a "comfortable" place to hold a serious conversation. Places and names might change, but labs had a tendency to remain the same, world to world.

She motioned for them to sit at one of the tables. "Can I get you anything?" When they refused, Kane ordered an enormous cup of coffee and two aspirin from the servitor in the corner before sitting across from Spock. She popped the aspirin, knocked back a mouthful of the steaming black beverage, and sighed. "It may be ersatz coffee, but at least the caffeine's real." She toyed with the cup, running a finger around and around the damp rim. "Sometimes I think it's the only thing keeping me functioning."

"Perhaps sleep would help," Spock suggested diplomatically.

A corner of her mouth quirked with a sad little twitch. "It's a precious commodity around here right now. I don't know of anyone who's had a whole lot of it lately. Too much has been happening."

"Why don't you start wherever's easiest?" Kirk said.

"Nowhere's easiest." Kane slumped back, fingers clasping the coffee cup. "Suffice it to say that several weeks ago some of our staff began acting erratic. We've learned over time that a certain amount of odd behavior is normal in the people on long-term company assignments, particularly when the planet is as nasty as Nordstral. But this was like nothing we've ever documented. We currently have over a dozen personnel in residence at the medical center."

McCoy pursed his lips in a silent whistle. "What kind of behavior are we talking about, Doctor?"

Kane held up one hand and ticked down the fingers as she talked. "Paranoia. Hallucinations. Hysteria. Violent mood swings. Suicidal ideation." She snorted. "You name it, we've had it." Her fingers twisted, lacing together like mating spiders. "And then it got weirder."

Spock tilted his head. "Could you be more specific?"

She put aside her cup and stood. "Come with me and I'll show you."

Kane tapped a short identification code into a recessed panel beside a high-security door. A tone sounded, and the indicator light flashed from gold to blue. She pressed another button and the door silently slid apart down the middle.

"Home, sweet home," she said, ushering them before her. "This is the psychiatric section of our complex." She made certain the door was secured, then preceded the three men down the hall.

A young med-crew staffer sat behind a station, back bent over her work. She looked up at the sound of footsteps and smiled in greeting, obviously glad for the opportunity to take a break.

Kane returned the young woman's smile. "This is the help Starfleet promised us." She indicated the men beside her with a short sweep of her hand. "They're finally here."

"Thank God," the medtech commented without rancor. She rubbed her eyes and stifled an enormous yawn. "These late hours are killing me."

"How's the gang tonight?" Kane asked.

The medtech rested her chin in one hand. "I

6

checked them an hour ago and they were quiet—watching vid and playing cards."

"Well, that's promising, at least." Kane snagged a chart from the rack beside the work station and tucked it under her arm.

"Be forewarned, though," the medtech added in a lower tone. "Mr. Personality is looking for you."

Kane's expression of bitterness and utter contempt startled McCoy. "What did the . . . what did he want?" she amended, her eyes shifting only slightly toward her guests.

"He didn't say." The tech splayed one hand across her chest. "*I'm* just a lowly peon, remember?"

"Right." Kane sighed with such irritation that McCoy, beside her, felt her whole body shudder. "Well, let's hope he's given up and gone to bed. Gentlemen, if you'll follow me?" She started down the hall.

"'Mr. Personality'?" Kirk queried when they were out of the medtech's earshot.

Kane's lip curled. "Nicholai Steno, Nordstral's station manager. If you haven't met him, you're in for a singular treat. He makes you hope the old adage of everyone having a twin somewhere in the universe isn't true." She stopped beside a door and keyed in another code. The smile she flashed over her shoulder momentarily eased the tension around her eyes. "Come on in and meet the gang."

The community recreation room was similar to many McCoy had seen in his long tenure as a doctor. Colorful and well-lit, the walls were decorated with what appeared to be native handicrafts. Better than a dozen people dressed in generic spacers' civvies were in attendance. Some read from viewers in secluded carrels, while others sprawled in comfortable-looking

7

chairs and watched an old movie on a wall-mounted vid. A card game was under way at a table in the center of the room.

"Hey, Dr. Kane!" A stocky, dark-haired man involved in the card game greeted her with a wide grin. "Care to try your luck?"

She toggled a finger at him. "Not tonight, Bracken." She rested a hand on another patient's shoulder. Her genuine affection for these men and women was obvious. "How's everyone feeling?" From around the room came responses in the affirmative.

"Are you doctors, too?"

McCoy looked down at the gentle-eyed man at his elbow. At Kane's nod of encouragement, the ship's doctor smiled. "Well, I am, at least. This is Captain James Kirk and First Officer Spock."

"Are you here to help us?" A slight woman, curled in a chair, had spoken up. Her hands tussled nervously in her lap. "We'd all like to know what happened. Why we went so crazy."

"You're not crazy," Kane stressed in the uncomfortable silence that followed the woman's remark. "You have to believe that."

"Then what happened to us?" someone else asked.

Kane appeared stymied. Before McCoy could frame a reply to the patients' fears that wouldn't sound condescending, Kirk jumped in.

"We don't know yet. But we'll do everything in our power to discover what happened." Kirk's voice fairly rang with assurance. He stood in the center of the room and, one by one, caught each person there with his eyes and drew them in.

With pride in his friend and something bordering on amazement, McCoy saw every set of shoulders in the room relax. Even among people other than his crew—people with no idea who he was or what he'd accomplished in his lifetime, people who had no reason whatsoever to believe in him—Kirk won instant trust. If he said it was so, then it would be so, or he'd die trying to make it that way. Somehow McCoy knew these patients had picked up on that and would believe in Kirk when they'd lost the ability to believe in themselves. McCoy shook his head in gentle wonder, supremely glad for his friend's presence.

Dr. Kane cleared her throat, obviously moved by what had just occurred. "We've got work to do, so we'll say good-night." She glanced at the chronometer on the wall. "Lights out at ten," she reminded them, and headed out the door.

Down the corridor and two turns later, they followed Kane into her spacious, pleasantly appointed inner sanctum. She urged them to pull up chairs around her desk, then leaned between them to key into the computer system. "Watch the main screen on the far wall."

The screen flared to life. It was obvious they were watching from the viewpoint of a wall camera situated somewhere to the side and above the subject. McCoy immediately recognized the slender man who'd first spoken to him. The man sat cross-legged, arms outstretched, fingers crooked and plucking the air.

"He's playing a harp," Kane murmured by way of explanation when Kirk made a confused-sounding noise. "Or thinks he is, rather. Said he was Rory Dall Morison. The computer identified the name as belonging to a Highland harper who died on Earth in 1713."

The view changed to the woman who'd asked whether the *Enterprise* crew were going to help them. A man sat to her right, watching her intently. She chattered animatedly, aiming most of the conversation to the empty area on her left. She was so frenetic, Kane keyed down the volume. "That's Risa. She started talking to saints." She shrugged when McCoy glanced sharply at her. "This particular discussion took place between her and Saints John Bosco, Raymund Nonnatus, and Dympna."

"Who's the man with her?" Kirk asked.

"Captain of the *John Lilly,* where Risa was stationed. When she demanded to see a priest, he filled the bill until they could get her topside."

"What kind of ship is the *John Lilly?*" Spock inquired. "One of your orbital fleet?"

Kane shook her head. "Oh, no. It's one of the submarine plankton harvesters that work under the ice sheets on Nordstral. The other two are the *Cousteau* and the *Soroya.*"

"Were all of these occurrences on the *John Lilly?*" Kirk asked, not taking his eyes off the screen.

"No." Another scene change, this one so abrupt and startling that McCoy lurched in his seat as a close-up of Bracken's face filled the screen. He paced the confines of a tiny room with lurching strides, arms swinging spastically and colliding with the walls. Abruptly, Bracken lifted his shirt and distended his stomach as far as he could. *"I call this my monument to an unsung hero!"*

"Bracken was stationed on the harvester *Soroya,* and had never met either Risa or Davis. In fact, almost none of the affected staff had any contact with each other."

The scene shifted again. Another room, with all the appearance of having been hastily padded. A woman stood in one corner, face to the wall. She turned abruptly and staggered to the center of the room, legs trembling. She straightened as much as she could without losing her balance, and lifted her hands toward the ceiling. She'd scored her arms with her fingernails, and blood streaked her flesh like gory comets' tails. Head thrown back, eyes clenched like fists, she began to shriek.

"That's Baker." The sorrow in Kane's voice made McCoy look up. "We didn't get to her in time." Kane's hand slapped down, cutting off the video and consigning the room to darkness. "She suicided in a very ugly manner shortly after what you just saw. Incidentally, fifteen minutes before this was recorded, she'd been given the highest dose of Valazine considered safe."

The lights abruptly came up and McCoy blinked painfully in the sudden brightness. "That's impossible!"

"You're so right," Kane agreed. "She should have been flat on her back and snoring. I've been over it a million times and it beats me all to hell." She shoved the chart into his hand. "So you figure it out."

Kirk stared at the empty screen, lips pursed, while Spock steepled his fingers in thought. "Those people . . ." The captain waved a hand vaguely toward the distant rec room. "They seem sane and lucid . . ."

"*Very* sane and *very* lucid, Captain. There's not one who's crazy."

"The drug protocol worked, then?" McCoy flipped through the chart. "What did you use?"

"That's the whole point, Dr. McCoy. Beyond the use of drugs to calm them enough to get them to our sickbay, there hasn't been any drug protocol because there hasn't been any need for one." She waved a hand toward the silent screen, her voice tight. "The patients seem to be healing themselves without the benefit of psychotropic drugs and, so far as we've been able to determine, without any lasting deleterious effects."

Spock looked at her. "Mental illness does not usually cure itself."

"Oh, you're correct, Mr. Spock. But this illness does, whatever it is, and we have absolutely no idea how it's happening. And believe me when I say we've tried every angle we can think of."

McCoy flipped through the chart, eyes racing over the lines of small, tight print. "These are all the personnel who have been affected?"

"So far." She didn't sound hopeful that it would stop with these hapless few.

"Did any of these people have anything to do with the shuttle explosion that stranded Dr. Stehle and his team?" Kirk asked.

Kane's short, bitter laugh seemed out of place with her dismissive wave. "No. That was just a common Nordstral accident. We've been losing equipment to the planet since the day we set up shop here."

"Given that Nordstral's magnetic field is many times stronger than normally found on a class-M planet," Spock remarked, "such losses are not surprising."

Kirk frowned, drumming his fingers on the table. "The *Enterprise* was told you lost that shuttle because of sabotage. Are you telling me Nordstral Pharmaceuticals lied to Starfleet about what's going on?"

Kane sighed. "According to our station manager, sabotage is always a possibility. He says other pharmaceutical companies would love to get their hands on our concession with the native Kitka." She waved a hand at the screen. "But I don't see how it could be related to these mental problems."

"Are there other records we could see?" McCoy interjected. "I'd like to check their personnel records, to see if there's some medical risk factor they all shared."

Kane shrugged. "Certainly." She leaned across her desk to swing the computer console toward McCoy. "Be my guest. I don't mean to sound short, but I've run out of ideas."

"That's what we're here for," Kirk assured her as McCoy began to work. "Sometimes all a problem needs is a new set of eyes."

"I hope you're right."

McCoy accessed the personnel files and sent the computer searching for corollaries between the sick crewmen. Anything had to be considered because nothing seemed likely. Despite hope that he might find a common home planet or education or a genetic link like eye or hair color, there was only one match he felt had any credence.

"Did you know that all your sick personnel came off surface installations and harvesters? None of them is from your orbital fleet or from this station."

She leaned over McCoy's shoulder and followed his finger as he traced the corollary. "My God . . . you're right!"

"So whatever's happening is confined to the planet's surface." Kirk turned to Kane. "We'll need to investigate this at the source. Can my people go down to visit one of the company's permanent installations?"

"That won't be easy. Our contract with the native Kitka limits us to only a few employees at our harvester docks. We might be able to find you space to stay on a harvester, but they're hard to reach by radio. It's those damned magnetic storms." She reached across to blank the computer screen and bring up further information. "You're in luck, though—the *Soroya*'s due for a brief stopover at Byrd Station midday tomorrow. I can call ahead to have Captain Mandeville expect you."

"That would be fine," Kirk agreed.

"Jim . . ."

Kane sighed. "Is there anything else you need me to arrange?"

"Jim . . ."

Kirk cocked his head thoughtfully. "You could transfer Dr. Stehle's plankton research files to the *Enterprise* for Mr. Spock to analyze. It might turn out to be useful."

"Jim—"

"After all, I— What *is* it, Bones?"

McCoy's stomach felt awash with bile. "I hope I heard wrong, but when you said 'your people' would go down to the planet surface, you didn't include *me*, did you?"

Kirk looked confused. "Of course I did. You have to examine the workers down there for evidence of illness."

"I don't like water, Jim."

Kirk blinked and stared at his friend. "It's not water, Bones, it's ice."

"Under that ice is a lot of water, and I don't like water unless it's surrounded by a glass and mixed with Kentucky bourbon."

A chime sounded, cutting them off, and Kane looked up in irritation. "Come."

McCoy heard her heavy sigh when the door opened to admit a tall, angular gentleman with blond hair. "Dr. Kane." His voice was heavily accented—Swiss, or Swedish, or something like that, McCoy couldn't be sure. "You're a hard woman to track down. I'd like some infor—"

"Mr. Steno," Kane coolly cut him off. "May I present Captain Kirk, Mr. Spock, and Dr. McCoy of the Federation starship *Enterprise?* Gentlemen, this is Nicholai Steno, *Curie* station manager for Nordstral Pharmaceuticals." There was no mistaking the undertone in her voice.

Steno either hadn't picked up on her dislike or didn't care. He came into the room as though he owned it—which, McCoy mused, he technically did. "So, Captain. Report to me."

"I beg your pardon?" Kirk asked with far more politeness than was deserved.

"Report, report! Tell me what you've found."

Kirk's gentle hand squeezing McCoy's shoulder stilled the doctor's tongue. "Nothing as yet, Mr. Steno. We've only just arrived."

"Don't waste my time, gentlemen. I hate when my time and money are wasted. Dr. Kane's been virtually worthless coming up with a solution to our difficulties. I was told the Federation could do better. Now I'm not so certain."

"We will do our best." Kirk's voice, low and calm, displayed the best of the diplomacy and tact drummed into him at the Academy, when, McCoy suspected, he'd really like to drive Steno's teeth down his lanky throat.

"I certainly hope so," the station manager sniffed. "We're planning to get an early start down to the planet's surface tomorrow to hunt for Dr. Stehle and his team. I don't want to be kept waiting."

"You don't . . .?"

"I'm heading the rescue team, Captain. You didn't think I'd leave it in the hands of amateurs, did you?"

"Captain Kirk and our security force can hardly be considered amateurs," Spock commented.

Steno snorted. "They're amateurs on Nordstral. This is a dangerous planet—and with the magnetic storms we've been having lately, you can't just beam off it when you get yourself in trouble." He glanced at Kirk. "Fortunately, my people will be along to keep you and your rescue team from doing anything stupid."

Kirk's body practically thrummed with irritation. Caught between his captain and Dr. Kane, McCoy felt like a tuning fork. "I'm sure my rescue team will appreciate that, Mr. Steno," Kirk said tightly. "But I'm afraid I'll have to miss out on the expedition."

Steno struck a pose apparently meant to convey righteous indignation. "But I thought you came all this way to find our missing shuttle crew. Are you going to look for them from orbit?"

"No." Kirk glanced over at Kane. "Judging from what I've just seen, your missing shuttle crew is the least of your problems on Nordstral. I've decided to send Lieutenant Chekov with the *Enterprise* search and rescue party, while I investigate what's causing the mental instabilities on the planet."

"I see." Steno sniffed. "And just who is this Lieutenant Chekov? Your second-in-command?"

"No." Kirk sounded amused. "He's chief of security aboard the *Enterprise.* My second-in-command is standing right next to you."

Steno scowled at the silent Vulcan, thin mouth pulled into a frown of displeasure. "For goodness sake, Captain. If you refuse to see to your own duties, I at least expect your second-in-command to take over for you."

"In case you haven't noticed," Kirk stated in tones

so clipped McCoy expected them to draw blood, "Mr. Spock is a Vulcan. If we send him down to a glacial planet like Nordstral, he'll freeze."

"Is that true?" When Spock nodded, Steno rolled his eyes with a subvocal sigh. "Isn't that just like Starfleet? They always find a reason to do exactly what they want."

Kirk favored the businessman with a smooth, if chilly, smile. "Then it's good for both of us that Starfleet wants to help Nordstral Pharmaceuticals. I think you'll find Lieutenant Chekov's very good at what he does. He'll find your missing research team."

Steno huffed. "He will if he has the sense to stay out of my way and do what I tell him. And I'll expect timely reports from you as well, Captain. You can be sure I'll report your change of plans—and obvious lack of desire to cooperate with Nordstral management—to Starfleet." Without saying goodbye, Steno left the room.

"I hate that man," Kane rasped angrily.

"I can't say I blame you," Kirk replied. He looked down at McCoy's snort of laughter. "What is it, Bones?"

The doctor's blue eyes danced. "So, Chekov's leading the shuttle rescue team now, eh? Does *he* know this?"

"He will shortly," Spock replied. "In fact, I will deliver the message personally upon my return to the ship."

McCoy chuckled. "Spock, you get to have all the fun."

Kirk shared his friend's smile. "Not all the fun, Bones. We get to beam up with him, long enough to pack and catch the shuttle down to Nordstral."

"Some fun." McCoy tried to hide the wash of fear

that flashed through him, suspecting he wasn't too successful. "First I get to have my particles spread all over the known galaxy, then I get to drown under billions of metric tons of water."

"Would you rather not come planetside?"

McCoy looked away when concern flicked over Kirk's features, knowing he'd do it if only because Kirk wanted him to. "No, I'll come. But I promise to hate it."

Chapter Two

"CHIEF? I THINK we've got company."

Pavel Chekov glanced up from his work station, quelling a twinge of irritation at having his hurried landing party preparations interrupted for what felt like the hundredth time that evening. Ensign Michael Howard, young and bearded, hung through the office doorway with his hands on either lintel, looking apologetic for barging in with a message after the chief specifically ordered he be left alone. "I can ask her to wait out here, sir, if you don't want her brought to your office."

Chekov leaned back in his seat without setting aside his note-taking stylus. Even so small a gesture of abandoning his work bothered him, and he was determined to finish these arrangements before morning, despite having to plan on such short notice. "Tell whoever it is to talk with Ensign Lemieux." He flicked eyes to the chronometer on his desk even though he

19

already knew the time, then caught himself kneading the back of his neck—more from frustration than because it actually helped anything. "I haven't got time to see anyone before we go planetside tomorrow, and Lemieux will be in charge while I'm away."

"Uh . . ." Howard tossed an uncertain glance over one shoulder, and Chekov heard voices approaching from the outer room. "This is kind of a 'now' thing, sir," Howard said. "I don't think she wants to see Lemieux."

"You keep trying to have these boys stall me, Lieutenant Chekov, and I'll just pull rank and force them to let me come through."

Chekov smiled tiredly at Lieutenant Commander Uhura as she leaned through the doorway beneath Howard's arm. Her black eyes, as bright as the silver disks on her earrings and necklace, matched her brilliant smile and playful tone.

"You could try," the security chief allowed, "but it wouldn't do you any good. I've a loyal crew—they'd never disobey my orders." He threw a mock-threatening glare at Howard and Publicker, now behind Howard's shoulder in the doorway. "Would they?"

Both guards fidgeted abruptly, drawing themselves a little straighter, their hands coming down to their sides. "Oh, no, sir." "Of course not, sir." The red on Howard's cheeks stood out nicely above his dark brown beard.

Chekov shrugged. "See? They would die for me."

Uhura's musical laughter lifted his spirits, just as it had from the moment he'd first met her. Chekov didn't think he'd ever known anyone so truly pleasant. Suddenly willing to be interrupted at least for the moment, he tossed his stylus to the desktop and pushed back his chair. "So—what brings you down to security? I'd think you'd be seeing enough of us tomorrow."

"Well, that might be." Hands behind her back, Uhura slipped past Howard with the delicate grace only available to the very small. "But there's one of you I haven't seen quite enough of lately." She brought her hands forward to reveal a small tray, packed with ice and bits of what looked to Chekov like uncooked cat food. "You weren't in the rec hall for dinner tonight."

Chekov leaned over his desk to peer at the bundles of grayish mess, wrinkling his nose at the distinct odor of raw seafood. "If this is what they served, I'm glad I wasn't there."

Uhura reached out to swat him atop the head. "You haven't even tried it yet."

"That's all right—I don't intend to."

"Pavel!" She slid the tray onto his desk, pushing aside what papers and diskettes he didn't snatch out of her way. "I'll have you know this is authentic native cuisine. The Nordstral natives survive almost entirely on a diet of seafood, and I went to a lot of effort to dig up these ingredients." She plucked a small sample from among the bed of ice and offered it to him between two slim fingers. "Try it."

Chekov looked at the tidbit, looked at her, and slowly shook his head. "It's raw."

Uhura sighed dramatically—the same sigh she used every time Chekov refused the various native foods she felt the need to foist upon him—and popped a piece into her mouth as though to prove it was edible. Chekov assumed she'd someday believe him when he told her he wasn't interested in being experimental about what he ate. So far, it was eight years and counting. "Be brave," she persisted when she'd finished chewing. "They don't have sophisticated cooking facilities—the Kitka live in an arctic environment."

Chekov rotated his chair to face his terminal again, feeling about for his stylus. "So do the Siberians, but we don't eat raw fish."

"No," Uhura snorted. "You eat forty versions of baked and boiled cabbage."

"What's wrong with cabbage?" He made a note to bring additional food rations for himself and his squad. Let Uhura eat the native fish if she wanted to.

Pursing her lips in wry annoyance, Uhura turned to offer the morsel to Howard. "Come on, Ensign Howard."

The guard glanced up from the slim reader screen he'd been scanning, his face a study in apprehension. "Sir?"

"Prove yourself a better man than your boss."

The ensign's eyebrows shot up nearly to his hairline and he slipped the reader back into his pocket. "That's all right, sir. It's his job to be the better man."

Chekov kept his eyes fixed on the notes in front of him, trying to recapture his train of thought while he counted supplies and played with mental images of the arctic terrain they would scour for Dr. Stehle and the missing shuttle crew. "Go ahead, Mr. Howard. You and Mr. Publicker assured me you'd be willing to die for me." He flicked both ensigns a crooked smile. "Now's your chance."

Uhura scowled playfully at the lieutenant while handing both Howard and Publicker a small sample. "You must be in a bad mood because you haven't eaten."

The computer inserted a flag into Chekov's list:

additional power packs for the thermal units couldn't be expected to maintain their effectiveness due to Nordstral's strong magnetic fields; shielded packs within the units should be fine. "I'm not in a bad mood." Scratching a quick delete through the packs, he tallied the mass allotments again for what they could leave behind in favor of additional thermals. The only things in the running were the smaller communications equipment and lanterns.

"You're just overworked and overtired." Uhura moved up behind him to rest her hands on his shoulders. He could feel her attention shift to the terminal screen, scanning his collection of lists and scribbled notes. "Other officers sleep before planet landings, you know. I'd think you'd appreciate the need for alert security personnel."

"I do." The accusation still stung enough to burn his cheeks, though. He was only willing to cut their lanterns by a third; not enough to add an appreciable number of thermals. "Other officers also have longer than twelve hours to prepare. If Mr. Spock had told me sooner that the captain had assigned me this rescue mission, I'd have had all this done by now."

Her hands tightened briefly on his shoulders. "He didn't have a lot of choice. That's why they call it a Priority One emergency."

Chekov sighed. "I know." As if knowing Nordstral's desperate situation should somehow make him feel better about outfitting a landing party at the next to the last minute. He hated planning planetary rescue parties, especially when he had every reason to believe the rescuees were already dead. He could think of few things worse than stumbling across the pitiful remains of people who died believing help would come to save them. "Do you think the

Nordstral shuttle pilot will complain if I make him strip the interior?"

"I suspect so. Call it a hunch." Uhura leaned forward to frown over his shoulder at the screen. "Did you remember to include my special suit translators? I want to be sure I can talk to the Kitka, and I can't read your handwriting well enough to tell if you've got them."

He didn't have the heart to tell her that was probably because he tended to note-take in a random mixture of Cyrillic and English. Keying the terminal to translate his notes into text, he switched screens so she could see the more readable version, pointing to the notation for sixteen grams worth of translators for the insulation suits.

Uhura nodded her satisfaction, then reached out to tap one entry with a fingernail. "Why all the lanterns?"

"It's winter in the northern territory—that means it's probably dark there, as well." It always was in Siberia. He remembered visiting his uncle during school break as a boy, getting up in the dark, running about all day in the dark, going to bed in the dark. It stayed like that for six months, his uncle told him, with six months of unbroken, watery daylight to follow. Chekov hated the thought of hiking Nordstral's ice sheets in perpetual night, especially with no allowance for lost or broken or malfunctioning lanterns.

"Oh, no, Chief, we've got normal night and day." Howard, Chekov noticed, took the opportunity to spit his raw fish into a napkin under the pretense of talking more clearly. "It says here"—he fished out the reader again, waving it in one hand—"that Nordstral doesn't have an axial tilt. That means no seasons, and no arctic night."

"Just one big, long ice age," Publicker added. He was still close to the door, his own reader now open, and no sign of Uhura's fish sample about him. Chekov wondered if he'd actually eaten it, or if he'd managed to otherwise dispose of it without Uhura seeing. He had to give both men points for being sneaky, that was for certain. "The Kitka are apparently the only sentient species known to have developed in an environment like this. It says here their biology is so tied to Nordstral's unique ecology, they can't even go off-planet for more than a few hours at a time. Nobody's sure why yet."

"Now you see why I keep them around," Chekov told Uhura as he recalculated the number of lanterns and replaced their mass with thermal units. "They're a font of random information."

Howard quirked a little smile, stuffing his wadded-up napkin in the disposal chute. "It's the random part that makes it easy."

"Is that why you're keeping these boys up late with you?" Uhura leaned to one side and helped herself to another piece of fish. "To be random fonts?"

"No." He still had nearly five kilos of allotment—too much for additional food, too little for another thermal. "They stay because they love me." He ordered an emergency medikit for each of the security officers, two more insulation suit repair sets, and one solar-powered winch—just in case.

"The chief has us doing research." Howard displayed the reader screen for Uhura, holding it so she could read the title beneath the shimmering Nordstral Pharmaceuticals logo: NORDSTRAL: A PLANETARY STUDY.

"We usually do this, just to make sure everybody knows at least a little about what we're going into." He shrugged and lowered the reader, thumbing through the screens. "It ends up that we all remember different things, which means the group of us together usually remembers just about everything. That works pretty well."

Uhura crossed the office to inspect the screen more closely over Howard's right arm. "Can't you just take the readers with you? That's what I'm doing with most of my native liaison tapes—there's no way I'm going to remember it all."

"It's not worth it," Publicker explained with a shrug. "You need the knowledge most when you're in the middle of a crisis, and then it's kind of hard to stop and take time to look things up."

"True."

Drumming his fingers on the terminal, Chekov let Uhura force another serving of uncooked seafood on his ensigns while he called up stat files on the security landing force. He'd requisitioned insulation suits and body slips for five immediately after hearing from Kirk—the computer verified only three suits and four slips. He could match up his and Publicker's, but the last suit wasn't anywhere near big enough for Howard, and the size listed for his third security ensign, Tenzing, came as close as it could to fitting her without actually matching.

Catching Uhura's attention, he pointed her toward the listing. "Is this your suit size?"

She pushed the food tray aside and perched on the edge of his desk, twisting a little to look at the screen. "Oh." Her voice sounded distinctly disappointed. "Do we have to use the insulation suits?"

Chekov twisted a look back at her, a little surprised

by her reaction. "If you don't want to freeze to death we have to."

"I mean can't we use parkas?" She rushed ahead over his impatient sigh. "Arctic peoples have worn parkas for centuries."

"Insulation suits are lighter than parkas," Chekov pointed out. "More flexible, more efficient. Why would you want to wear a six-kilogram bundle of synthetic fur when you have the option of something more comfortable?"

The intercom in the front office shrilled, and Uhura jumped with a startled gasp. By the time Chekov had waved Publicker out to take the message, she'd slid off the desk to clean up her half-eaten dinner offering, blushing lightly.

"Besides," he went on, "parkas are too massive. We don't have room for them."

"That's all right. I was just curious." She smiled her stunning smile and nodded toward the screen. "Yes, I'm a size five."

That meant Tenzing and Howard still needed full suits. Publicker turtled his head around the doorway while Chekov was typing in the new requisitions. "Lieutenant Chekov? That was Commander Scott, sir. He'd like to see you in engineering about the phaser modifications, if you have time."

He didn't, but he needed the phasers too badly to refuse. His mind darting ahead to the next few hours' work, Chekov committed his lists and powered down the terminal.

"Phaser modifications?" Uhura asked as Chekov got to his feet and kicked his chair beneath the desk.

He slipped past her, wishing she'd thought to bring some more conventional fare for dinner, his stomach now twinging with remembered hunger. Maybe he could grab something portable on his way to engineering. "Nordstral's strong magnetic field could interfere with our power supplies and incapacitate our phasers." He handed the disk with both requisitions to Howard and nodded him out the door. "Get these from the quartermaster. Burglarize supply, if you have to, but don't come back without them."

"Yes, sir."

He continued his explanation to Uhura as Howard ducked out the office door. "Mr. Scott is trying to find a way to make our phasers at least minimally operable." Retrieving his duty jacket from the back of his chair, he shook his head and shouldered into it. "It's not proving easy."

Uhura stacked the last of the napkins atop her tray, apparently not caring that the ice would ruin them. "Can't you just go without them?"

Chekov paused in latching closed his uniform. With all the things he could possibly say to placate her, he decided on a simple "No."

Uhura stopped her own cleaning to stare up at him in surprise. "Chekov, we're talking about a primitive village, the closest thing Nordstral has left to an aboriginal tribe. We don't need phasers to feel safe among them. What is it you expect them to do?"

"We're talking," he answered very carefully, "about a tribe who may very well be responsible for the disappearance of an entire team of researchers."

"You don't know that."

He fought hard against an impulse to stubbornly cross his arms. "Uhura, they were probably the last to see those scientists alive—the shuttle landed within walking distance of one of their villages. In any murder investigation, that has to make them the first suspects."

She let her food tray clap to the desktop with a ring of tinny thunder. "We don't know that anyone has been murdered."

"But we *do* know that one of Nordstral's two shuttles detonated while making a planetary survey. We know that in their last communication the survivors from that shuttle said that they'd arranged to meet a Kitka hunting party within the hour. We know that every last one of the survivors is now missing, and the Kitka are denying any knowledge of the accident. If nothing else, we know that communications with the *Enterprise* will be severely limited—that communications between landing parties will be impossible altogether. With the magnetic storms making it impossible to use our transporter, that means I can't even expect a quick pull-out if things turn ugly. No." He strode past her for the door, all his tiredness, frustration, and worry twisting together to feed a headache he'd been hoping not to have to nurse. "I will not go into a situation like that with absolutely nothing to use as protection."

"Pavel . . ."

He stopped, poised in the open doorway. The silent industry with which Publicker sat at his table, reading, assured Chekov the ensign had heard everything just fine, and was officially prepared to claim otherwise.

"You really don't like this," Uhura said gently from behind him, "do you?"

Chekov tightened one hand on the edge of the door. "I don't like retrieving dead bodies, no."

She stepped up beside him, close enough that she could tip her head and see his face while still talking softly enough to not be overhead. "We may not even find anything, you know." Her hand on his arm urged him to turn and face her. He acquiesced after only a little pulling, stepping around to let the door hiss shut behind him as she slid her hand down to slip it into his. "Not even why that shuttle went down, much less the crash site itself."

He nodded unhappily. "I know." Not that the prospect of never locating a crash site or bodies made him feel any better about the assignment; there could be few things worse than leaving a family without even anything to bury.

He shifted his gaze back to her face, not wanting to leave her on such a harsh note after she'd gone to the effort to look in on him. "You know I hope that nothing happens while we're planetside," he said, wanting her to believe that, and understand it as well. "I hope the phasers never matter. But I have to be so careful."

"Of course you do." She smiled gently and patted him on the cheek. "That's your job." Then, leaning around him, she keyed open the door and let go of his hand. "Go talk about your phasers. I promise to stay out of your hair until tomorrow."

He smiled down at her wryly. "And then you'll be in my hair for the entire mission. I know you." Her laughter relieved at least one small knot of worry; he couldn't stand the thought of her thinking badly of him, even if only for the duration of one mission. "Thank you for coming by tonight. I do appreciate the food."

"Even though you didn't eat it."

"Even though I didn't eat it," he acknowledged, nodding despite his embarrassment. "I promise—when we get back, I'll treat you to dinner." He hooked a thumb at the abandoned tray. "I'll even make sure they cook the food."

Laughing, Uhura planted both hands on his chest and shoved him out the door. "All right, Lieutenant. It's a date."

McCoy stared out the narrow shuttle window beside his chair and made no attempt to hide his disgust. Beyond the thick, protective material, Nordstral's icy landscape stretched to the horizon.

It set his teeth on edge. Even after decades aboard a starship, McCoy was still too much a southerner to have much of a liking for snow or cold. His blood had thinned in the lizard-baking heat of New Orleans and the gentle, balmy breezes of Georgia's sunny peach orchards, and never thickened again, no matter how many different climates he'd experienced as a member of the *Enterprise* crew.

He recalled a handful of vacations spent at the home of an uncle who'd braved the cooler climes of the North American continent. As a child, Leonard enjoyed the novelty of cold days, fire-warmed nights, and being tucked under so many thick blankets he could barely move. He remembered the snow being soft and delicate on his upturned face, feather-light against kicking boots bent on creating their own blizzard, bright white against the tumbling gray sky.

The memory bore no resemblance to the sculpted landscape before him. Here the snow was harsh, packed hard by the searing cold, and molded into fantastic shapes by a slicing wind that could cleave flesh from bone and freeze blood in its heated passage. The snow and ice didn't even look white here; more a pale blue shading to indigo in the deepest, most secret hollows, which McCoy had absolutely no desire to explore.

His crewmates weren't as jaundiced, and expressed

their delight when the Nordstral Pharmaceuticals shuttle cleared enough outer atmosphere for them to see properly. The sun glared off a sheet of trackless white and would have blinded the pilot but for the polarized screen.

"Oh, it's *beautiful!*" Uhura drew their attention from the interior of the cramped shuttle and the monotony of one another's faces to the wasted landscape visible below them. The passengers, Kirk included, jockeyed for position around the windows for a first look at the planet's surface, excited as always by someplace new and different. McCoy took one look and pointedly returned to his seat. He found no beauty in Nordstral's skeletal starkness. The wind-carved designs and unending white seemed sinister to him, like a large beast playing dead.

While the shuttle pilot traded information with ground-crew radio, repeating waves of wailing static rendered their conversation almost unintelligible to McCoy's ears. "Does the radio do that often?" the doctor asked one of the Nordstral techs working near him.

The younger man shrugged and glanced toward the cockpit. "Most of the time, at least. Annoying, huh?"

McCoy grunted. "Only if you have to use your communicator."

Kirk's deep voice captured McCoy's attention, and he turned back to the others just to give himself something to do. Kirk, just like McCoy, looked like a bulky burgundy snowman in his fleet-issue parka and heavy boots, especially compared to the sleek, dark lines of the security crew in their insulation suits. Chekov reminded him of a compact, slender, watchful predator. Shoulder to shoulder with his security force, the dour young Russian did more than just admire the scenery as his serious eyes skated the territory below the lowering shuttle. Howard looked even taller in the ebony clothing, one foot tapping frenetically as a giveaway to his excitement or nervousness. And there were also obvious delights in watching Uhura in her close-fitting insulation suit.

McCoy's cheeks reddened and he looked away, feigning interest in whatever it was the pilot was up to, not that anyone was watching him to notice his discomfort. If Uhura knew what he was thinking, she'd read him the riot act, and rightly so. A long time ago, the doctor had learned great respect for this lovely woman who was as delicate as ten-penny nails and as defenseless as a cornered tiger.

To clear his thoughts, McCoy glanced over the remaining members of the landing party and suppressed a grin. Tenzing looked as comfortable and calm as her Sherpa ancestors. Publicker, with insulation suit goggles pushed up onto his forehead, looked like a tadpole. Steno had been so rude before takeoff, McCoy didn't even glance in the direction of him and his men.

"Take your seats, please." The shuttle pilot's voice sounded tinny over the small, recessed wall speakers. As smoothly as oil over water, the joking crew became Chekov's well-disciplined security force. Without comment, they returned to their seats and began a final check on their insulation suits. The Russian lieutenant spoke briefly with each of his officers before taking a place beside Uhura.

Kirk jostled McCoy's leg with his knee. "You're awfully quiet, Doctor."

"Nothing much to say, I guess," he replied, and tried a smile that felt like a rictus. He turned away, pretending interest in the sweeping passage of snowfield beneath their rushing shuttle, and felt Jim's eyes on him.

The shuttle landed smoothly, and McCoy and Kirk disembarked. Kirk hunched into the coat collar as frigid wind tugged his hair, dusting it with fine snow crystals. McCoy cursed and pulled the hood up to shield his face.

"Lieutenant Chekov . . ." Kirk steadied himself with a hand on the frame of the open hatchway as a gust of wind threatened to knock him off his feet. Loose snow skirled around them like a tangible fog, and briefly obliterated the long, oblong, Quonset-type building nearby. "Good luck to you and your crew." He nodded, briefly touching each of them with his eyes and the reassurance of his smile in a way that made them all sit a little straighter. "I have every confidence you'll find the missing research team."

"We'll do our best, Captain."

"Lieutenant Commander Uhura, keep me posted on your progress." Kirk patted the communicator at his hip.

Uhura nodded. "Mr. Scott modified the communicators, sir, but he wasn't completely certain how they'd operate under the magnetic fluctuations of the planet. He may be able to reach you via the *Enterprise*, but I'm not sure we can make contact between landing parties."

"Noted."

The shuttle pilot grinned at them over her shoulder. "If that engineer of yours *does* make 'em work during the storms, Nordstral Pharmaceuticals may just buy him off you."

Kirk smiled in return. "He's not for sale."

"Jim." McCoy nudged him with one arm rammed

stiff into a pocket to keep his fingers from freezing. "You're leaving the refrigerator door open."

"Right. Good luck, everyone." McCoy and Kirk stepped back with a final wave. The shuttle hatch slid closed on their good-byes and secured with a reassuring thump. The pilot waved them back out of range, watching until they were within the security of the Quonset vestibule, then lifted off and headed north.

McCoy had never known a wind to feel so cold.

Chapter Three

THE BRIGHT STREAK of the Nordstral Pharmaceuticals shuttle burned across the horizon and left its roar hanging in the clouds behind it. The slate-gray sky rumbled with echoes for a while, then faded down to a silence that seemed too deep to be real. Uhura lifted a hand to the ear mike embedded in the hood of her insulation suit, wondering if the superinsulating plasfoam was muffling its sound pickup. A quick adjustment shot the volume upward until she could hear frost crackling in the air, but otherwise the ice sheet stayed dead silent.

A footstep crunched snow behind her, painfully loud. Uhura hurriedly dialed her mike volume down again, then turned to find a night-black figure with huge opalescent eyes staring down at her.

"I don't see any natives," Chekov said, his voice sober, slightly muffled by the insulation suit's breath filter. The reflective goggles protecting his eyes also

36

hid any trace of expression, but Uhura knew the security chief well enough to read the tense set of his shoulders under the sleek-fitting suit. "The company official said that some natives would meet us here."

"Maybe we're not at the right place." Uhura glanced at the area around them. It was mostly flat, with occasional spoon-shaped mounds of dirtier ice strung across it in parallel lines. To her untrained eye, the mound on which the company shuttle had dropped them looked no different than any other. "Why don't you ask Mr. Steno?"

Chekov made an irritated noise. "I would, but as far as I can tell, he's busy unpacking his lunch."

"What?" Uhura turned to see a cluster of men in ice-green insulation suits huddled over an untidy pile of gear, muttering as they rummaged through it. Their iridescent Nordstral Pharmaceuticals insignia glistened like fallen shreds of aurora on their shoulders as they moved from one open pack to another. Beyond them, the three black-clad security guards from the *Enterprise* stood quiet and watchful, their own gear neatly loaded onto a gravsled. "What on earth are they doing?"

"You mean, besides making a mess?" The angle of Chekov's jaw tightened in disapproval as he watched. "I have no idea."

"Well, hadn't we better find out?"

"I'll send Tenzing over to check." He sent a quick hand signal to one of his attentive security guards, just as the tallest green-clad figure straightened with a pistol-shaped object in one hand.

"Chekov!" Uhura gasped, but the security chief was already moving. His hand signal turned into a chopping wave that sent *Enterprise* guards diving forward even as he leapt toward them with what looked to

Uhura like recklessly long strides. Four sleekly muscled black figures converged on the company official. He vanished beneath them, but not before a blast shattered the icy silence.

Uhura blinked and tipped her head back, watching as a sulfur-yellow flare feathered its way up into the clouds. It burned there for a moment, then sizzled out just as a rising growl of voices drew her attention back to the landing party. She squared her shoulders and headed for them.

". . . what right you have to interfere?" The Nordstral officer scrambled to his feet as the *Enterprise* crewmen moved apart, shoving his hard plastic face mask back so Chekov could see his scowl. Uhura recognized the jutting features of *Curie*'s station manager, and winced. Captain Kirk had warned her that Nicholai Steno was not an easy man to deal with. "Just who the hell are you anyway, mister?"

"Lieutenant Pavel Chekov, Federation Starship Security." The Russian sounded calm enough, but Uhura could hear suppressed dislike in his deepening accent. "Captain Kirk put me in charge of security for this landing party."

"The hell he did! All he put you in charge of were those goons you brought with you!" Steno waved at Chekov's security personnel, two of whom had swung to face their startled Nordstral counterparts while the third cradled the confiscated flare gun. "As of this moment, I am the senior planetary officer of Nordstral Pharmaceuticals. *I'm* the one in charge here!"

"Begging the senior planetary officer's pardon." Chekov's voice had turned so cold, Uhura barely recognized the undertone of sarcasm in his words. "Federation articles clearly state that in a Priority

One emergency, starship personnel outrank their equivalent planetary authorities. Sir."

"I'm not your equivalent authority, you bug-eyed idiot!" It amazed Uhura that the company man would snarl into Chekov's face like that, as if he couldn't see the readiness in the younger man's stance. Despite the half-meter difference in their heights, she had no doubt who would win if this came to a fight. The possibility made her pick up her pace. "You deep-space jockeys like to think you run the universe, but I'm not going to let you—"

"You have no authority—"

The snarled braid of voices rose to a roar. Uhura skidded the last few feet down the rocky ice slope, hurriedly tapping a dial on her insulation suit's translator as she went.

"Gentlemen!"

Both men swung around as her amplified voice cracked through the frigid air, Chekov with a swift pivot, Steno with a jerk and a curse. Uhura tapped her volume adjustment down again and faced them, trying to project as much calm patience as she could.

"Lieutenant Chekov, Mr. Steno—please try to remember that we're here to rescue people, not to fight with each other."

"Yessir," Chekov muttered, ducking his chin against his chest. Steno snorted scornfully, and Uhura turned toward him, flipping up the goggles covering her eyes so he could see her frown. The sudden unshielded brilliance of the ice sheet made her eyes burn, but she kept the goggles up anyway.

"For your information, Mr. Steno, Lieutenant Chekov is entirely correct about Priority One emergency rules. In point of law, his rank may not make him your equivalent in authority, but *mine* certainly does."

The snap in her voice must have gotten through to the station manager. A muscle jerked in his cheek as he blinked down at her, his frost-whitened eyebrows lifting in surprise.

"Thank you, Commander." Chekov put a little more stress than usual on Uhura's title, and she heard Steno grumble a reluctant acknowledgment. With a sigh of relief, she lowered her goggles and blinked as the polarizers brought the white blur of the ice sheet back into focus.

"Now, Mr. Steno," Chekov said, very politely. "Would you care to explain to the lieutenant commander what you were doing with that flare?"

The Nordstral official grunted, wrestling his old-fashioned plastic visor back down over the coating of frost that had gathered on the edge of his foam suit. "It's standard procedure," he said curtly. "That's how we tell the Kitka to send out guides for us."

Uhura scanned the barren expanse of ice around them. "Do the natives have a settlement near here?"

"Who knows? They're nomads, they follow fish around from one open crevasse to another as the ice sheet drifts. When they do stop, they burrow down inside the ice like moles. It's easier to let *them* find *us* when we need guides."

"Do we need guides?" Chekov still made an effort to sound polite, but the undertone of skepticism in his voice must have gotten through to Steno. The taller man scowled through his frost-clouded visor.

"Listen, Lieutenant—this planet has more transient magnetic fields than a galactic core! You try finding your way around it alone, and you'll find out real fast how well your fancy Starfleet instruments work in a mess like this. We don't even have any decent maps, the way the ice sheet keeps cracking and moving—it's like trying to map the scum on a stagnant pond." Steno snorted, blowing a cloud of mist out his breath filter. "Trust me, starboy. When the boreal winds kick in this afternoon, you'll be damn glad to have a Kitka here to guide you to shelter."

"Will I?" Chekov's voice sounded grim. "I wonder if your missing research team was glad of it."

The Nordstral officer took a step back, almost bumping into the tall *Enterprise* guard behind him. "What's that supposed to mean? You think the Kitka had something to do with us losing that research team?"

The sheer amazement in Steno's voice surprised Uhura—was the man so stupid he'd never even thought of that possibility? She didn't consider it very likely herself, but if twelve years in Starfleet had taught her anything, it was never to discount the improbable on unknown planets.

Chekov muttered in Russian, then said quietly to Steno, "You have no idea how your research team vanished, sir. All we know is that they probably sent up a flare just like this one, and you never heard from them again. We have to consider every possibility."

"Not that one." The station manager snorted out another cloud of mist. "Of all the stupid things I've heard today, blaming the Kitka for this mess is the worst. Listen, Lieutenant Checkers or whatever your name is—you just mind your goons and do what your little lieutenant commander tells you to. Leave the thinking on this trip to me."

Uhura watched speechlessly as Steno turned and strode back to his messy sprawl of equipment, swerving awkwardly around the security guard behind him.

The tall, black-suited figure swung to follow him, then glanced back over his shoulder when Chekov snapped out, "No!"

"But, Chief!" Michael Howard's voice sounded oddly fierce through the breath filter. "He called you—"

"Being rude does not make him a security risk, Mr. Howard." Chekov sent a quick signal to the rest of his crew, and they left the uneasy Nordstral men they had been guarding to gather around him. "This is a Code Three situation. Potentially dangerous ground parties are now aware of our location and converging on this site. I want perimeter guard at twenty meters, with surveillance cross-checks on anything that looks suspicious." The security chief glanced around. "Positions clockwise starting from that tall rock: Publicker, Tenzing, Howard, me. Phasers on stun."

"Yessir." The three guards scattered outward without another word, leaving Uhura and Chekov standing together. She lifted her eyebrows inquiringly at him, then remembered he couldn't see the expression through her goggles.

"Is there anything you'd like me to do?" she asked instead. "You know I haven't got a real job here until the Kitka show up."

"I was hoping you'd ask." Chekov jerked his chin toward their gravsled. "How about keeping an eye on the supplies?"

"Is that really necessary?" Uhura asked, peeking under the gravsled's cover to see what was hidden beneath it. "What's going to happen to a few kilograms of tents and—" Catching sight of a bundle snuggled near the bottom of the load, she angled a look up at him. "A solar-powered *winch,* Chekov?"

He shrugged, obviously not put off by her amusement. "We had extra room and I like to be prepared." He tugged the cover back into place as though to forestall any further comments. "I'd rather have you on perimeter with the rest of us," he admitted, "but if we leave our gear lying around unwatched, it might get ransacked by these Nordstral—"

He paused, evidently searching for a word. Uhura smiled and supplied one. "Goons?"

"Goons." A flicker of his usual wry humor surfaced for a moment in his voice. "That's not exactly what I'd call them in Russian, but it's close enough."

Kirk stopped pacing the land station's narrow confines when a technician's voice rang out. "Yo, Clara!"

A short woman had entered the other end of the docking hut from a rabbit's warren of tunnels connecting it to the other buildings. She was dressed for outside in pants, knee-high boots, and a parka that appeared twice as thick as the Federation-issued garb. A large, bulky pack lay secured across her shoulders, and goggles hung around her neck.

She turned at the docking technician's call and waved a mittened hand. She tossed back the jacket hood and set free a wealth of multibraided hair that reminded McCoy of Medusa's snakes. "Don't be yarpin' at me, Tootsie. I got mail-run, and you know how them sailors hate to be kept waiting."

The tech jerked a thumb in their direction. "Two for the *Soroya.*"

She nodded. "Ah, yes." She smoothly shrugged out of the cumbersome pack and left it leaning against the wall while she approached the Starfleet officers, pulling off her mittens as she walked. She offered a strong

43

handshake first to Kirk and then to McCoy, and smiled broadly, her perfect teeth very white against her chestnut-colored skin.

"You'd be the Federation men," she said in a lilting, singsong accent. "I heard you were coming."

"Captain James Kirk and Dr. Leonard McCoy," Kirk replied briskly. "You're our guide? You'll take us to meet Captain Mandeville?"

Her grin broadened, puffing her cheeks up like a squirrel's. "Ah, yes. I'm Clara." The vowels were broadened to "ahs" in an almost southern-sounding dialect. She jerked her head toward the door. "Come on, then." She strode across the room without waiting to see if they'd follow, reshouldered the pack, and opened the outer door.

The frigid air made McCoy hiss. Clara cast a dark eye toward him over her shoulder while she adjusted her goggles and watched the men do likewise. "You don't sound used to this weather, Doctor."

"I'm not," he grumbled, securing the hood soundly around his ears as he walked. The snow and ice screamed and squealed under his boots and made him feel like he needed a good scratch. "I'm a southerner."

She chuckled as though she understood. "Me, too."

"You're not a native?" Kirk asked, sounding surprised.

Clara hooted with good-natured laughter. "You must never have seen a live Kitka to be saying that," she said, still grinning. "Bandy little folk, they are— square and squat, not like this skinny body." She slapped herself in the stomach, but didn't seem displeased with her proportions. "More yellow than brown, too, with eyes that sparkle like fish scales. Blue- or green-eyed, most of them, going whiter and whiter as they get old. You'll never take a human for one, once you've met them."

Kirk nodded, glancing nervously around them. "But I'd heard Nordstral Pharmaceuticals hired native guides to lead everyone across the ice."

"Oh, that was in the beginning, when we first arrived. This area's as stable as anything gets on Nordstral, so we're all used to it by now. They still have to use guides out on the pack ice up north, though. Bad, dangerous stuff, that. Grab you up and swallow you whole without a trace. Whatever mystic ways they have, those northern Kitka are the only folk can walk around safely up there." She grinned when the men exchanged looks; or it might have been a continuation of the same grin, McCoy wasn't certain. She seemed to smile more than anyone he'd ever met, except for maybe Sulu. "No need to worry, though. I'll take care of you. As for being native, well, I thank you for the compliment, and I'm probably the next best thing, having been here as long as I have. I'm from Earth—Jamaica, to be exact."

"How did you end up here?" McCoy asked, curiosity getting the better of him.

Clara shrugged one shoulder and dipped the other for further emphasis. "Oh, that's a long story. I'll tell it to you, maybe, sometime."

"Can you tell us a little about the company?" Kirk asked, sounding as though he was just making conversation.

Their guide turned around and walked backward as easily as she had facing forward. "I'll do what I can," she replied agreeably.

"I'm curious. How do you harvest plankton on an icebound planet?"

"Only partially icebound. The Kitka hunting holes are open, as are various areas where the action of the glaciers calving has kept free water. And there's a good, sound band of open water around the equator." She pointed down as she walked. "Which is here."

"Doesn't plankton need sunlight to bloom?" Kirk asked. The tips of his ears and nose were red with cold, and his breath steamed and curled about his face.

"To get the biggest and heaviest blooms, sunlight always helps. But most of the plankton's energy comes from the planet's magnetic field, and that's present everywhere."

McCoy frowned. "It's not too cold under all that ice for plants to grow?"

Clara shook her head. "The ability of marine plankton to thrive under heavy ice sheets was first discovered on Earth by Russian fleets. They brought ice cutters in to catch the schools of fish that fed off the plankton." She cocked her head and studied McCoy. "What's so funny?"

He pursed his lips around a smile. "I was thinking about one of our crewmen. He's Russian, and he'd be proud as punch to hear you tell this."

"He should be. If not for the Russians, we probably wouldn't be on Nordstral now." Again, the grin. "Then again, maybe I don't exactly owe them a debt of thanks for that, eh?"

Clara swung her arms and shifted the pack across her shoulders. "Anyway, what the Russian fleets found under the ice where they'd previously thought plankton could not exist was an abundance of wildlife, all subsisting on plankton or plankton feeders. Fortunately for this company, Nordstral proved to behave exactly the same way, only on a much greater scale. Using submarine harvesters makes it fairly easy to gather the plankton."

"Indigenous life?" McCoy asked.

"Well, there's the Kitka, of course. And lots of marine life." She waved a thick arm at their surroundings. "Not much else can stomach what Nordstral has to offer."

"And the Kitka serve on the harvesters?" Kirk queried.

"Quite a few of them, yes." She winked playfully at the captain. "Don't let all those glaciers fool you. They've got quite a tech level in the cities that are strung along the equator."

"Are they hostile? Upset by the harvesting or having their skilled people drawn away to the harvesters?"

"Not to my knowledge. They don't seem to much care what we do, so long as we don't dirty up the place and we pay our rent. And it's not just the skilled working the harvesters. We've got plenty of young folk looking for good money, not to mention Kitka well into their middle years, with plenty of hunting and ice experience behind them." Her eyes twinkled. "That's to our advantage."

"What about Captain Mandeville?" Kirk squinted against the glare and turned the full force of his gaze on Clara.

She didn't seem particularly affected. She shrugged, turned about-face again and trudged forward. "What do you want to know?"

"What kind of man is he? How is he with his crew? Do they like serving under him?"

The pack shifted under the movement of her shoulders. "As much as sailors ever do. Somebody always complains about something, Captain Kirk. Such talk isn't worth much."

"Isn't it?" Kirk pressed, obviously expecting that *any* captain, even one as good as he, would have disgruntled *someone* somewhere down the line.

"I can't know it all, obviously, but nothing's come to these ears worth discussing, and I do have a talent for hearing most things that go on around here."

"You wouldn't say that just to protect him?"

Clara stopped and turned to face him. For a change, her expression was completely serious. "Captain Mandeville doesn't need protecting from anyone. That much I can tell you." Without giving him an opportunity to respond, she turned away and continued toward the harbor.

McCoy, hunched as deeply in his parka as he could go without curling into a fetal position, looked at his friend. "So much for round one."

Kirk's eyes were pensive as he watched Clara trek across the ice ahead of them. "It's only the groundwork, Bones. Just because she doesn't know anything or is pretending she doesn't, doesn't mean someone else won't talk. I want to check out this Captain Mandeville close up. I think Clara's protecting him for some reason, and I want to know what it is." He followed Clara's retreating back.

McCoy watched him for a moment, then let his gaze drift beyond Kirk's broad shoulders. A cold fist clenched around his heart and he swallowed hard. He'd been so caught up in the conversation between Kirk and the guide, he hadn't realized how close they'd come to the water. The tiny ribbon visible from the hut had widened into an enormous channel of black, seemingly thick water. Icebergs as small as a child's snowman or larger than a shuttle floated majestically on the surface. He murmured and hurried to catch up with Kirk.

"What did you say?" Kirk barely glanced at him.

McCoy shook his head, finding it odd the way his hood stayed still and his head moved around inside it. "Nothing. Just something from an old song I once heard about the *Titanic.*"

"You'll have to sing it to me sometime." Kirk glanced sideways and gave McCoy a tolerant, lopsided grin.

"In your dreams, Captain."

Clara trotted back to meet them, her breath streaming in the air behind her. "We'd best stop here. *Soroya's* due up any time now, and sometimes there's a backwash in the rise. We don't want you being flooded off the ice into the water, now, do we?"

McCoy took one giant step backward. "What are we here to investigate?" the doctor muttered. "I'd be nuts, too, if they locked me in a submarine."

Kirk sharply nudged McCoy's arm. "You saw for yourself, they're *not* nuts. That's what makes this whole thing so weird." He watched the smooth surface of the water for several moments. "What's the matter, Bones?" he asked quietly. "We're going to be in a ship."

"If you poke a hole in a ship, water rushes in." McCoy glared at the icebergs and tried hard not to imagine what kind of damage they could inflict on a vessel.

Kirk laughed gently. "If you poke a hole in a starship, space rushes in."

McCoy scowled at him. "It's different and you know it!" He suddenly gripped Kirk's arm, gloved fingers tight around the biceps. "You feel that?"

"Yes." The ice quivered faintly under their feet. McCoy shot a frightened look in Clara's direction. Her eyes flicked from the sea to the sky and back. She looked altogether far more comfortable than McCoy felt anyone had a right to, given their surroundings. It annoyed him, which was better than feeling scared, and it certainly kept him warmer.

"Here she comes," the woman drawled.

First, the surface of the water moved. Eddies built and swirled, humps of water ebbed and receded. McCoy was reminded of a bass rising from the depths of a lake and not quite breaking the surface. Then the ship was suddenly *there*, emerging out of nothing like a khaki-green magician's rabbit out of a top hat.

The turret rose like an oblong head sheeted with water. The rest of the harvester followed, surfacing in an almost stately fashion, as though aware of scrutiny. Water rushed and roared, falling off its pocked sides and cascading back into the bay.

"We're actually going to *board* this rust bucket?" McCoy growled under his breath, eyes wide.

"You'll be fine, Bones." Kirk's eyes roamed the harvester. "I thought it would be sleeker," he mused. "Less worn."

"What for?" Clara snorted. "The money men don't care what the ships look like so long as they do the job. This tub's in pretty decent shape, given her age and the wear and tear she's seen." She pointed one long finger at a dent running a third of the length of the long ship. "You see that? Surfaced too close to a 'berg, didn't judge its drift right. It's hard to, sometimes. Those damned magnetic storms screw up everything."

"Is Mandeville careless?" Kirk asked innocently.

Before Clara could reply, the *Soroya* settled at the surface with an enormous sigh and a wash of water that nearly reached their feet and had McCoy backstepping nervously. A top hatch opened with a

50

clang. A man with thick, iron-gray hair emerged to waist height and leaned on the hatch rim. Even from this distance, McCoy knew the man must be a Kitka. The heavy bone-lines of his cheeks and jaw swept his features into a broad, exotic circle; his eyes showed a clear and frosty green against the turbulent waters behind him. When he smiled, his copper-skinned face creased into a million lines. "Yo, Cap'n. You bring in the mail?"

McCoy thought at first he was addressing Kirk. Obviously, so did the *Enterprise*'s captain, until Clara raised one hand and caught the rungs of a metal ladder welded to the side of the ship. She snorted. "As though your family ever needs to write. You crazy Kitka talk through the ice." She turned, one foot on the bottom rung, and speared Kirk with a hard look. "No, Captain Mandeville is *not* careless." She started up the ladder, shrugged out of the heavy pack and tossed it to the waiting crewman. At the top she paused only long enough to clap the dark man on the shoulder. "Those are the Federation men. Show them where to bunk. I'll be up front." She didn't even favor McCoy and Kirk with a look before she disappeared down the turret like Alice down the rabbit hole.

Kirk stared after her, jaw working and hazel eyes blazing.

McCoy's eyebrows rose and a smile tugged up one corner of his mouth. "You're looking a little hot under the collar, Captain."

Kirk glared at him. "I don't like being deceived."

"She didn't deceive you." When Kirk's expression didn't ease, McCoy stepped closer. "Jim, she never once denied being Captain Mandeville. You just didn't ask her if she was."

From below came Mandeville's voice. "Get them in

here! Dammit, Nuie, we're a harvester ship, not a damned trundle cab!"

The gray-haired crewman smiled with encouragement. "There's nothing to it. One, two, and you're up and in."

When Kirk gestured for McCoy to ascend the iron ladder ahead of him, the doctor obediently took the first water-slicked rung in a hand gone clammy inside its glove. Both feet still firmly grounded on the ice, he looked back at his friend and found a smile despite his fear of the ship and the ebon water. "What you don't like, Jim, is being outfoxed. Mandeville was just being careful with her words around a stranger, just like you would." He leveled a finger under Kirk's nose. "And don't tell me you'd have done it any differently, because I've *seen* you do it a million times."

"Maybe." Face still flushed with embarrassment, Kirk waved a hand for McCoy to get a move on. "I just hope Chekov's having a better time of it than we are."

The boreal winds arrived without a rustle of warning. One moment the ice sheet lay wrapped in its usual dead silence, its noon brilliance slowly dimming into a gray-green afternoon. The next, Uhura heard a distant, high-pitched shriek and saw the security guards stop pacing their careful quarter circles to look around. She stood from her seat on the gravsled just in time to be buffeted back into it by a fierce slam of cold air against her insulation suit.

"Boreal winds," shouted Steno across the three-meter distance separating them, with just a note of smugness in his voice. The wind's shriek rose to a howl, one that went on and on without remorse. Uhura winced and dialed the volume on her ear mike down as far as she could, then tried clicking on her insulation suit's communicator channels. She got only the same strange static she'd heard on the shuttle radio, a falling whistle that repeated itself as monotonously as the wind's howl.

It occurred to Uhura that the planet Nordstral was about as close to a communications officer's vision of Hell as she could imagine. She shivered and tried to huddle deeper into the shelter of their piled gear as the wind bit through her insulation suit. With her sound input damped, the first hint she had of company was the tap on her shoulder. She jumped and swung simultaneously, not seeing the familiar black insulation suit until too late. Her fist rebounded from hard stomach muscles, just as Chekov's faint voice said, "It's only me."

"Sorry." She rubbed her knuckles with a wince, then tapped her ear mike's volume back to normal. "Are the Kitka here?"

"No. I don't know if that's good or bad." He lifted a hand to rub at the back of his neck. "Uhura, can you do anything about these suit communicators? I can barely hear my guards past the static."

She shook her head. "It's planet-wide interference. I think Nordstral's magnetic field is so strong that it spins off magnetic storms as well as auroras when it gets hit by solar wind. Our communicators can't distinguish the radio output of the auroral storms from real transmissions."

"That's what I was afraid of. We'll have to rely on our hand signals." He glanced down at her, expressionless under the bright shimmer of his goggles. "Are you all right here?"

She shrugged and rubbed her arms. "Just a little cold, now that the wind's blowing. I'll survive."

"It's warmer if you keep walking." Chekov glanced at Steno and the other company men, huddled close around their hastily repacked gear. "With this wind blowing, I don't think we have to worry about the, ah, goons."

"All right." Uhura scrambled to her feet beside him, swaying a little when the wind buffeted her. "This is another thing I don't like about insulation suits," she complained as they headed out to Chekov's section of perimeter. "They don't break the wind."

"That's because they're designed to reduce wind friction. You'd be getting hit twice this hard if you were in a parka."

"But I wouldn't feel it half so much." She noticed that he put himself on the windward side as they started patrolling, and smiled without saying anything. Chekov hated to be caught doing something gallant.

"What's the first thing?" he asked after a moment.

"Hmm?" The wind was stirring up fine snow into a knee-high mist that hid the ground around them. She didn't bother to look up from her feet, since she wouldn't have seen Chekov's expression anyway. "What first thing?"

"You said that the wind was another thing you hate about insulation suits. What was the first thing?"

"Oh, that. It's nothing important." Uhura lifted a hand wistfully to her throat. She was too embarrassed to admit that she felt lost without the comforting brush of polished metal against her skin. An insulation suit's skintight construction didn't allow her to wear anything as nonessential as jewelry beneath it. "So—you haven't seen any sign of the Kitka?"

"Not a whisker." Chekov turned a slow circle as

though her question had reminded him to look again. "Assuming that the Kitka have whiskers. You should know, you're the expert."

"On their language, Chekov, not their facial hair." She sighed. "And to be honest, I'm not even an expert on that. The information that Nordstral Pharmaceuticals gave us was awfully sketchy."

"Our suit translators will work, won't they?"

"Nordstral says they'll catch most of the words for most of the Kitka, most of the time." Uhura shrugged. "The Kitka distinguish words by pitch, and that makes it hard to translate into English. God only knows what happens when the machine tries to translate from English to Kitka."

"Great." Chekov blew an exasperated breath out through his filter. "We're expecting possibly hostile natives, and we may not even be able to talk to them."

"Chekov." Uhura reached out and caught his arm as they turned to head back the way they'd come. The wind was swirling snow mist around them at shoulder height now, making it hard for her to see. "You don't have to worry about the Kitka so much, honestly. They're a tiny remnant of the pre-ice cultures that lived on this planet before the glaciers pushed everyone else down to the equator. All available information says they're isolated nomads, dedicated to preserving their environment, so peaceful they won't even harpoon a fish without asking its forgiveness first."

Chekov made a frustrated noise, nearly drowned by the rising wind. "And do you think that they understand what the fish say back to them any better than they'll understand us?" He turned his back on a particularly severe gust, pulling Uhura around to stand in the shelter he made. "Commander, I'm not trying to say that they're evil people. I just think that we should be . . ."

The shriek of the boreal wind stopped as suddenly as it had started, dropping the snow mist like a curtain to reveal what had been hiding inside.

Uhura stared in silent shock at the circle of needle-sharp harpoons surrounding them, held by a circle of burly figures in ragged white furs. The tip of each harpoon head looked as if it had been dipped in ruby-dark blood.

". . . careful," Chekov finished grimly.

Chapter Four

CLAUSTROPHOBIA SHUDDERED McCoy's insides as he stepped off the iron ladder's final rung and put both feet firmly on the harvester's inner deck. He bit down on the fear, forcing it to bay. The inside of his mouth tasted filmy and bitter, and he was briefly reminded of the unsweetened lemon drops his grandfather had favored.

The corridor walls curved closely around him, not even wide enough for two men to walk abreast. The floor was a straight lane as far as he could see, riveted metal covered with some nonskid material. The ceiling was low, heightening the sense of closeness, of being shut in an iron coffin. He was grateful for the open hatch above his head, the touch of breeze snaking down the entry to stir the fur of his hood and bring the freshening scent of saltwater.

"I'd hate to end a promising surgery career."

Kirk's teasing voice broke into McCoy's thoughts. The doctor tilted his head back and peered up at his captain, standing halfway down the ladder. "What's that supposed to mean?"

Kirk bent one knee and nudged McCoy's knuckles with the toe of his boot. "It means that if you don't let go that death's grip on the ladder, I'll be forced to tramp on your fingers. Starfleet might never get over the loss."

"Oh." Doubly embarrassed at not only having been caught holding the rungs for support, but not even realizing he was doing so, McCoy released the smooth worn metal, crammed his hands into his pockets and stepped back to afford Kirk room to climb down. The *Enterprise* captain's feet had no more touched the decking than the hatch above closed with a resonant clang. There was the muffled thud of catches being thrown, insurance (McCoy hoped) against an inwash of seawater, and Nuie landed lightly beside them. He pulled shut the inner hatch and turned the locking wheel as far as it would go, then faced them.

In the overhead lighting, McCoy saw that Nuie's eyes were silver-green, a striking contrast against his weather-roughened copper skin and sleek, thick gray hair. He was shorter than them both by several inches, boxy and squarely built. He smiled now, as broadly as his captain had, and jerked his head. "I'm Nuie, first mate on *Soroya*. Come with me, please."

They followed him to a lozenge-shaped door several meters down the corridor. Nuie dogged it open and stepped aside to allow them entrance, but remained in the doorway, one hand curved around the jamb. "Captain Mandeville offers her quarters to you," he stated formally, as though in recitation. "She asks that you remain here until we're under way. I'll be back to fetch you then, and give you the . . ." His face screwed up in concentration. "Ten cents tour?" He appeared confused by the idiom.

Kirk smiled. "That'll be fine, Nuie, thank you."

The crewman paused with the door halfway closed to bob a quick nod before he was gone.

Kirk crossed the room and checked the door. It was unlocked and opened at his touch. He closed it again after glancing down the corridor in each direction. "Well, we're not being watched." His eyes hunted the corners of the room.

"What are you looking for?"

"Surveillance. Cameras of some kind."

"Would you know them if you saw them?"

"I don't know." Kirk tabbed open his parka and spread it wide, hands perched on his trim hips. "I'd like to get a look at that bridge."

"You'll probably get your wish. I don't recall you ever being comfortable with strangers on the bridge when you're coming out of dock, either."

"True."

McCoy crossed his arms over his chest and looked around. The walls, floor, and ceiling were the same monochrome color. A metal storage locker was bolted in one corner, presumably for Captain Mandeville's clothing, toiletries, and personal effects. A tiny desk was hinged to the wall and depended from two chains. The chair before it was bolted to the floor but could swivel freely above the pedestal of its legs. Two pictures vied for space on the wall above the desk. The one on the left was a reproduction of an oil painting. It showed a large ship, its bow awash in a sea pocked with icebergs. The tiny brass plate at the bottom of the frame read, "Maiden Voyage of *Titanic.*"

"That's not very damn funny!" McCoy jumped

back, afraid that studying the painting too closely might just tickle the Fates into bringing it back to life, starring the *Soroya*. He knew he was being foolish, but that didn't change the face of his unhappiness or the macabre fascination that made him step closer again to peer at the painting, searching the *Titanic*'s decks for the faces of the doomed.

"Hmmm . . . what did you say, Bones?" Kirk frowned at the other picture, an ancient photograph of a man with short, dark hair, a round, cheerful face, and wire-rimmed glasses, posed before an old-time submarine. "Who do you suppose this is?"

"I don't—" McCoy's hand seizured out and clutched Kirk's arm as movement threw him momentarily off balance. The blood drained from his face and, for all he knew, disappeared into the bulkhead. He was suddenly cold all over and slick with sweat.

Kirk eased him onto the edge of the bed. "Come on, Bones. Out with it."

Embarrassed, McCoy looked up from the floor beneath his feet. "Out with what?"

"With whatever's bothering you."

"What makes you think anything's bothering me?" McCoy made the effort to look his captain right in the face and smile sickly.

Kirk snorted, but the doctor couldn't tell if it was in disbelief or annoyance. "Well, for one thing, you're not displaying your usual sterling personality."

McCoy returned the snort. "I don't have Spock here to serve as inspiration." He burrowed his hands under his armpits on the pretense of crossing his arms.

Kirk surprised his friend by leaning down and placing a firm hand on the bed to either side of McCoy, effectively trapping the doctor where he sat. "What's eating you?"

"Nothing's—"

"Bones." He spoke quietly, without annoyance, and drew McCoy's attention like steel filings to a magnet. Blue eyes met hazel ones of an intensity the doctor had never experienced with any other single human being. "I need you *with* me on this one. I need your way of looking at things to help me figure out what's happening on Nordstral. I can't do it by myself."

Staring into those eyes, McCoy found himself wondering just *when* he decided he would die for this man. He felt a flush of shame for pulling away, even momentarily, from the friendship and understanding he knew Kirk constantly offered. "I'm with you, Jim," he murmured, then nodded his head firmly. "I *am.*"

"Then what's wrong?"

McCoy's eyes strayed across the cabin's narrow width to the wall opposite. The picture of the *Titanic* showed much the same view as Nordstral's surface, a ribbon of black interspersed with lurching chunks of white. The scene reminded McCoy of the harbor area where they'd waited for the *Soroya* to come for fuel and supplies, where all the harvesters came to discharge their loads of plankton. McCoy couldn't remember the last time he'd seen something that looked so evil.

When he finally spoke, his voice was very soft. "When I was, oh, seven or eight, my family had a reunion, a picnic along the banks of the Chattahoochee River." The memory did not elicit a smile, even though McCoy could still hear his relatives' voices, still smell the glorious food, still feel the breeze off the river ruffling his hair. "The men pitched green and yellow pavilions to shield the ladies from the sun. There was all kinds of food, and I remember drinking a lot of lemonade because it was so hot. The men played horseshoes and smoked horrible cigars. I spent most of the morning catching frogs with my cousin David and throwing them at the girls." His lips curved gently. "Some of the older cousins had gotten together earlier and built a raft of logs, like something out of Mark Twain. The Chattahoochee's nothing like the Mississippi, but it served our purposes. In the press of people, with so many children running around, I guess every adult assumed every other adult was keeping watch. Nobody thought it prudent to make certain all us kids knew how to swim." Before McCoy's unfocused eyes, the *Titanic's* ages-old fate vanished, replaced by a wide expanse of grass and a deep, slow-moving river glinting in the sun.

Something that tried to be a laugh, and died as a short gasp of air, hitched McCoy's chest. "There must have been a dozen of us kids on that thing, maybe more. I guess my cousins weren't as smart as they thought. We got out to the middle of the river and the raft just fell apart. I went down like a stone." His eyes squeezed closed, drawing the memory closer with morbid fascination. He ran a hand across one cheek. "I don't know how long it took them to figure out little Leonard wasn't with them, or who pulled me up. They said I was blue and that my grandfather walloped me sound and got me breathing again." He opened his eyes and focused on a blank area of wall beyond Kirk's left shoulder. "I remember being scared. I remember looking up as I sank, and seeing the whole sunlit world fading to a distant spot of color on the surface of the river. I remember my lungs filling with water."

His gaze jerked sideways to Kirk's astonished face. McCoy's hands felt cold despite the room's heat and he curled his fingers into his palms. Someplace deep inside him a pit shivered open after all these years and a wailing cry echoed where only he could hear. "I wasn't the only one who didn't know how to swim."

McCoy looked across at that damned picture. No grass. No sun-dappled water. Just chunks of ice like dancing mountaintops, bobbing on the ocean's black surface. "They didn't bring David up until after dark." He closed his eyes again and dropped his face into his hands.

Chekov stretched out one arm to tuck Uhura behind him, instinctively wanting to shelter her from the Kitka. She resisted slightly with a hand on his shoulder; he shrugged it away, afraid of being distracted.

The Kitka blended into their arctic landscape with fluid, natural ease. Thick, ice-silver parkas obscured faces already hidden behind carved ivory masks, the wind corkscrewing frost-flower patterns in the long animal fur. Their bodies were uniformly square and small, their limbs short and strong from generations of trudging across barren tundra. When they jostled amongst each other like a band of disturbed foxes, Chekov caught himself restlessly squeezing his hands into fists.

The Kitka fluttered back to either side, harpoons swinging to their shoulders. From behind them a single native—taller and more slimly built than the rest—swept forward through a swirl of glittering snow. Stiffened feathers clattered faintly against a chest plate sewn of native bone, and gloves almost as supple and thin as those on a Starfleet insulation suit made his hands seem infinitely delicate in contrast with the bulky Kitka parkas and mittens. For some reason, the fact that he didn't walk or stand like the others bothered Chekov more than the foot-long bone knife at his waist. Knives Chekov understood and could deal with—disparity hinted at danger.

Steno, however, apparently lacked the same reservations. "Alion! My old friend!" Dancing around the end of his untidy gravsled, Steno popped open his faceplate on his way across the ice to greet the feathered man. Chekov noticed that Alion didn't reciprocate the gesture. "How has life been at your village?"

The first fluting words to pass between Steno and Alion were too faint to pick up on Chekov's translator. Even body language could not be trusted—Steno was as insincere and erratic as they came, and Chekov hadn't observed enough Kitka yet to know what any of Alion's movements might mean. From Steno's effusive reactions, though, Chekov was forced to assume Alion hadn't offered to murder the station commander. Too bad. He was probably the first person to meet Steno who hadn't. Chekov would have liked a peek past Alion's ivory mask with its temple-to-temple eye slit, though, if only to judge whether Kitka grimaced over Steno's blabbering as readily as humans did.

"See." Uhura placed both tiny hands at the small of Chekov's back and delivered a playful shove obviously not intended to disturb his stance. "I told you they were friendly. You worry too much."

Chekov twisted a look over one shoulder, unsure whether or not she'd intended that remark to be funny. Even without seeing her expression, he could read the eager interest in her body's balance when she leaned around him to study the natives. "You must be joking." He glanced back at Steno and Alion while the businessman tried to thaw the ice statue with his words. "They don't look friendly to me."

Sunlight flashed white across Uhura's goggles when she tipped her head up to sigh at him. "You're paranoid."

Chekov turned his attention back toward the natives without letting Uhura know how much her comment stung. It was his job to be paranoid, to make sure the rest of a landing party could go about their duties without worry—it annoyed him to be criticized for being careful.

Steno turned neatly to bring himself shoulder to shoulder with Alion, head still inclined in a very political display of interest. Chekov watched the two men start toward his group across the ice, and his stomach tightened with apprehension. He liked Alion better at a good stone's throw away.

"Chief?" Howard's voice came very quietly over the suit communicators. Chekov answered him by moving one hand behind his back to signal the squad into a four corners watch. Uhura glanced up at him, then behind her at the others, as the three remaining officers pulled together into a diamond with Chekov at the head and Uhura near the center. Chekov almost expected her to say something further about his paranoia, but she only stood close beside him in silence. He never knew when he'd be most surprised by her—when she agreed with him about something, or when she didn't.

Alion came to a halt just more than an arm's length away. His carved ivory mask shifted to look downward at Uhura, then lifted again to angle at the guards behind Chekov's left shoulder. He stood even in height with Chekov—not tall by human standards, perhaps, but impressive enough among the Kitka if the natives around him were any example. When he straightened his shoulders to stare straight at the lieutenant, something about the ease with which he dismissed the other officers left Chekov certain Alion assumed him to be party leader. "I am Alion, the Speaker to Fishes."

Chekov wondered if these were the same fishes who didn't answer when the Kitka asked permission to kill them.

"I'm Lieutenant Commander Uhura." Voice pleasant with friendliness, Uhura stepped out in front of Chekov—not far enough to panic him, but just far enough to make his hands itch with an urge to pull her back a step. "I speak to other peoples for our leader. This is Lieutenant Chekov." She gestured behind her without turning. Alion's expressionless mask made it impossible to tell if he shifted his gaze even once throughout the exchange. "He and his people provide us with protection when we travel."

Steno pursed his lips and snorted.

Alion nodded, lifting his ivory face to the sky. "You come from houses above the aurora." The English words came through Chekov's translator well behind the sound of the native's throaty ululations. Long pauses disjointed the phrasing, hinting that the translator was having difficulty choosing words and deciphering meanings. "You come to search for your broken airship."

The meaning of that seemed clear enough, though. "You know about the shuttle accident?" Chekov wondered if he should have tried to phrase things more simply when the translator sang back an extended string of verbiage only after a noticeable delay.

Even so, Alion seemed to understand. He lifted one delicate hand to indicate Steno. "Only what he tells me."

"Apparently"—Steno folded his arms with a

business-weary sigh that would have frosted his face-plate had he left it down—"our idiot company pilot landed the shuttle's life-pod in some sort of Kitka ceremonial ground. Alion and his people have been reconsecrating the area all week."

Chekov turned back to Alion, found that the native was still focused on him, waiting. "What about the survivors?" he asked.

Alion offered nothing, but Steno shrugged as though not particularly concerned. "Alion says they saw none—only the explosion where the shuttle went down."

Chekov frowned in irritation. "Can't your native friend speak for himself?"

"Lieutenant!" Uhura's startled exclamation made Chekov glad for their goggles, if only because they protected him from what he was sure was a killing glare from the communications officer.

"No. I understand." Alion put up one hand to placate Uhura, his dispassionate translator voice giving no clue as to whether he felt anger or amusement or irritation at this treatment. "I have lived with humans at the equator, so I know some of how they think. Lieutenant Chekov believes some man must always be to blame for things that happen, so he wishes I should prove myself blameless." Stepping away from Steno, Alion brought himself so close that Chekov could see reflections from his own goggles dance light patterns on the Kitka's ivory cheeks. "My hunters saw the flash of your airship's landing. It came to rest in a holy area, and none of my hunters could cross the spirit boundary to go to it."

"What about your holy people? The ones who consecrate the grounds?"

"They have not yet been made ready."

67

"So you haven't made contact with anyone from the accident?" Chekov could almost see the color of the native's eyes inside the shadowed eye slit. "No radio contact? Not even a flare?"

"He told you no!" Steno blurted.

"He's told me nothing." Chekov put out one hand when Steno made as if to come forward, warning him back from where he didn't belong. "Let him answer, Mr. Steno, or I'll have my people remove you so that I don't have to put up with your interruptions."

Steno slapped at the restraining hand, exposed cheeks flushing from more than wind when his blow had little effect on Chekov's barrier. "I'm not afraid of you."

"That's your problem."

"Listen, you pompous little son of—"

Mister Steno!" Uhura flashed forward to snatch Chekov's extended wrist. He let her push his arm back to his side, recognizing her stern grip as a reprimand, although she kept her face and voice directed at Steno. "If you're unhappy with how Lieutenant Chekov conducts an interview, then I ask you to express your opinions in a polite and professional manner, or not at all." The brief tightening of her fingers on his wrist obviously said, *And you, too!* "Am I understood?"

Steno slapped his faceplate back into place—not specifically an answer, but a retreat, at least, from what Chekov could tell. The lieutenant, meanwhile, kept silent. Uhura would no doubt have plenty to say to him as soon as they weren't in front of civilian personnel, and he was perfectly willing to wait for that lecture.

"If we're finished here," Uhura went on, releasing Chekov so she could chafe her hands against her arms, "can we go someplace a little warmer to finish our discussion?"

Steno fidgeted openly, kicking his heel into the ice to watch the spray of glittering shards it rained across his shadow. Alion simply waited, blind ivory face looking at nothing, while Chekov's stomach knotted with worry. "Mr. Steno?" he prodded.

The sound of Chekov's voice seemed to remind Steno that his job was to be decisive and impervious, not to sulk like a four-year-old. Clasping his hands behind his back, he stated bluntly, "Before they take us to their village, you'll have to hand over your phasers."

That was easy enough to deal with, at least. Chekov crossed his arms. "No."

Alion actually responded in what Chekov almost recognized as surprise, jerking his chin as though to avoid a sudden blow.

"You must understand." Uhura patted the phaser on her hip. "These things are our only means of protection."

Alion made a harsh sniffing noise, and a curl of steam feathered past the bottom of his mask. "I thought he was your protection." He pointed a slim finger at Chekov.

Uhura glanced up at the lieutenant, hesitating. "These things belong to him," she said at last, obviously thinking carefully before saying each word. "The way those harpoons belong to your men."

"He knows what they are," Chekov said, peering at Alion. "He lived at the equator, worked around technology."

Alion answered Uhura as though Chekov had not interrupted. "Harpoons are for fishing," the Kitka told her. "For hunting, for food. Our village will gift you with all the food you need—nothing and no one can harm you if you stay with us." He fluttered impatient fingers at the phaser under her hand. "These weapons are not necessary."

Very aware of the dozen native harpoons still surrounding them, Chekov touched the casing of his own weapon behind the cover of his folded arms. "Then why do you have to take them from us?"

Steno brought his hands together in front of his waist. "It's a trust thing, Lieutenant—something you wouldn't understand." He shot a quick look at Uhura before she could say anything, and added, "I was polite."

Chekov still wanted to tear Steno's voice mike out if he did one more thing to undermine negotiations.

"Our spirits do not allow us to bring another tribe's hunters onto our holy grounds." Alion kept his face close to Chekov's, ignoring Steno in favor of fingering the hilt of his knife in mimicry of the lieutenant's uneasy gesture. "We cannot purify you to travel to our holy places to find your missing crewmen if you carry your weapons."

Without being able to see eyes or even hear a real voice, Chekov couldn't tell how much of Alion's words and mannerisms should be taken as a threat. He decided that being accused of unfair paranoia was preferable to overlooking dangers just because he wasn't certain.

"Howard." He waited for his second-in-command to slip up beside him, then unclipped his phaser and slapped it into Howard's palm. Alion's mask shifted position ever so slightly, following the path of the weapon. "Stay with Tenzing and Publicker," Chekov went on, not taking his eyes off the native. "I'll go with Lieutenant Commander Uhura—"

"No." Uhura pulled her own phaser from her belt, checked its charge, and handed it across to Alion. "We're not splitting up the party."

Chekov nearly lunged in front of her to intercept the transaction. "Commander—"

"Lieutenant." She put the back of her hand to his chest, an ages-old signal to halt, and Chekov was forced to stand maddeningly immobile while Alion took the gun and slipped it into some carry place beneath his cover of feathers. "If I was safe enough with only you and no phasers, I'll be plenty safe with *four* of you and no phasers." She clicked off her outside mike and added over their private channel, "We don't even know if the phasers will work down here—Scotty said he wasn't certain."

"That isn't the point."

"That's entirely the point." Steno cocked his chin a fraction higher when Chekov shot a sharp glare in his direction, assuming he knew their full conversation, although he'd only heard Chekov's part of it. "Begging Federation Starship Security's pardon"—he echoed Chekov's earlier platitude with a sneer—"but your lieutenant commander's right. We're not going into a combat zone. We've sent visitors to the Kitka at least a million times in the last ten years, and—every time—we've complied with their religious tenets and walked among them as honored guests."

"Have they always taken your phasers?" Chekov asked.

Steno sketched a little shrug, obviously a little put off by the question. "Not until recently. But I don't see how that matters. They still haven't cooked us for dinner, or shrunken our heads, or anything else similarly dramatic."

Chekov considered suggesting that Steno could stand to have his head shrunken, but bit back the comment to avoid igniting the already volatile feelings between them. "In the past," he said reasonably, "you haven't been among them searching for shipwrecked personnel."

"Missing personnel don't affect how much I trust them," Steno countered, "any more than standing here arguing brings you one step closer to finding those people." He appealed to Uhura, hands outspread in hopeless submission. "Alion won't budge on this matter, believe me."

Uhura nodded, her breath filter hissing on a tiny sigh. "Lieutenant, give him your phaser."

Her acceptance of the conditions struck Chekov like a physical blow. "Sir . . ." He stiffened beside her, bringing his hands to his sides and schooling what he could of the annoyance from his voice. "I would rather not."

"I think that's obvious." She lifted her goggles to squint first at Chekov, then across at Alion. "They'll give the phasers back when we leave. Yes?" Alion nodded slowly, and Uhura echoed his gesture with faint smile creases crinkling at the corners of her dark eyes. When Chekov didn't move right away, she turned her gaze back up to him. "I can make it a direct order, if you want me to."

For an instant he thought about going on record as objecting to her decision, then clenched his jaw with disgust that he'd even considered that course of action. The responsibility for what he did was his, and he refused to shirk that responsibility by either lodging some formal complaint or by forcing Uhura to pull rank. If he had more to go on than an abstract gut feeling, even her direct order couldn't compel him to surrender their weapons—he would do what he thought best for the safety of the party, and deal with the consequences later. With no concrete threat before them, though, he couldn't justify disobedience, and so had no choice but to comply with his commanding officer's wishes before she was forced to turn them into law.

Turning to Howard, he collected back his phaser, then tugged the ensign's weapon from his belt as well. "Go get the others' phasers," he said, his voice as neutral and even as possible. "Bring them here to me."

Howard nodded shortly. "Aye, sir."

Steno chuckled as Howard trotted between the other two guards, gathering up both their phasers and extra power cells. "Well, Lieutenant Chekov, what a pleasant surprise."

Chekov looked around to find the station commander drumming his fingers together with unconcealed satisfaction. "You almost had me convinced you hadn't a reasonable bone in your body," Steno purred. "Perhaps this trip won't be a total loss after all."

Chekov didn't need a warning from Uhura to know he should keep his mouth shut. Still, he saw her head angle to glance over at him as he took the phasers from Howard and handed them across into Alion's waiting hands. The negligent ease with which Alion signaled two of the waiting natives forward to take charge of the weapons made Chekov's stomach ache.

"Many thanks." Alion turned back to Uhura with a deep, reverent bow. "Now we go to our village and make you ready to meet our gods." He pivoted to face his people, one hand circling the air above his head, and the group sprang into motion with a burble of untranslatable sound.

While Steno's people labored to secure their gear for transport, Chekov motioned Tenzing to bring the *Enterprise* gravsled into line with the column Alion's people had already begun to form. He kept himself close to Uhura's side while supervising the lineup, serving as sentinel until Howard could take over and leave him free to shadow Alion. When they finally fell into step beside Tenzing and the gravsled, Chekov thumbed off his outside mike and touched the insulation suit communicator by his ear. "You know," he commented privately to Uhura, "where I come from, 'going to meet your gods' usually entails some kind of dying."

Uhura laughed, punching him on the arm in friendly admonition. "Don't be so gloomy. Sometimes, I think you'd consider your own mother a danger to starship security."

"My mother never asked me to give up my phaser."

"Maybe she should have." She angled her head up at him in a gesture he assumed meant she was smiling behind all her insulation suit gear. "You're being paranoid again."

He wasn't sure how to tell her that his greatest fear of all was that he wasn't paranoid enough.

Chapter Five

To Uhura's eyes, the Kitka village looked no different from any of the other mounded hills of ice Alion had led them through for the last few hours. The fading arctic sunset painted the west face with rose-violet streaks of light, leaving the other sides charcoaled with shadows. It wasn't until one of the Kitka hunters lifted his face shield and let out a fluting cry that she could see the stir of movement in one of those shadows.

The dark patch resolved into an ice-carved doorway as they came closer, a small cluster of fur-clad Kitka climbing out of it. They called back across the ice, a questioning note clear in the rise of their high-pitched voices.

"Uhura, can *you* tell what they're saying?" Chekov's voice sounded oddly metallic through her communicator, distorted by the static-filled distance between them. The security chief had kept pace with

Alion on the long walk from their landing site, staying so close that he could have been a thin, dark shadow cast by the native's paler bulk. Steno trudged a half meter behind them, eyes trained on the uneven ground. He didn't seem to have heard Chekov's question. Uhura guessed that Chekov had turned his voice mike off so the Kitka wouldn't know he was talking.

"My translator didn't pick up anything definite," she replied. Howard glanced at her, his goggles a shimmering bright spot against the dark expanse of ice behind him. He'd stayed about as close to her as Chekov had to Alion, on what Uhura suspected were direct orders from his chief. "I'm increasing sensitivity on my unit. I'll let you know if that helps."

"Right."

The cries across the ice cut off abruptly as Alion answered with a long, falling howl, eerily similar to the radio interference generated by Nordstral's auroras. Uhura wondered if the natives had actually picked up the purely electromagnetic signal. Was it possible the Kitka were even more in tune with Nordstral's environment than her reference materials hinted? Once again, though, her translator stayed stubbornly silent. She let out her breath in a quiet sigh of frustration.

"They may just be exchanging voice signals, sir." Howard must have heard her through the open communicator channel. "After all, we didn't have any trouble translating when they talked to us before."

"I know," Uhura agreed. "But Alion was being careful to speak slowly then, so our translators could distinguish each word and hear them clearly. If their normal speech pattern is as rapid as this"—a chorus of rising and falling wails now volleyed back and forth between the villagers and the returning party—"the translator may not be able to separate out individual words." She turned one gloved hand upward to indicate her helplessness. "I'd hate to think we could only translate their language when they wanted us to."

"You'd hate it?" This time it was Chekov's voice in her ear, a distant growl through the static. "If we can't even understand—" He cut off abruptly when Uhura saw Steno close the distance between them. A moment later the security chief spoke again. "Commander, the planetary officer wants to go inside the village for the night. I think you'd better come talk to him."

"I'll be right over." Uhura took a deep breath, hoping Steno would have enough sense to be polite to Chekov. Her second-in-command was getting understandably short on patience with him. "Coming with me, Mr. Howard?"

The tall security guard glanced over at the swarm of Kitka villagers heading out toward the gravsleds. "With your permission, sir, I'd like to go help Publicker and Tenzing guard our gear."

"Good idea." One of the small fur-clad natives was already poking with childlike curiosity at the Nordstral sled, ignoring the company guards' attempt to shoo him away. The gentle Kitka seemed to have no fear of Steno and his men, although Uhura noticed that they parted ahead of her like startled fish when she walked through them. Natives clustered around the *Enterprise* sled in a cautious halo of windswept fur, pointing and whistling to each other in what sounded like surprise. None of them made any attempt to approach the gear, however.

". . . I'm telling you, the equipment will work better down in the tunnels." Steno's sudden bellow dragged Uhura's attention away from the natives and back to her own party. The planetary officer was glaring down at Chekov, who was busy blocking the taller man's access to the ice-carved entrance. She bit her lip and hurried forward. "Can't you get it through your foam-insulated head that there's nothing to be afraid of here?"

"Mr. Steno." The intensity of Chekov's accent told Uhura he was probably talking through clenched teeth. "May I remind you that we still have a missing research team out on the ice sheet? I don't see how sleeping unprotected inside a native village is going to help us locate them!"

"That's because you're an idiot," said Steno unwisely. Uhura saw muscles jump in Chekov's shoulders as he clenched his fists, and she hurried forward to put a hand on his arm. It felt rock-hard beneath her fingers. Steno switched his unshielded glare to her, his cheeks mottled with frost and anger. "Lieutenant Commander, would you please explain to your chief goon that electronic equipment functions better above minus thirty degrees than below it?"

Uhura winced and quickly tapped her voice mike off, dialing her communicator to a coded channel that Steno couldn't overhear. "Chekov, he's right." Static crackled in her ear as she paused, waiting for a reply. "Even a ten-degree difference will enhance our reception by a hundredfold. It could make all the difference in hearing a distress call from the shuttle."

"Sir." The strain in Chekov's voice when he finally spoke surprised Uhura. "I understand that, but I still don't think we should enter this village. Not with our phasers in the natives' control and no assurance that our translators will allow us to speak with them."

Uhura glanced over at Alion, waiting with stoic patience for them to follow him down into the village.

His mantle of feathers stirred in the evening wind, with a faint sound like chattering teeth. "I think you're overestimating the danger, Lieutenant." Chekov started to protest, but she overrode him. "However, I'll grant you the right to be cautious. You'll keep our security guards out here on the ice, while I help Mr. Steno set up his communications center down in the village. If we encounter any problems, I'll let you know."

"But, sir . . ." Chekov sounded distinctly unhappy with this arrangement. "You're the one we're here to guard!"

"No, Lieutenant." Uhura shook her head, giving him a little push away from the doorway. He didn't move. "You're here to guard all of us—including the shuttle survivors we were sent to find. And our best chance of doing that is to let Mr. Steno into the village."

The security chief looked down at her, his masked and goggled face expressionless, but he yielded to her push and stepped aside. Steno gave him a scornful look on his way past, signaling his men to come with him. Chekov caught Uhura by the wrist when she turned to follow.

"I'm sending a guard down there with you," he said grimly. "Don't argue with me about it."

Uhura gave him a concerned glance, although she knew he couldn't see it. "I'm not the one arguing, Chekov." One of the Nordstral men brushed by her, equipment case balanced on his shoulder. Two fur-clad Kitka danced around him with excited whistles, so tiny they had to be children. Uhura watched them with a smile. "I really don't see anything to worry about."

"I know." Chekov hadn't noticed the children. He

was staring at something over Uhura's shoulder, and when she turned to look, Alion ducked away from the doorway to disappear deeper inside. "That's what worries me."

Soroya had been under way for approximately half an hour when Nuie returned to Kirk and McCoy with another crewman. While the captain was escorted to the bridge to meet with Mandeville, McCoy followed Nuie to *Soroya*'s sickbay.

The door to the medical section stood open when McCoy and Nuie arrived. "This is our infirmary," the first mate explained, ushering the Federation officer in ahead of him. "Dr. Muhanti's probably in back, in his lab. Come with me."

McCoy looked about as they crossed the room, comparing it to the sharp, clean lines of the *Enterprise* infirmary and finding it adequate, although lacking in what he considered a "healing" atmosphere. He was proud of his sickbay, proud that it didn't have the notoriously sterile smell and look of so many hospitals on so many planets. Here the walls were bland, the riveting undisguised by color or wall hanging. The few tall beds were narrow and gray-sheeted and looked hard as hell.

"Dr. Muhanti?"

"One moment, Nuie."

McCoy stopped just behind the short first mate's shoulder and looked into the lab. Vaguely familiar experiments ran at two of the three work stations. Sticky-looking dried areas spotted the lab table, and used beakers and test tubes layered with crud were piled near the sterilizer. A dark-haired man perched on a stool at the center work station, his back to the door and his hands in his hair. McCoy at first thought they'd caught the doctor in a moment of frustration, and felt a pang of sympathy. He knew how hard it would be for him if the *Enterprise* crew was suddenly afflicted and he could find no way to help them. Then he noticed the odd, systematized way the doctor felt at his head, and he frowned in puzzlement.

Muhanti abruptly pivoted the stool to face them. Fingers still probing the depths of his hair, the Indian doctor blinked at McCoy with surprise on his dark-featured face. "Who is this?"

"Dr. Muhanti, Dr. McCoy of the Federation starship *Enterprise.* He and Captain Kirk have come to aid us."

"Indeed." Was there veiled malice in that tone, or was it just McCoy's imagination? Muhanti's face abruptly split into a friendly, but almost condescending, smile. "How nice of the Federation to notice us." His hands dropped into his lap. "You look confused, Dr. McCoy, by my actions. Could it be that the knowledgeable Federation has yet to discover the new science of phrenology?"

Caution alone halted McCoy's derisive snort before he could vent it. This was becoming strange. "Phrenology?" he queried politely, mind running scattergun.

"Ah! It's somewhat comforting to know that the Federation is not first in all things." He took a pose that put McCoy in mind of several of his professors back when he'd been a lowly first-year med student. "Phrenology is an analytical method based upon the fact that certain mental faculties and character traits are indicated by the configurations of the skull. I have mapped the contours of my own skull as an experiment and found the science to be highly exacting in its diagnosis. I intend to use it as the basis of my research

81

into the aberrant behavior of my fellow crewmen. Within a relatively short amount of time, I believe I'll have a cure for their various psychoses."

"Really?" McCoy replied dryly.

"Do I detect a tone of disbelief, my good colleague? I find that skeptics are often those most afraid of what a new science will illuminate. Perhaps you'd allow me a small experiment?" He stepped toward McCoy, hands lifting to feel the doctor's skull.

McCoy was saved by Captain Mandeville's voice over the intercom. "First Mate Nuie to the bridge. Bring Dr. McCoy with you. I think he'd like to see this."

McCoy looked curiously at Nuie. "See what?"

The first mate was grinning. "I think I know what it is, and she's right." He bowed shortly to Dr. Muhanti. "If you'll excuse us."

McCoy spread his hands wide in mock apology. "Duty calls."

"Of course," Muhanti sneered down his nose. "Perhaps another time." He turned away, fingers already worming back under his hair, and McCoy followed Nuie into the corridor.

McCoy resisted bringing up Muhanti's strange behavior. Maybe this was normal for the Indian. Maybe all the crew was skewed a little left of center by whatever had caused the abnormal behavior in those crew taken up to *Curie*. He didn't want to bring it up unless Nuie did so first, and since he didn't, McCoy prudently kept his mouth closed.

He followed the silent crewman through the harvester and to the bridge. Here, as elsewhere in the ship, areas for personnel had been trimmed as much as possible to allow maximum cargo space for harvested plankton. McCoy gave the crew points for maintaining what sanity they could during long dives in such cramped quarters.

McCoy spied Kirk immediately and moved among the colorfully clothed Nordstral employees to his captain's side. "What's this all about?" he murmured.

Kirk shook his head. "I don't know." He didn't appear worried, and that alone was enough to make McCoy relax his cautious stance somewhat.

Kirk's hazel eyes scanned the viewscreen, and McCoy followed his gaze. Water granulated with tiny floating particles of sediment or something like it surrounded the ship, lit by the sub's running lights to a murky green. An amazing abundance of sea life flourished here under the ice sheet. Beyond the reach of the lights was a darkness even deeper than that found in space. McCoy understood why the ocean had truly been mankind's last unexplored frontier.

Kirk's head tocked sideways toward a young woman hunched over a radar screen, one hand to her tiny earphone. "They've picked up something, but I don't know what it is," he said quietly. "Nobody seems upset, though."

That was true. In fact, everyone seemed slightly excited. McCoy's eyes hunted the murky depths to no avail. "Is it always so dark?"

"Ah, yes." Captain Mandeville strolled across the cramped bridge to stand between them. "Under the ice sheet it's very dark, indeed, Dr. McCoy. That's the seaman's night. Only for us, night lasts a good deal longer than you're used to." She chuckled.

McCoy couldn't see what was so damned amusing. He'd almost managed to forget they were underwater, let alone submerged under several meters of ice. Now the reality of their situation returned and a shiver of fear took a meandering stroll from his ankles to the top of his head. He suppressed the desire to reach up and feel if his hair was standing on end.

"Where is it?" Mandeville spoke over her shoulder to the radar tech.

"Dead on, Captain. It's holding in one spot, so it must be a mater." She looked over her shoulder, face lit expectantly. "If we up the floods, we should be able to see something."

"Hit floods," Mandeville said.

"Aye-aye, Captain." A Kitka crewman several years younger than Nuie shifted at his station and flicked a bank of switches. The floodlights illuminating the ship's path suddenly brightened considerably, banishing the darkness for several hundred meters ahead. Something writhed in the near distance. Something large and looking like nothing McCoy had ever seen before. At the same moment, an eerie ululation reached them. The throaty cry rose and fell, ending in a ponderous sigh of sound.

McCoy's eyes bugged. "What the hell's *that?*" he gasped, grabbing Kirk's arm.

"That," said Mandeville dryly, "is a kraken."

"No." Nuie's voice was reverent. "That is god."

The Kitka village was cut from tunnels barely taller and wider than the Kitka themselves. For once, Uhura's smallness was an advantage. She took some unrepentant pleasure in watching Steno try to navigate the narrow warren, his curses booming off the icy walls when he banged against them. There wasn't much illumination beyond the glow of their small flashlights and the occasional flicker of a native oil pot.

"What are they burning in those things, Tenzing?" Uhura asked softly as they passed another of the small lights. A drift of spicy fragrance stole through her air filter to tickle at the back of her throat. Beside her, the security guard Chekov had assigned her pointed a tricorder at the pot and called up a quick analysis.

"Some kind of fish oil, sir." Tenzing's voice sounded surprised. "It sure doesn't smell like fish to me."

"No." Uhura glanced at the fur-clad Kitka walking behind them, wondering if the translator was actually working. She'd set it for maximum sensitivity and was trying to choose her words carefully, but the Kitka equivalent still came out in unsteady rushes and stops. "What kind of fish makes this oil?"

The small native looked up at her, then ducked away from her glance with a muffled warble of sound. The translator hummed, then supplied a single word: "Kraken."

"Kraken?" Uhura blinked. The word conjured up an image of mythical monsters from Nordic legend, not an alien arctic fish. "What is a kraken?"

The native looked up at her again, face and gender hidden behind a plain bone face mask. Still, uncertainty was easy to read in the tilt of the native's head. This time the warble was longer, and deliberately slow.

"Kraken hunter under ice," said the translator. "Kraken eyes like your eyes."

"My eyes?" Uhura repeated, puzzled. The little Kitka couldn't possibly see her eyes through the reflective goggles over them. Then she laughed, realizing that the native couldn't know there *were* eyes under that bright shine. "Those aren't my eyes," she said, and pulled off the goggles.

A startled wailing sound was her reward. Uhura squinted against the bite of frigid air, wondering if she'd managed to frighten the little native even more with the sight of her dark skin. The Kitka answered her by pouncing forward and patting at her arm excitedly. "Kraken eyes gone," said the translator, after sorting through the native's rapid whistling squeaks. "Kraken eyes gone!"

"Yes." Uhura glanced over at Tenzing, unsure whether the security guard's less complex translator could handle the Kitka's sudden rush of speech. "The goggles seem to remind the natives of something scary, Tenzing. Would you mind taking yours off, too?"

"Not at all, sir." Tenzing lifted her goggles, revealing Asiatic eyes and pale brown skin. She looked curious. "Is it this kraken-thing, sir?"

"Apparently." Uhura looked back at the small native standing next to them in time to see the bone face mask fall from a young girl's eager face. Her eyes were dark blue and thickly lashed above oddly flattened cheekbones. The coppery tone of her skin deepened to amber around her lips and eyes, paling upward into a mane of shining silver hair. "Is this better?"

"Better," the young Kitka said, and touched her mittened fingers to her lips in a gesture of what looked like thanks. Then she reached up to pat curiously at the reflective plastic of Uhura's goggles. She seemed to have no shyness now that recognizable eyes could be seen. "Kraken eyes not real?"

Uhura smiled back at her, delighted. "The kraken eyes are a mask, just like your mask." She reached out to touch the thin bone plate now dangling around the girl's strong throat. "They keep the wind out of my face."

Amber lips parted in a snow-bright smile. "Mask

for going outside," she agreed. "Not wear mask inside."

"No." Uhura glanced around as they turned a corner and emerged into a junction of several tunnels. The roof was higher here, allowing Steno and his men to move around a little more freely. They promptly began unboxing their communications console. Uhura frowned and moved over to watch them, her little native friend skipping beside her.

"Mr. Steno, is this where you usually set up your equipment?" she asked quietly. The two Nordstral guards emptied the last of the insulated boxes and left, presumably to bring in the rest of their gear. Most of the accompanying natives went with them, except for two of Alion's harpoon-bearing hunters and Uhura's small friend, who still hovered by her arm. Tenzing was making brief forays into the darkness of the surrounding tunnels, taking some kind of measurements with her tricorder.

The planetary officer grunted. "It's the only place in this damned snake nest where I can sit without hitting my head on the roof. What's wrong with that?"

Uhura glanced at the dark mouths of tunnels gaping in silent emptiness around them. "It doesn't seem very well protected," she said at last, feeling as if some of Chekov's suspicions had rubbed off on her. "For the equipment," she added hurriedly, as Steno glared down at her. "Won't there be a lot of natives coming back and forth through here?"

"No, of course not." He snorted and bent to plug his amplifier units into the main receiver. "Alion will tell the other natives to leave us alone."

Uhura bent to help him run the cable to his transmitting disk, her slender fingers untangling the cold wire faster than his bulky gloves could manage.

She got an ungracious grunt in response. "Is Alion the Kitka's leader?"

"He must be—they all seem to dislike him enough." Steno slid a packing case over to make a seat in front of the console, then dropped onto it and began to warm up the central processor without even bothering to consult her. Uhura felt her lips tighten involuntarily. She was the communications specialist here, not this glorified corporate policeman! Now she knew how Chekov must have felt when Steno ignored his security precautions.

"Personally, I'm not sure the Kitka really have leaders," Steno continued absently, watching the monitor spit out its start-up codes. "That's one of the reasons they're so damned hard to cut a deal with. You talk to one group and think you've got everything straight, then some other group comes in and gets hysterical because you're walking around on their sacred icebergs."

Uhura stifled an urge to reach out and slap off Steno's translator, which was still emitting its unsteady equivalent of native speech. She glanced down at the Kitka girl and saw that she looked puzzled but not particularly offended. With luck, Steno's rudeness was being lost in translation.

"Then what is Alion?" she inquired, keeping her voice soft with an effort.

"Some kind of religious guru, I think. Like a witch doctor or a shaman. Maybe he hears their confessions and makes them do penance, I don't know." Steno scowled as the communications console buzzed and flickered an error message at him. "Damn those idiots! They forgot to put the signal equalizer in. I'd better go make sure they don't leave it sitting out on the sled."

Uhura stepped back as he surged angrily out of his chair, making the little Kitka skitter out of his way. The planetary officer scowled when he saw her. "Don't let her touch anything!" he snapped at Uhura as she started to speak. "And don't you touch anything, either. This isn't Starfleet equipment."

Uhura frowned but stayed silent until he left, the Kitka hunters trailing after him like quiet drifts of snow. She glanced down at the young native girl, who was watching her with wide eyes, then up at Tenzing, who had come back into the main room in time to hear the last exchange. "If I'm not allowed to touch anything," Uhura said, thoughtfully tapping on a small box hidden in the clutter of unwrapped insulation, "I suppose that means I can't install this while he's gone." She saw Tenzing's puzzled look and added, "It's his signal equalizer."

Tenzing's eyes crinkled into slits a moment before her gruff laughter filled the frigid air. Uhura burst into laughter with her, letting out her frustration with the shared joke.

The Kitka girl made a quick hooting noise that sounded remarkably like laughter, too, and she tugged at Uhura's hand. "Time for dinner now."

"Is it?" It certainly was for her, Uhura thought. It had been a long time since she'd eaten on the ship. She wondered if Chekov would remember to eat something, with no one but his well-trained guards around to remind him.

The native girl tugged at her again, harder. "Time for dinner," she insisted. "Kraken Eyes come home with Nhym."

Uhura glanced up at Tenzing with a smile. "I seem to have a dinner invitation. Are you in the mood for raw fish?"

"Uh, no, sir. But I've got the lieutenant's orders." Tenzing slung her tricorder over her shoulder. "Good thing I remembered to bring ration packs."

McCoy canted his head back to look at Nuie, torn between wanting an explanation and the desire to watch the magnificent creature suspended in the murky depths ahead of them. "I beg your pardon?"

Mandeville laughed. "Gentlemen, meet the planet's largest predator. When Nordstral Pharmaceuticals first came here, the initial survey crews saw these creatures and wanted to learn what they could about them, so they asked the Kitka. The natives told them how their heroes dream of coming back to life as pieces of 'god,' and how the planet punishes wrongdoers by sending them this visitor in the night. The closest the translators could come for a human word was 'kraken.'" Her mouth twitched. "I guess it's as good a word as any."

McCoy slid into a vacant seat at the console and intently watched the creature as it circled. It was impossible to divine its true color under the harsh glare of the floodlights. It might have been gray or brown or the same green as the water. The color was milky pale over the length of its body, unmarked by variation except around the head. The skin didn't appear leathery, but rather like that which whales were supposed to have had. The animal was huge, nearly the size of the harvester, as far as he could tell at this distance and with the weird properties of water coming into play. Its head was small, suspended on a long, graceful neck. Large, iridescent eyes sat close together on the front of the head, above two slitted nostrils and in front of what appeared to be gill-like membranes of brilliant white that resembled stiff, water-buoyed feathers. The four limbs were short and broad, but tipped with claws. The tail was short, broad, flat, and set perpendicular to the body's general orientation.

"It's amazing," Kirk murmured, and McCoy became aware once again of his surroundings. "What does it eat?"

"Kitka," someone replied, and the crew laughed.

Nuie shook his head as though with long tolerance. "They like to make jokes about it, Captain Kirk, but you don't see anyone going for a swim, now, do you?" He glanced around the bridge, and the crew shifted and looked aside, embarrassed. "The kraken feed on the same sea creatures as the Kitka. It may be the largest predator on Nordstral, but the Kitka are the strongest." He said it with great pride.

"I've got another blip, Captain!" The radar tech's excited yelp captured everyone's attention. "Looks like the show is on!"

"The show?" Kirk queried over the rising murmur of the crew's voices.

"Mating fight," Mandeville replied, excitement coloring her tone.

"Mating *fight?*" McCoy asked, unsure he'd heard her correctly.

She nodded and took the seat beside him, motioning for Kirk to take another. "Quick biology lesson. Kraken are water breathers. They can also breathe air for short periods of time, usually when they're busy munching Kitka. They bear their young underwater, and the young are independent from birth. In fact, they have a set period of time—something between six and twelve hours, as we've judged it—to get the hell away from Mommy or be eaten."

A sound was building outside the ship. McCoy felt

it first like a pressure deep within his ears. It grew, becoming fully audible, like the roar of an approaching comber. Something huge and pale flashed by above the ship, arrowing straight for the kraken, which had stopped its haphazard circling and turned to face the newcomer.

"Kraken spend the majority of their lives asexual, androgenous," Mandeville continued. "Until mating rapture strikes. Then they meet in pairs and battle to the death."

"Doesn't that kind of forestall any type of mating?" Kirk asked, eyes intently following the converging pair.

"The victor becomes female, Captain, and steals what she needs." Mandeville leaned forward. "Here they go."

The roar of the meeting leviathans was enough to make McCoy cover his ears. Double-hinged jaws gaped wide, whipping about on lean necks like lethal snakes, seeking a stranglehold or a major vein. Dimly, he heard Mandeville call for a full stop at a safe distance.

The water roiled where the two giants collided, obscuring the view. Clawed appendages raked unprotected sides and underbellies. The kraken twined their necks, lurching from side to side in an effort to snap vertebrae. One pulled back in an effort to improve its hold, and the other slashed forward, using its opponent's weight against it. They collided hard, rolling in the swell, and were suddenly obscured by a brilliant blooming, like an underwater flower. Bright arterial blood swirled in the saltwater as the victor sliced her enemy from neck base to tail and dragged forth a large, yellow sack. She rent the sack and gobbled the contents greedily, then caught the dead kraken in her claws before it drifted away on the tide, and began to feed.

Mandeville's hand clapping down to dim the floods startled McCoy, but it was the strident whistle over the ship's communication board that made him jump. The communications tech listened for a moment, then turned to the group of officers with confusion on his round Kitka features. "Captain Kirk, I'm receiving a transmission from the *Enterprise*. It's secured on a Priority One channel, sir, and flagged emergency."

Kirk exchanged looks with McCoy. "Put it through," he ordered, striding toward the comm station.

"Captain, this is Spock."

McCoy moved up quietly behind Kirk, not liking this particular lack of expression in the Vulcan's voice.

"Spock," Kirk said in acknowledgment, "fancy hearing from you. What's the matter?" So he hadn't missed the stillness in Spock's voice, either.

"Captain, I am afraid I have grave news." Spock paused, and McCoy glanced over at Kirk in time to see the captain steel himself. "We have just been informed by orbital station *Curie* that the Nordstral shuttle bearing the remainder of the *Enterprise* landing party exploded while in transit."

Kirk's jaw hardened, his eyes very bright. "Exploded." It wasn't even a question. "You're certain?"

"Indeed. At this time, we do not know if it was on its way to the northern rendezvous point or returning. It is unknown if there are survivors."

McCoy didn't realize he'd sat until he felt the chair's hard seat under him. His entire body felt numb, the way a foot does if you sit on it too long. It seemed a long while before his eyes sought Kirk.

The captain stood with his arms held rigid at his sides. The muscles of his shoulders and back stood out in relief under the close fit of his white shirt, knotting and relaxing like a fist. "Have you attempted to raise Chekov or Uhura?"

"I have. No contact has been made."

"But the planet's magnetic interference is devilish, sir," Scott's voice interjected, strained and emotional against Spock's stoic report. "Being unable to reach them might not mean a thing."

"I know that, Scotty." Kirk's voice sounded husky. "Thank you." He took a deep breath then, shoulders pulling back in a stance McCoy knew all too well. "Spock, I want Scotty to start the necessary modifications to one of the *Enterprise*'s shuttles. I want a team at the crash site as soon as possible."

"May I remind the captain that Lieutenant Commander Uhura already headed such a rescue team for another shuttle's crew?"

"I hear you, Spock. But I won't just leave them." He pursed his lips in fierce thought. "Two shuttles in such short order . . . We can't rule out internal sabotage. I want the next shuttle to come from our fleet so we can guarantee its integrity. Besides . . ." A tiny, sad smile flashed across his face. "Nordstral Pharmaceuticals doesn't have Mr. Scott."

"Thank you, sir." Scott's broad accent came over the comm. "I'll do my best."

"You always do, Scotty. Keep me posted on when that shuttle's ready. And I want updates on any information you get."

"I shall do so. Spock out."

94

McCoy watched Kirk close his eyes, hands wound into fists of frustration. He thought the captain would say something, or the *Soroya*'s crew would do something to shatter the illusion and make it all not so real. Instead, the silence on the tiny bridge only grew, until it finally made a sound all its own.

Chapter Six

NHYM'S HOME proved to be nothing more than a deep alcove hollowed along one tunnel wall, curtained with the leather skins of sea mammals and lit with several oil-pot lamps. The spicy smell of kraken oil filled the enclosed space, masking over the muskier scent of unwashed Kitka. Uhura took a step inside the curtained area, Tenzing following cautiously at her heels, then stopped to blink sudden moisture from her eyes. The faint trapped warmth of the oil fires had melted the frost off her eyebrows and lashes.

Nhym threw back her fur hood and shook water off her hair, the thick silver strands falling into place as neatly as a seal's pelt when she was done. The three Kitka inside the alcove greeted her with a chorus of rising trills, although their voices sounded thin and whispery compared to Nhym's. "Granddaughter," provided the translator for two of them, and "Great-granddaughter" for the last, a tiny huddled figure in smoke-dark furs.

"Grandmother, Grandfather, Great-grandmother!" Nhym skipped around a long, carved-bone table to pat affectionately at each of them. "Guests come for dinner! People from above the aurora who wear kraken eyes for masks!"

The two Kitka kneeling behind the table looked up at Uhura and Tenzing, surprise turning to delight in their pale blue eyes. Their response was so fast and excited that Uhura's translator couldn't catch it, but the slower whistle from the huddled older woman came through clearly. "Alion's guests?"

The distaste in the old woman's voice was obvious, and Nhym gave Uhura an uncertain look. "We prefer to be the guests of all the Kitka," the communications officer said in reply, hoping the translator had some way of expressing that. It seemed to work well enough. The oldest Kitka made a fluting sound of satisfaction and rose from her huddle of furs. She moved strongly despite the age that yellowed her face and made her eyes bone-white.

"Welcome, Hunters of Stars. I am Ghyl of Chinit Clan."

"I am Uhura of the starship *Enterprise*." Uhura tried to keep her introduction in the same format. She took a chance and touched her gloved fingers to her lips. "I thank you for sharing your dinner."

"It is our honor," said the old Kitka, her amber lips lifting in a smile that looked a lot like Nhym's. "Please sit at our table. You came with Nordstral's Steno?"

"Yes." Uhura settled herself on the thick leathery skin that covered the floor, folding her legs gracefully beneath her. Tenzing squatted silently beside her, tricorder discreetly scanning the alcove to record the Kitka in it. "We came to look for people from one of our ships. They are lost somewhere on the ice north of here."

Ghyl's answer was a falling wail that sounded grim. "Not good," said the translator after a pause. "The ice sheet hurts too much to hunt on it now."

Uhura wasn't sure how to answer that. Fortunately, Nhym interrupted, pushing a carved bone platter across the table to her. "Special dinner for guests," she said, looking anxious. "Kraken Eyes eat?"

"Um . . ." Uhura looked down at the seaweed-wrapped bundles. Instead of the gleaming raw fish she'd seen them chopping before, these contained translucent blobs of something that glistened like wet gelatin. "What is this?"

"Tail blubber." The young Kitka smiled at her brilliantly. "Very best part of sea mammal!"

Uhura's nose wrinkled despite herself. She heard Tenzing choke over what sounded like a laugh and knew if she refused to eat, Chekov would never let her hear the end of it. She took a deep breath and lifted one quivering bundle.

"Lieutenant Commander Uhura!" The shout came muffled through the skin curtains, but it still sounded urgent. "Lieutenant Commander Uhura, where are you?"

"Here!" She dropped the food and headed for the door, ignoring the fluting cries of the Kitka. Tenzing was already ahead of her, scanning the outside tunnel warily. A pale green insulation suit glimmered at one end. "What's the matter?"

One of Steno's men scuttled toward her, obviously trying to hurry despite the cramped space. "We're getting some kind of signal on the monitor, but Mr. Steno can't make any contact. He wants to know if you can help us."

"Of course I can." Uhura turned back to the alcove and found Nhym already sliding out after her. "I have to go away now." The girl's disappointment showed in her dark blue eyes. "For a little while," Uhura added quickly. "May I come back later?"

"Yes!" The Kitka's answering trill was emphatic. "Nhym comes with you to show the way back."

"All right." Uhura didn't have time to explain that Tenzing's tricorder could have guided them just as easily. She followed the Nordstral guard back to the junction of tunnels where Steno sat glowering at the communications console.

"If you don't mind, Mr. Steno . . ." Uhura pushed past him without waiting for a response and crouched in front of the console. A familiar contact code flickered across the screen and sang in her ear like a mother's call when she picked up the transceiver. "No wonder you couldn't make contact! That's not the shuttle party, that's the *Enterprise.*"

Steno looked disgruntled. "What would your starship be calling us about?"

"I don't know." Her fingers ran across the control panel, automatically adjusting their output from wide surface band to a narrow skyward beam. *"Enterprise,* this is Lieutenant Commander Uhura. Do you read me?"

There was a pause before a familiar calm voice came through the console's falling howl of interference. "We read you clearly, Lieutenant Commander Uhura," said Spock. "And it is gratifying to know that you are still alive."

For some strange reason, the static behind him sounded like Sulu cheering.

"The shuttle exploded?"

When Chekov asked the question, it was in the desperate hope Uhura would laugh and tell him that wasn't what she'd said at all.

Instead, she stood in the open doorway of their dome tent with her hands on a young native girl's shoulders and nodded miserably. "I just got the message from Spock."

Publicker, sitting on the edge of the gravsled next to Howard, looked up from his half-finished dinner with blond brows knit in confusion. "You mean the shuttle we're looking for, don't you?" He had the top of his insulation suit unsealed and peeled back, just like the other men in the tent, and the bright white of his suit's body slip highlighted the muscle tension in his shoulders and neck. "Not our shuttle."

Chekov crumpled together the remainder of his own rations and paced across the tent to jam them into the disposal unit. "She means our shuttle."

"But . . ." Publicker glanced anxiously at Howard, at Uhura, up again at Chekov. "But that means we're stranded."

"Yes, Mr. Publicker." Sighing, Chekov ran both hands through his hair. "We're stranded."

"Only temporarily."

Chekov turned, hands locked behind his neck, and frowned at Uhura. "How temporarily?" He'd allotted a certain amount of extra rations and gear, but not enough to survive on Nordstral indefinitely—not even to attempt a hike to the equator, if the situation came to that.

"Mr. Scott's working on modifications to one of our

shuttles," Uhura explained, making a point, Chekov noticed, to turn a reassuring smile on Publicker. "He thinks we can look forward to a pickup within thirty-two hours."

Howard looked up from policing his own dinner area. "I thought the company shuttles were already modified specifically for use here on Nordstral." He reached over and gathered Publicker's things together with his own. "What's to keep our shuttles from having the same problems?"

Old navigator knowledge filtered to the surface even as Chekov paced the four-stride width of their tent, tallying their options. "Our shuttles have to tolerate warp speeds, so they're better shielded. Nordstral's magnetic disturbances are less likely to disrupt their engines." Not that those magnetic disturbances hadn't already disrupted plenty. Chekov wondered how Steno had reacted to this news, and if the planetary official intended to abort their rescue mission now that his own skin could be in danger. Chekov wouldn't put it past him, and, in fact, more than half expected word to come up at any moment.

"The magnetic fluxes have been a lot worse in the past couple months." One of Steno's young retainers ducked his head past Uhura's so he could look into the tent from where he waited behind her, out in the snow. Pushing his visor away from his face, he glanced among the Starfleet occupants until he caught sight of Chekov to his left, then continued earnestly to the lieutenant, "The Kitka say it's their god, raging in his sleep about some sacrilege. All I know is, the pilots say it didn't used to be this bad. And now, losing two shuttles so close together . . ." He shrugged apologetically, as though the rest were obvious.

Chekov paused in his pacing to look at the boy. He

was half as dark as Uhura, maybe all of nineteen, with a narrow face and huge, soulful brown eyes. He was also the first Nordstral employee to speak civilly to the Starfleet contingent. That in and of itself made him noteworthy. "What's your name?"

"Jimenez, sir. Emilio Jimenez."

He waved the boy inside, catching Uhura's eye to nod her in as well. "Well, there's no sense standing there with the door open, Jimenez. We may not have a shuttle, but we can at least hold onto our heat."

Publicker gave a half-hearted grunt. "Such as it is."

Chekov ignored the ensign's comment. He and Publicker had already had their discussion about what temperature they would keep the tent's interior. Chekov's memories of poorly insulated houses sunk into quagmires of melted permafrost had finally prevailed over Publicker's loving reminiscences of his native California, so the automatic thermal units were set to maintain the tent's air temperature at no higher than ten degrees centigrade. That was positively tropical by Nordstral standards, and less likely to melt them through to the bottom of the ice sheet by morning.

Little native girl still clinging to one hand, Uhura stepped out of Jimenez's way when he turned to seal the doorway. Chekov stood behind Uhura's shoulder to look down at the girl, with her mass of silver hair and curious violet eyes, and found himself suddenly uncomfortable with how the other Kitka might react to one of their children being locked up in a tent filled with unfamiliar human men.

Leaning over Uhura's shoulder, Chekov said quietly into her ear, "Maybe your friend had better wait outside."

Uhura turned to look at him in surprise, her lips

pursed in disapproval and annoyance. "Chekov, she's just a little girl, and she's as cold as the rest of us. She's not going to do anything."

He started to protest that what the little girl might do wasn't his concern, but stopped himself with a sigh. Uhura had spent hours before planetfall studying the Kitka culture, and she'd already been walking among them down below for at least an hour. If there were anything about this situation that might upset the native elders, she was in a better position to know than he. He nodded, smiling down at the little girl when she tipped her head back to blink up at him.

"All right," he said softly to Uhura, "I'm sorry. I didn't mean for it to sound that way."

Uhura reached back to squeeze his arm, smiling to prove he'd been forgiven.

Officers shifted and gear was shoved aside as everyone congregated toward the center of the now-crowded tent, where the automatic thermal put off its soothing waves of gentle warmth. Uhura took a seat on the gravsled between Howard and Publicker, her native companion squatting comfortably at her feet. Jimenez settled himself on their stacked sleeping gear across the thermal from the others, and Chekov—feeling oddly like the family watch dog—sat on the floor to Howard's left, more or less between his people and Jimenez. Warmth from the silent thermal felt good as it soaked through the open front of his insulation suit and into the body slip beneath.

Without being told, Publicker dug out an extra ration pack and tossed it across to Jimenez. The Nordstral employee caught it between both hands with a grin and a sincere, *"Gracias.* The food here isn't exactly what I'm used to."

Uhura only made a little sound of amusement, but

the *Enterprise* security force laughed aloud. "We brought extra," Chekov assured Jimenez, and the young man thanked them again.

Howard, meanwhile, had slipped out one of his breakfast packs and liberated a honey compress to dangle in front of the native girl's nose. She sniffed at it, a bit cautiously, then furrowed her brow with concern when no scent reached her past the airtight seal. Fumbling inside his pushed-back hood, Howard activated his translator and said slowly, "Go ahead— you can eat it."

Chekov watched the girl cross her hands on the flooring between her feet, cocking her head to half watch Howard while his translator struggled with the alien phrasing. Although she tried to keep her wide face expressionless, the lieutenant recognized the sharp brightness of fear in her twilight eyes and felt a pang of regret. The price of eternal vigilance, he thought while Uhura coaxed the girl to take Howard's offering—having native children be as frightened of us as we are distrustful of their elders. He wished they'd have longer to stay with the Kitka, time to learn from them and learn with them so that no side would have to be afraid of the other. Wouldn't Uhura just laugh to hear him thinking that.

A shrill Kitka whistle and the sound of humans laughing called Chekov's attention back to the doings in the tent. Uhura's native friend had apparently divined the workings of the ration air seal and now sat, eyes wide and lips pulled into an amazed smile, while she chewed the first bite off her honey compress.

"See?" Howard reached behind Uhura to swat at Publicker's shoulder, inciting another round of laughter. "Love of sweets is universal. I told you."

Apparently responding to whatever Howard's

translator made of his remark, the little girl broke a fingerful off the compress and passed it over her head to Publicker. He accepted it with a blink of surprise and a short, untranslated, "Thanks." Pieces followed for Uhura and Howard, but when the girl stretched her hand out to offer a clump to Chekov, he only grinned and shook his head. "No, thank you. I'm not hungry."

Chekov saw Uhura roll her eyes, as usual. Apparently, she didn't care whether he'd just finished his dinner; she believed hunger had nothing to do with eating, as far as Chekov could tell.

Reaching around the back of his collar to locate the unit in his hood, he depressed the button with his thumb. "I'm not hungry," he said again, waiting this time for the slow, stilted translator to finish its wailing. "I don't need to eat—you can keep that."

That only seemed to reassure the girl marginally. She sank back against Uhura's legs, retaining what remained of her honey compress but frowning at Chekov in that way children do when they suspect they're being made fun of. Laughing, Uhura stroked her hair and leaned over to report, "Don't feel bad, honey—he does the same thing to me all the time."

Chekov snorted. "You just don't give up so easily." Propping his elbows on his knees, he folded his hands between them and leaned his chin on his fists. "Thirty-two hours?" He sighed, his mind sliding quickly back to their predicament.

Uhura shrugged. "Maybe sooner. You know how Scotty is."

Chekov nodded. Careful but quick, and the best chance they had of safe rescue, even hoping for some sort of Nordstral ground transport.

"Is this going to keep us from bringing in that shuttle crew?" Howard asked.

Chekov glanced up at him, shook his head with a frown. "No. We came down with everything we need to locate the survivors." All the same, his brain started sorting through mental lists of equipment and supplies, pondering how far they could stretch all of it. "They still need to be found, even if we can't lift them off-planet immediately."

"The Kitka tunnels are warm, at least." Even mentioning the native race prompted Uhura to unconsciously brush the little girl's hair. "If all else fails, I'd think the company could send a harvester north for us."

Jimenez shook his head emphatically, struggling to swallow a mouthful of food before speaking. "The ice sheet's almost five hundred meters thick around here. Even if they wanted to, I don't think they've got a ship that can crack through."

"Ground transport, then," Publicker suggested, looking hopeful, and Jimenez nodded.

"It takes a while," the Nordstral man admitted, "but, yessir, they've got sledges that could make the trip."

"A while?" Chekov prompted.

Jimenez shrugged. "A week, sir. Maybe two."

They wouldn't starve or freeze to death, then, although they might have to cut back to two meager meals a day. Uhura would hate that, Chekov thought. "All right." He glanced around at them, trying to seem decisive and sure. "Come first light, we'll set out looking as we originally planned." He cocked a questioning look at Jimenez. "Has Mr. Steno had any luck contacting the survivors?"

106

"No, sir. And that's not good." Jimenez sounded genuinely apologetic, and Chekov felt a surge of annoyance with Steno that the man could make his own people feel guilty about something none of them had any control over. "We've found in the past that if we don't locate missing personnel on the ice sheets within twenty-four hours, we usually don't find them at all. That's why we depend so much on sending up flares for the local Kitka." He cast helpless eyes toward the food in his lap. "Dr. Stehle's group has been missing almost four days."

"We'll find them."

Jimenez looked up at Chekov, face open and hopeful, and relaxed without even seeming to realize he did so. The lieutenant fought off a faint, uncomfortable twinge. This must be how Kirk did it, he realized. You say the words as though nothing made by God or man could make you break them, then worry later about whether or not you can make them come true. "We'll find them," he said again, as though repetition would help.

"Not if our children continue to bother you while you're working."

The words over Chekov's translator startled him, but not nearly so much as they did the young Kitka girl at Uhura's feet. Leaping upright, Nhym stuffed the remainder of Howard's treat into Uhura's hands and spun to face the doorway. The seal whisked open and fluttered aside, and a broad, unmasked Kitka face appeared in the opening, surrounded by brilliant feathers and swirls of windblown snow.

"Go back, Nhym, to your grandparents. These people don't want you here."

Chekov recognized the arrogance of the Kitka's

words even though he couldn't recognize the face. "We asked her to be here, Alion. She may stay."

Alion kept his stare fixed steadily on Nhym. "She may do as I tell her, and I tell her not to bother you. Go, Nhym."

Uhura rose, keeping one hand on the girl's shoulder as she fitted her insulation suit hood back over her head. The young girl was obviously scared. "I'll go with you, honey," she offered. Her voice was comforting, but Chekov could read the flashes of anger in Uhura's eyes. "You promised me I could come back."

"Oh, yes!" Nhym reached up to tug at Uhura's hand. "Yes!"

Chekov flicked a glance at Tenzing. She nodded silent understanding, an overnight pack already tucked beneath one arm.

"I'd better get back down, too." Jimenez stood, looking awkwardly about with the empty ration pack in both hands. Howard leaned across to take it from him, passed it to Publicker for disposal. "Mr. Steno said he didn't want us spending time with you, either," Jimenez explained with a shrug as he followed Uhura toward the door. "I guess he's afraid we'll get smart or something." He bobbed a nod to the security force. "Thanks for the food."

Chekov acknowledged him with a wave. "No problem."

"I'll be back up before morning," Uhura promised from the doorway.

Chekov caught her eyes with his, knowing he didn't have the authority to stop her, but wanting her to see his displeasure with her decision. She conceded his feelings with a nod, but still slipped out past Alion, with Nhym and Tenzing in tow. The hiss of gusting wind drowned out even the crunching of their footsteps on the frozen snow.

Alion stepped a little to one side when Jimenez moved to squeeze past him, but didn't relinquish the doorway. The Kitka's persistent lingering bothered Chekov, made him uneasy about being down on the floor with an entire tent between the two of them. He pushed to his feet to join Alion at the doorway. "Can I help you with something?"

The Kitka's round, flat face was slit by a narrow smile. His weird eyes—a white-ice green in contrast to Nhym's brilliant indigo—danced in what might have been either laughter or secret malice. "No one here needs help, Lieutenant—either from you or your Federation. I am in control here."

Hearing the native's voice come straight from his mouth in fluid English snatched Chekov's breath like a sudden slap. So much for the northern natives not being able to speak human language. Alion must have learned English during the time he claimed to have spent at the equator. When one of the men rose restlessly behind him, Chekov thrust a hand back without turning to keep the crewman in his place. "I'm glad you chose to come to us this way," he told Alion in a tone held carefully neutral. "In fact, I rather prefer it."

"Yes." The native glanced over Chekov's shoulder at whoever stood toward the back of the tent. "So do I. It grants one a great deal of insight." His eyes darted back to Chekov's, and he commented dryly, "For example—among my people, dark eyes are considered a sign of youth and stupidity."

Even Publicker—the only blue-eyed human in the tent—uttered an indignant protest to that.

"Among my people," Chekov told Alion without responding to Publicker's grumble, "your value isn't judged by the color of your eyes."

Alion's smile twisted wryly. "Then you'll be the ones at a disadvantage here, won't you?"

Chekov wished he'd thought to record this conversation before it started, if only to prove to Uhura that not all paranoia was unfounded. "We'll see who's at a disadvantage."

"Yes. I'm sure we will." Alion backed out the door with hands held out to either side, as though proving he carried no weapons against them. Chekov had a feeling Alion's greatest weapon would be all the things about him that Chekov had no hope of discovering until far, far too late.

"You know," Howard remarked conversationally from the rear of the tent, "I don't think I like that guy."

Chekov resealed the door flap, shivering a little despite the resurgence of inside warmth. "If you can convince Lieutenant Commander Uhura to feel the same way, Mr. Howard, I'll put you in for a promotion."

Chapter Seven

McCoy STARTED to run his fingers through his hair, then thought better of it. The gesture reminded him too much of Muhanti's fixation on phrenology. He settled for pressing the palms of his hands tightly over his eyes. The insides of the lids felt like coarse-grain sandpaper against the tired irises, and he wondered if they were as red as they felt.

He'd spent the last couple of hours since the kraken fight alone in Muhanti's lab, cleaning. The accumulated waste and clutter made quite an impressive heap, which he jettisoned into the disposal unit, all the time wishing irritably that he could do the same with the *Soroya*'s doctor. No self-respecting scientist would ever let his or her work station deteriorate to such a degree. That Muhanti had allowed just that to occur was only further evidence in McCoy's mind of the Indian doctor's instability.

111

At least now the place was clean enough to begin to do some work without something heinous contaminating the results, McCoy reflected. He'd left Muhanti's noxious experiments alone, and only hoped he could ignore the fumes and tune out the happy bubbling long enough to build up some concentration.

His mind replayed the last few hours since Spock's soul-numbing call. He and Kirk had met with Mandeville in her quarters. "Captain," she said somberly, closing the door behind them. "I'm sorry about your people."

"Thank you." Kirk managed to sound gracious despite his own turmoil. "This is asking a lot—but there may be injured survivors. I'm requesting that the *Soroya* detour from her present heading to the crash site and cut through the ice in an attempt to pick up the survivors."

Mandeville shook her head, braids lashing like cats' tails. "That's impossible."

McCoy stepped nearer, convinced Kirk would not be able to stop from shaking the woman. He was relieved to see Kirk's hands merely curl into fists at his sides. "This is an emergency, Captain Mandeville." Kirk's tone was under tight control. "You may not care about your rescue team, but *I* care about mine. If they're alive and injured, they won't last a day unprotected on the ice."

"If they're injured and on the ice without protection, they won't last an hour." She wasn't being flippant. Her expression was gravely serious. "I appreciate your concern, but there's nothing I can do." She held up a hand to forestall any argument. "Not because I *won't,* but because I *can't.* Or, rather, the *Soroya* can't. The ice sheet in the north is almost five hundred meters thick. There's not a ship in the fleet that can bust through that without damaging itself and probably killing everyone up on the ice or in the ship to boot."

"So where does that leave us?" McCoy asked after a long, painfully silent pause.

"It leaves us," Kirk said decisively, "with doing what we can from this end. We'll have to rely on Nordstral ground personnel and Mr. Scott to take care of the shuttle crew." It was a wish and a prayer rather than a confidence. McCoy saw that at once. But it wasn't the first time he'd seen Jim Kirk want something to *be* so badly that he brought it into existence by sheer force of will. James Kirk carried his own brand of magic with him, and Leonard McCoy had learned a long time ago to place a great deal of faith in it. Things just had a way of turning out, if Kirk wanted them to badly enough.

"What can I do to help?" Mandeville asked.

Kirk glanced at McCoy. "Bones?"

"Well, I'd like your permission to use the lab. I want to take some samples from the air filtering system, waste disposal, that sort of thing, to see if I can get a handle on what might be causing the aberrant behavior we were sent here to track down."

Mandeville nodded sharply, hands sliding into her back pockets. "That's fine. I can assign one of the crew to help you."

"If you don't mind, Captain Mandeville, I'd like it to be Nuie or no one at all. It's not that I question their integrity," McCoy hurriedly added. "It's just that I want to keep the variables as small as possible. And I've already decided Nuie can be trusted."

She answered his smile with one of her own. "All right. What else?"

"That'll do for starters," Kirk said. "Let me start discounting things before I put too much on my plate." He quirked a not-quite-happy grin. "Maybe I'll get lucky on my first shot."

"I'll start praying to the kraken if you do," she vowed. She held the door open for them to pass into the corridor ahead of her. "And, listen, Dr. McCoy. About the aberrant behavior? Just remember that harvester workers will do almost anything to break the monotony. That's just to give you some kind of rule to judge them by." She peered more closely at him, and he felt like a bug under a glass. "Have you seen something?"

He reluctantly nodded, his eyes flicking to Kirk's first for approval. "I suspect another of your crew might be falling victim to whatever this sickness is."

"Who?" Mandeville asked anxiously.

"I'd rather not say."

"Dr. McCoy, if my people are in danger because of an illness one of them has contracted, I need to know."

"I appreciate that, Captain Mandeville. And as soon as I know for certain that this person *is* ill and not just . . . eccentric, you can be assured I'll come to you immediately. I have no desire to put you, your crewmen, or your ship at risk."

She studied him for a moment, obviously not entirely happy, then nodded. "All right." She pulled the door shut behind her. "You know your way to the lab, Doctor? Good. Nuie's on the bridge. I'll send him down to help you. Captain Kirk, you can come with me." Her teeth flashed whitely against her dark skin. "You can be first mate in Nuie's place."

A smile graced the *Enterprise* captain's lips. "I'd be honored."

They went their separate ways. The first mate arrived in the lab and listened seriously to what it was McCoy wanted. He then patiently led the doctor from one end of the ship to the other, holding supplies as bidden, shining probing lights into dark corners and along damp filters and conduits. Snippets of remembered conversation played across the back of McCoy's mind as he wiped the counter a final time, methodically hunting out the last bits of dirt and sticky residue. He felt almost as though he could traverse the submarine blindfolded. Certainly, he could ace a test on how often the filters were cleaned and the waste disposal units cleared. He'd hunted out every speck of mold he could find, uncertain what he thought he'd discover, and afraid he wouldn't know it when he saw it.

He bowed his head, mentally preparing himself for the work at hand, forcing sleepiness to bay. He'd contemplated a nap, but the noises of the ship through the water, the disquieting creaks and snaps of a vessel under enormous pressure, kept him uneasy and awake. He wasn't going to sleep until he got back aboard the *Enterprise*.

A deep, distant sound reverberated through the ship's metal hull, and McCoy raised his head, staring at the wall with eyes a little wider than normal. Another kraken? Or something else he didn't want to know anything about? He shifted his shoulders, feeling the tension. "Get a grip on yourself, McCoy," he ordered under his breath. "You're acting like a kid at his first autopsy." He reached for the nearest vial of sample, this one labeled, *Center conduit; crews quarters; aft*.

"What are you doing here?"

Already more jittery than he probably had a right to

115

be, McCoy jerked and spun about. The disk of the petri dish fumbled against his fingers, slid from his grasp and shattered on the floor. Green gobbets spewed in a bright sweep.

McCoy glared at Muhanti, unsure which he was most angry about—being frightened or losing the sample. "Don't you ever knock?"

"At the door of my own lab?" Dark spots of color shaded Muhanti's cheeks as he advanced into the room.

McCoy bent to pick up the shattered glass. "You always go around sneaking up on people?"

"Only people I feel have no right being where they are." The Indian doctor stopped, the sole of his boot almost brushing McCoy's busy fingers. "Leave it alone, or I'll crush your hand."

McCoy froze, a long sliver of glass between two fingers. He'd learned the art of reading tone and nuance at Jim Kirk's knee. He didn't have to look into Muhanti's face to know that if he didn't stop immediately, there was every chance Muhanti would carry out his threat. He gently replaced the shard where it had lain, slowly brought his hands close to his knees and stood.

Muhanti's eyes were white-rimmed and angry. "You've made a shambles of my lab."

McCoy goggled. "This lab's never been so clean," he rasped.

If Muhanti heard him, the insult had no impact. "Who gave you permission to use my facility?"

"Captain Mandeville."

"Captain Mandeville," the other doctor mimicked, his voice a sneer. "She would. I suppose it never occurred to her that it was common courtesy to *ask* if I minded."

"Then let me apologize." McCoy strove to make his voice as sincere as possible. "I take full responsibility. I should have asked your permission before I ever approached her."

"Yes. You should have." Hands on hips, Muhanti pivoted slowly, eyes scanning the room, always between McCoy and the door. When he looked back, he was more furious than he'd been before.

McCoy's mind singsonged *madness* in a babble of hysterical bird voices, like a flock of sparrows driven into sudden, terrified flight.

"Bad enough my good captain was so rude as to give you access to my laboratory without my consent. But I don't believe she's stupid enough to give you permission to tamper with my experiments."

"I never touched them, Muhanti." McCoy tried hard to keep his voice neutral, gentle. "But those are rudimentary experiments, and we both know it. Child's play. If it's your way of letting Mandeville think you have a handle on things, that's your business. I won't say anything. But we need to work together to—"

"I don't need to do anything! I had everything under control! I was this close"—his fingers spanned a tiny distance—"to breakthrough. I could have saved hundreds of crew the fate of madness, but you had to intervene. The great Federation doctor comes to lead the savages out of darkness." He spat, face angry as a cat's. "You just want the glory for yourself! Well, you aren't going to get it with my help!" He bent, graceful as a stooping crane, snatched a shard of glass from the floor, and lunged for McCoy's throat.

McCoy jumped back from Muhanti's attack and cracked his backbone against the rigid edge of the lab table behind him. The sharp, unexpected blow momentarily numbed him from the waist down, and his knees felt rubbery. His feet skidded on the spray of shattered glass and he collapsed onto one knee, cutting open the pant leg and the skin beneath it. He raised a hand in awkward defense, balance lost, and felt a blast of pain as Muhanti sliced into his palm.

Vision suddenly tunneled, McCoy stared at the hand as though it belonged to someone other than himself. Shock briefly numbed the realization of injury as he watched blood well from the gash like an encroaching tide.

Just as swiftly, pain returned, galvanizing him into action. He lurched sideways under Muhanti's second swing, shoving the Nordstral doctor back and leaving a lurid red cameo of his hand across the company logo on the doctor's chest. McCoy scrabbled across the floor, tiny splinters of glass digging into his hands and knees, gaining his feet as he ran. He clutched at the end of the lab table, reaching blindly for anything with which to defend himself. His undamaged hand curled around the neck of a bottle awaiting cleaning. He spun around and flung it at Muhanti. The Indian skipped aside with an unbelievable agility and came on, the glass shard held low and dangerous, in a hand slicked with its own blood where he'd cut himself and taken no notice.

McCoy's fingers felt wet and sticky where they curled tightly into his palm in an effort to staunch the blood flow. A whisper of thankfulness kissed his mind that his fingers could curl at all, given the suspected depth and angle of the slash. He backed up, eyes on Muhanti's taut features, his free hand flailing for a weapon of any kind, and brushed heat. Fingertips danced in rapid exploration of the hot surface. Muhanti's stupid experiments still bubbled, uninterrupted until now. Unmindful of the damage he might do his good hand, McCoy grabbed one of the vials and launched the contents at Muhanti's face.

The Indian doctor shrieked and ducked aside, covering his eyes with his arms as hot liquid sprayed over him. McCoy dove forward and tackled Muhanti around the waist. They crashed to the floor and McCoy twisted to get astride, kicking savagely at the hand still holding the blood-tainted shard of glass, knowing that if Muhanti got the chance, he'd slit him from neck to gizzard.

Blood-slicked fingers loosened and the shard went flying, striking the floor and spinning like a gory top. It skittered across the floor with an almost musical sound and slid under a bank of cabinets. McCoy was never so glad in his life to see something disappear.

He grunted as Muhanti attempted to knee him sharply in the back, and shifted, grabbing for the other man's hands, twining bloody fingers with those of his assailant and biting back on the pain that lanced up his arm from his lacerated hand. Muhanti rocked from side to side and back and forth, trying to dislodge McCoy, and all the time he was deathly silent, his eyes fixed solidly on McCoy's face as though burning it in effigy onto his pupils.

McCoy struggled in despair. His wounded hand was going numb, the fingers useless. His fingers slipped within the confines of Muhanti's, and the harvester ship's doctor lurched to the side, rolling, pinning McCoy beneath him. He freed his hands from McCoy's with a snap of his wrists and grabbed for the Starfleet officer's throat. His hands were warm and wet around McCoy's neck, his thumbs firm across the windpipe. McCoy bucked frantically, clawing desperately at the other man's hands with fingers that would not obey him. His vision began to blur and darken. There was a rushing and roaring in his ears, as of much water through a confining space, and a responding growl from somewhere outside the ship, echoing distantly through the hull and leading McCoy into oblivion.

A distant, bone-deep rumble crept into Uhura's sleep and woke her. She stirred, pushing back folds of cold-stiffened fur from her face to blink into the frosty darkness. The Chinit alcove was so quiet, she could hear the whispery breaths of sleeping Kitka and the low hum of Tenzing's insulated tent. The security guard hadn't tried to stop Uhura from staying inside the native village for the night, but she'd drawn the line at sleeping in her insulation suit under furs.

Another rumble edged the silence, so deep and far away Uhura could barely hear it. She frowned and sat up in her nest of furs. Originally, she'd thought it might be the approach of an *Enterprise* shuttle, but the noise was too irregular for an impulse drive. It sounded as if it came from somewhere deep in the ice sheet. Uhura put her gloved hand on the floor to feel for vibrations, then gasped as another hand closed hard over hers. She looked up to see ghost-pale eyes staring at her from the darkness.

"Ice hurts." Ghyl knelt beside her, almost invisible in her ancient dark furs. The elderly Kitka spoke in a quiet, falling hiss. "The ice hurts. You hear, Kraken Eyes?"

"Yes." Uhura spoke softly, knowing the translator would match its tones to hers. She could feel the thin tendons in Ghyl's hand shake when the native released her grip. "Does it do this every night?"

"No. Only when god is angry." Ghyl lifted her

hands and played with the blackened bone mask she wore around her neck. Beneath it, her face looked more lined than it had the day before, as if worry had aged her. "Great-granddaughter says you talk to god, Kraken Eyes. Tell me then, why ice hurts?"

"Um . . ." Uhura frowned, hunting for an explanation the Kitka could understand. "The god I talk to lives above the aurora. He doesn't know things like that."

"I know." The sudden bitter note in Ghyl's wail caught at Uhura's breath. "Only gods lived in deep water, before humans came down from auroras. Now Kitka live there, too, and hunt things gods don't want them to have."

"The plankton," Uhura said. She wasn't sure how the translator made that come out, but Ghyl grunted something that sounded like agreement.

The native fingered her mask, face crumpled in deep thought. "Gods give Kitka everything—light to see, furs to keep warm, weapons to hunt. Ask us only to go meet them, and apologize to hunted things before we catch." Ghyl looked up at Uhura, her bone-colored eyes sharp with suspicion. "Do men in deep water apologize to small swimming things before they catch, Kraken Eyes?"

"I don't know." Uhura put out her hand to touch Ghyl's shoulder reassuringly. "But there are Kitka who work under the water, too. Surely they'll remember to apologize before they catch the plankton."

"Some, maybe." Ghyl's voice wailed very softly, in what might have been despair. "Others maybe not know. Many Kitka, like Alion, come from villages in far south, where now no one goes to meet with gods. How can they know the proper things, growing up so?"

"Oh." Uhura pulled her hand back inside her furs, feeling helpless. The elderly Kitka sat huddled for another moment, lips working although no sound emerged. Around them the other natives slept, undisturbed by the quiet conversation, although a rustle of motion stirred inside Tenzing's tent. A third faint rumble gnawed at the silence, then died away again.

"Time to go." The sudden strength in Ghyl's rising voice startled Uhura and woke the other Kitka into sleepy murmurs of inquiry. The elderly woman ignored them, sliding her bone mask back over her face with hands that no longer shook. She stood and lit one of the oil-pot lamps with a quick strike of flint, then began to gather things from the carved bone chests lining the walls. Uhura heard the odd little keen she made under her breath, but the translator provided no English equivalent.

"Great-grandmother!" Nhym's slight form hurtled out of her sleeping furs almost explosively. Her whistle sounded shrill with fear. "What you do?"

"Time to go meet god, Great-granddaughter." The keening note in Ghyl's voice was stronger. "Ice cries, and no one goes to ask gods why. Kitka need answers before all things come to an end."

The young Kitka made a sound like a spitting cat. "Make Alion go!" She tugged at the older woman desperately. "Make *him* meet god and talk to him! Alion is the one who makes god angry!"

Ghyl shook herself free with a reproving whistle. "Alion does not meet gods as we do, Great-granddaughter. He thinks it helps to make others talk to god for him, but gods stay angry." She slid her gathered belongings—dried shreds of fish, a fistful of crumbled seaweed, and one small bone knife—into a fur-lined bag. "I do not trust his way. I will talk myself."

"No!" Nhym's voice had taken on the same keening note as Ghyl's, only stronger. Uhura realized it was the Kitka way of crying and felt her own throat knot in sympathy. "Chinit Clan needs you here, Great-grandmother, not gone to sacred place. You haven't told me kraken stories yet!"

"Your grandfather can tell them." Ghyl glanced over at the two older Kitka, who watched her in painful silence. "Hunt well, children. I will bless you all from Chinit's sacred place when I meet god there."

She turned, slinging her travel sack across her shoulder, and crossed the alcove with unhesitating strides. The furred skins marking the entrance to the tunnel barely quivered around her when she slipped through.

"No!" Nhym cried again. Her grandmother caught her when she would have followed the old woman, hissing a wordless comforting sound in her ear. The male Kitka merely bowed his head, stripping off one mitten and dipping his callused fingers into one of the unlit lamps. He brushed the clinging oil onto his face mask, streaking it with a dark film of wetness.

"All Kitka go to god." His wail sounded unsteady, but his hand moved without shaking until the entire mask was smeared with oil. "As god comes to all Kitka in the end. So it is."

"So it is," echoed the old woman, and dipped her fingers, too, rubbing the oil across Nhym's paler mask. The little girl was still keening, in short strangled gasps that sounded just like sobs. Uhura desperately wanted to comfort her, but she knew better than to interfere in what was clearly a native ritual.

"This doesn't look good." Tenzing's gruff voice caught Uhura by surprise, speaking through the insulation suit communicator channel without the background accompaniment of the translator. The security guard had emerged from her tent, fully dressed except for the shimmer of her goggles. "What happened, sir?"

Uhura took a deep breath that eased the ache in her throat a little, then turned to face her companion. A quick tap switched her own voice from mike to communicator, so the Kitka wouldn't be bothered by their exchange. "Nhym's great-grandmother just left on some kind of sacred journey. She said the Kitka gods were angry. She's gone to talk to them."

"I wonder if that means she's going to where the shuttle crashed—to their sacred place." Tenzing knelt and began to decompress her tent. "If Alion's right and it's safe to travel there now, we may be following her today."

"That's true." Uhura shook herself free of her furs, feeling a little better. "Maybe I can explain that to Nhym—"

But when she turned back toward the Kitka, only two fur-clad figures stood in the wavering lamplight. Uhura glanced toward the swaying doorway skin and her eyes widened. She tapped her translator back on. "Where is Nhym?"

The female Kitka's whistle sounded both resigned and puzzled. "She follows her great-grandmother, to watch her leave. It is not right, but the time comes too soon—"

A stronger rumble broke across her whistling voice. This time the sound didn't die away, but gathered itself up into an enormous slow roar like a shuttle rising. Uhura gasped and swayed as the alcove's floor rolled beneath her. She caught at the nearest wall to steady herself.

"It's a quake!" she shouted to Tenzing, who'd been thrown down into the folds of her collapsed tent. The roar tore the ice sheet apart around them, cracking the floor and shaking the skins down from the ceiling. A chorus of terrified Kitka shrieks echoed down the tunnel, and Uhura felt her heartbeat slam into her throat.

"Nhym!" She managed to stagger toward the alcove door, skidding and catching her balance as the floor thrashed in slow waves beneath her feet. "Tenzing, stay here and help the others. I'm going after Nhym!"

"Sir, don't—" Whatever else the security guard meant to say was lost beneath a fierce crackle of static across the communicator. All around Uhura ice splintered and cracked, fracturing the polished walls of the alcove. A chunk fell from the ceiling as she lurched into the tunnel outside, barely missing her as it shattered against the floor. She recoiled instinctively from the ominous darkness, then gritted her teeth and reached for her flashlight. The wavering circle of light caught a small furred figure up ahead, huddled in the angle where two passages met.

"Nhym!" Uhura skidded across the buckling floor of the tunnel, stumbling when one block of ice thrust up suddenly and caught her across the knees. She threw her arms up as she fell, trying desperately to protect her unshielded face from the ice. The roaring in the ice had become a thunder that made her bones shake with its growl. Dimly beneath the chaos, Uhura heard a frantic wailing, and small hands caught at her shoulders to drag her across the ice.

"Nhym?" Uhura managed to catch herself against a shaking wall of ice long enough to find her balance and scramble to a crouch. Nhym's small form plastered itself to her side, bone-masked face digging into her insulation suit with painful force. "Hold on tight, Nhym," she said as the icy ceiling above them groaned ominously. Flying shards of ice pelted them from above. "Just hold tight!"

With a crash that made her ears hurt, the ceiling fell.

Air rushed back into McCoy's lungs in a whooping roar that left his throat raw, accompanied by a loud voice over the ship's intercom. "Doctors Muhanti and McCoy to the bridge immediately! We have an urgent medical situation! Repeat, Doctors Muhanti and McCoy to the bridge immediately! Urgent medical situation requires immediate assistance!"

Muhanti let up the pressure on McCoy's throat at the intercom's intrusion. His fingers still coiled wetly around the Starfleet officer's neck, but they were loose, relaxed as he listened, captured by the sound. His weight shifted slightly, back onto his heels from the pressing confine over McCoy's abdomen. With his last reserve of strength, McCoy bucked fiercely and threw him off. Muhanti collided hard against a cabinet and sprawled, stunned.

Shaking, McCoy struggled to his feet and staggered out the door, turning left toward the bridge. He heard the clatter of Muhanti behind him in the lab, then the louder sound of running feet. McCoy was almost afraid to hazard a glance over his shoulder, certain he'd find Muhanti gaining on him, a murderous gleam in his eye and another shard of glass clutched in his lacerated fingers.

A flash at the edge of McCoy's vision—an arm

pumping in time to the running man, one dark hand clutched around a generic-issue medikit in a bright green Nordstral wrapper. McCoy's feet fumbled and he caught himself against the bulkhead, breathing hard, hand throbbing and welling fresh blood. He stared as Muhanti ran past, one arm waving. "Hurry, McCoy! They need us on the bridge!" He dashed through an interconnecting doorway and on down the corridor.

McCoy's chest heaved, adrenaline running so high as to give him the shakes. He tipped his head back against the cool metal and stared at the riveting overhead. "What the hell . . .?" he gasped. Groaning, he levered away from the wall and ran after Muhanti.

"Chief? Chief!"

Chekov rolled to all fours, spitting snow out of his mouth and shielding his eyes with one arm. Painful morning sunlight blazed like daggers off broken ice and snow, and bitter wind froze his tears to ice against his cheeks. Taking off his goggles to watch the morning auroras suddenly seemed an amazingly stupid thing to have done.

"Lieutenant Chekov?" Publicker's voice—clear and open, not across the insulation suits' communicator channel—sounded frantic and very nearby.

"I'm here." Covering his eyes with one hand, Chekov squinted between his fingers to cut the snow glare. It only helped a little, blurring everything to a fuzzy, white-laced patchwork that only hinted at the destruction wrought on the ice field around him. Still, he was able to sight the tent a few dozen meters away, as well as the waist-high upthrust that hadn't been there before a few moments ago. "Howard! Publicker!

Over here!" Maybe they'd be able to spot his missing goggles, or at least fetch a spare set from their sled full of equipment.

The guards hurried across the broken ice to him, arms pinwheeling for balance on the uneven terrain. "Are you all right?" Chekov asked, using one hand to lever himself up to their level.

Howard stooped to give him a hand, nodding. Publicker cast anxious looks all around them, his own goggles cracked and misted. "Just shook up," he admitted, sounding it. "What happened?"

"Some kind of earthquake. I don't know . . ." Chekov had crept out of the tent just before dawn, awakened by the sheeting brightness of auroras while the sun was still making its approach on the horizon. Then, the stark sameness of the rainbow-washed landscape had seemed almost beautiful in its stillness.

Now, the ice sheet looked like someone had tried to wad it into a ball, strata crumpled until icy layers flaked and shattered into rubble. Sunken trenches of broken snow sketched out the Kitka village with intersecting dotted lines—the legacy of caved-in tunnel passages between more sturdily constructed alcoves and inner rooms.

Chekov scanned the white-and-gray-clad bodies pouring out of the destroyed village, searching for some flash of human black among the natives. "Where's Tenzing?"

Howard turned to follow his gaze. "With Lieutenant Commander Uhura, sir."

Chekov felt the first twistings of panic in his heart. "Still down below?"

". . . Yes, sir . . ."

"Oh, my God." He broke into a run without waiting to see if the other men followed.

Natives milled around their damaged holes, howling in fear and confusion. Chekov started counting them in groups of three or four, then realized he didn't know how many lives this village harbored to begin with, so he couldn't assess the damage this way. Skidding to a stop beside a cluster of white-eyed elders, he flipped on his translator. "How many are still inside?"

They turned to stare up at him, their wide, flat faces registering only uncomprehending shock.

"How many?" His own taut worry made the words come out more harshly than he intended, but no Kitka words came out of his translator. He stared back at the natives, equally confused, until it suddenly struck him that nothing he said was being translated for the frightened natives to understand. And vice versa. *"Chortov!"*

The old man closest to him shied away, and Chekov caught at his arm to stop him as Howard joined them with already-assembled shovels in hand. "My people," Chekov insisted, trying to make some connection with the old man, if only through shared panic. "The two women who were with the little girl—where are they?" He ducked his head to wrestle his voice back under control. Even the insulation suit's communicator channel blew only deadly static. "God, can you people understand *any*thing I'm saying?"

One of the women answered in a complex flutter of whistles and whines that meant nothing more to Chekov than he knew his own pleading meant to her. Still, she pointed with one hand while plucking at his wrist to make him look behind. A sunken tunnel snaked away from them, still hissing with internal falls of ice and snow. Chekov felt nearly dizzy with grief. "They're under that?"

Her only response was to push him toward the collapse.

Howard climbed into the trench behind Chekov, handing his chief one of the shovels without waiting to be asked. Chekov tried to keep his shovel strokes rhythmic and steady, ignoring the brilliance of snow light in his eyes, ignoring the fearful trembling that wanted to shiver through him as they worked. The quake had broken much of the snow into heavy powder, the ice into manageable splinters that two men could easily enough heave out of their way. He tried not to think about the speed with which a phaser set on stun could melt past this jumbled blockage. If he had seen Alion at any time during their digging, though, he'd have been hard pressed not to turn his shovel on the shaman instead of the ice.

Kitka men gradually converged on their work space, keening softly among themselves but apparently understanding the uselessness of trying to communicate with the Starfleet officers just now. Chekov accepted their help in grateful silence. It was somehow reassuring to know translators weren't needed yet for all forms of sentient communication.

Howard turned over the first shovelful of bloody snow. He sank to his knees, one hand covering his breath filter. "Chief . . . oh, no . . ."

The pain in Howard's voice shot through Chekov like lightning. He threw down his shovel, scrambling past confused Kitka to land on his knees beside Howard. The young ensign had already scraped out a slushy pile of scarlet ice, and sat now with his hands on his lap, looking downward. Trembling, hands made clumsy by desperation and fear, Chekov leaned over the open hole without letting himself think about what he would find there.

Tenzing's goggles had been shattered in the earthquake, and meltwater sheened her golden skin in a glaze already frozen brittle by the wind. Chekov saw only enough of her eyes to confirm that they were dull and inanimate, then he rocked back on his heels and closed his eyes against the blinding whiteness of the snow.

McCoy dashed onto *Soroya*'s bridge at Muhanti's heels and nearly ran the Indian doctor down when he stopped quickly. Kirk and Mandeville knelt on the floor, Nuie stretched limply between them. Both doctors landed on their knees, one to either side of the unconscious crewman. Muhanti batted Mandeville's hands away. "Don't move him!" he ordered, digging into his medikit.

"What the hell happened to you two?"

McCoy looked up and met Kirk's baffled regard. Clotted blood wiped off on Nuie's clothing as McCoy routinely took vital signs the old-fashioned way, listening with one ear while Muhanti muttered over his equipment and ran a medical scanner above the Kitka. "It's a long story."

"I'll want to hear it." That was an order.

"Later." That was a *promise*. "What happened?"

"He fell. The ship hit a wave, or a current pocket, or something, and he fell and hit his head." Kirk gestured at a nearby panel.

"Is he going to be all right?" To McCoy's relief, Mandeville directed this question to her own ship's physician.

"I don't know, Clara." He met her eyes briefly, and McCoy got a glimpse of the kind of doctor Muhanti probably was when he wasn't influenced by whatever was happening on this godforsaken planet. Muhanti pressed a loaded hypo against Nuie's neck and shot it home. McCoy recognized the drug, almost unconsciously noting that it was the correct dosage for the Kitka's build.

"I'll need to examine him in sickbay." Muhanti grasped Nuie's arm and shifted to get an arm around his waist. "McCoy, get his other side and help me carry him. I want to run a battery of—"

His voice was cut off by an ominous rumble. They stared at one another, frozen by the rapidly growing sound. Suddenly, the *Soroya* heeled over on her side. McCoy slammed into the decking, crying out as he landed on his wounded hand. Kirk's fingers snagged his shirt and dragged at him as the helm fought for control.

"Icequake!" someone cried.

"Damn! Damn!" Mandeville moved along the canted interior of the ship, pulling herself from the back of one tipped chair to the other, her fingers tight and white-knuckled on the well-worn upholstery. "Take us down! Dive! Get us into a canyon!" Her eyes raked the map above the tech's station.

"Can't!" the pilot grunted, hands fighting controls. "There's no response! Radar's gone to hell!"

"Not good enough!" Mandeville snapped, reminding McCoy of a certain Starfleet captain he knew. "Get us upright if you have to go out and *push* her! Activate the cutting turret! Blast us a big enough hole that we don't breech her on the ice!"

"Trying, Captain!" His fingers ran scattershot over his controls. "Not responding, Captain! Mechanism seized!"

Mandeville swore explosively and snagged someone's jacket off the back of their chair. She flung her arms into it and hurled herself up a wall-clung ladder. "I'll do it manually!"

Kirk caught Nuie's rolling body and pushed him into McCoy's arms as he struggled to his feet. "I'll do it!"

Mandeville looked down at him from her perch. "Not your ship, Captain. Here, you're just cargo." She sped up the ladder and disappeared into the upper decking.

A moment later another shock, much worse than the first, rocked the harvester again. Rending metal sounded like the scream and tear of living flesh, and there was one short, loud cry from Mandeville. Kirk lunged toward the ladder and was blocked by another crewman hurtling up the worn metal rungs. An enormous roaring filled the air, and a fount of water gushed from the access, bringing the crewman's battered, lifeless body back down with it.

"Bones! Get out of here!" Kirk struggled forward into the gout of water. "We've hit something! Evacuate the bridge crew!" he thundered, physically hauling people away from their stations and shoving them toward the door. He grabbed the pilot's arm tightly. "Can we secure the hatches?"

Her reply was lost to McCoy in the surge and wash of thundering water. A klaxon began its raucous cry, alerting the rest of the crew to danger. McCoy hauled on Nuie's limp form, his hands locked across the Kitka's chest from behind. Where was Muhanti? One brief glance over his shoulder as he dragged Nuie toward the door showed Muhanti trying to get through the water rushing about his knees. He shouted something about trapped crew and Captain Mandeville, but McCoy couldn't make out the words.

Kirk clutched at Muhanti. The *Soroya's* doctor shoved him aside and disappeared.

Someone pushed McCoy into the corridor, Nuie still locked in his embrace. The *Soroya* rolled, driving him to his knees, and there was a sound like someone had pierced the ship's heart and ripped free her soul. The roar of water intensified, and McCoy looked up to see a wall of water bearing down on them.

Chapter Eight

UHURA WOKE with her face pressed against a hard, cold surface that blocked out half the light. Distant thumps and scrapes echoed around her, so muffled she couldn't tell where they came from. She lifted her head, but somehow the hard surface moved with her, refusing to go away. Her mind spun in dizzy circles for a moment, then focused enough to realize there was a leather thong tied around her neck, holding something onto her face. She lifted her hand and felt the curved bone contours of a Kitka mask, slipped over the head of her insulation suit.

"What on Earth . . .?" She sat up, bumping her head on ice. Through the narrow eye slits of the mask, she could see a dim blue light refracting through the shattered tunnel walls, with one bright sliver of glare overhead where the ceiling block had cracked away from the wall. The enormous slab of ice canted steeply down into the passage, meeting the floor just past Uhura's legs. She pulled in a startled breath, seeing how close she had come to being crushed. If Nhym hadn't tugged at her—

"Nhym!" Uhura looked around frantically, then saw the small, fur-clad body snuffled under her arm and released her.

"Kraken Eyes awake!" The little Kitka sat up and patted at Uhura, her face bright with pleasure. "Not hurt?"

"I don't think so." Uhura managed to get her feet under her despite the cramped space in which she had to move. One numb ankle complained about the return of circulation with tiny needles of pain, but otherwise she seemed undamaged.

"Face not hurt?" Nhym persisted, peering up at Uhura in concern. "Nhym's mask keep warm?"

"Yes. Thank you for lending it to me." Uhura put up her hand to untie the leather strings, but small mittened fingers caught at hers and stopped her.

"No!" Nhym's whistle sounded fierce. "You keep Kitka mask now. Better for you than kraken eyes."

Uhura glanced down at her through the confining slits of the bone-carved face shield. She ought to be wearing her own goggles, but hadn't thought to bring them when she left the Chinit alcove. "Do you have another mask to wear?"

The girl sat back on her heels, looking indignant. "Always have two," she told Uhura as she pulled a second bone mask from one of her parka pockets. "Need if first one breaks."

Uhura smiled at her in wry affection. "A child after Chekov's heart," she said, then looked around their ice-walled prison with a new determination. The comment had reminded her that she didn't know where the other members of her party were. "Nhym, can we get out of here?"

The little Kitka paused in tying on her shield. "Maybe," she said. "Lots of ice down in tunnel, but Nhym hears people digging through."

Uhura recalled the muffled thumping sounds she'd heard before. "That sounds like something Chekov would do." She reached up to tap on her insulation-suit communicator. The ear-splitting static was gone, she noticed thankfully. "Lieutenant Chekov, can you hear me?"

There was a pause, then a passionate burst of Russian in her ear. Uhura blinked as the translator dutifully transcribed it into English.

"Uhura!" Chekov's voice sounded rough with relief and some other emotion, hidden below the urgency of his words. "Where are you? Are you injured?"

"No, I'm fine. Nhym and I are trapped in one of the tunnels, about twenty-five meters away from the Chinit alcove. Tenzing can show you where—"

"Tenzing's dead." The relief vanished from his voice, leaving it grim with self-reproach. Chekov always took his squad's losses hard. "We just dug out her body."

"Oh, Chekov, no!" Uhura closed her eyes, remembering how she'd left the security guard without listening to her warning. She took in a shaking breath, feeling a chill creep into her despite her insulation suit. Gentle hands patted at her arm, and she heard a wordless hissing, the sound Kitka made to comfort each other. Uhura opened her eyes to see Nhym looking up at her, violet eyes worried behind her mask.

"I'm all right," she murmured to the girl, and saw her face brighten with a smile.

Chekov must have heard her, too. He cleared his throat. "Commander, I think we're near the alcove that you stayed in last night. Where are you relative to that?"

Uhura frowned, trying to remember the layout of the Kitka tunnels. "On the right-hand side of the alcove's opening, down where the tunnel bends to the right. There's a big block of ice slanting down from one side of the ceiling."

Uhura heard a shout that echoed through the ice as well as through her communicator. It sounded like Publicker. "Down here, sir! I can see her!"

Nhym yelped and pointed upward. Uhura tilted her head back to see a familiar shimmering mask peering down through the overhead crack in the ice. She reached her hand up into the narrow opening and felt gloved fingers close around it briefly.

"We'll have you out in no time, sir." Publicker looked up as thudding footsteps signaled the arrival of the rest of the squad. "Looks like the main slab's too big to move, sir, but there's a smaller chunk down to the left."

"Let me look." Chekov's masked face replaced his guard's for a moment. "Yes, that looks movable. Howard, stay up here and lever it back with the shovel while Publicker and I dig out around the base."

"What can I do?" Uhura asked as two dark shadows slid down the thick slab of ice above her. Nhym went to peer curiously around the edge of the block while metal scraped and thudded against the outer side.

"Just keep the little one out of our way," Chekov said. Uhura reached out to pull Nhym back to her side as the shoveling sound grew closer. "I'm afraid this block might—"

A splintering sound interrupted him as the smaller

block toppled outward without warning, letting a dazzle of arctic light into the tunnel. Uhura scrambled to her feet in alarm.

"Chekov! Are you all right?"

Another explosion of Russian answered her, and two snow-dappled black forms picked themselves out of a shattered mound of ice. Uhura sighed in relief, then bit her lip as the translator patiently repeated Chekov's words in careful English.

"I don't think you can do that," she said to the lieutenant, trying not to laugh. "Especially while you're dancing."

The chief security officer groaned, reaching out to pull her into a quick, fierce hug. "I forgot the translator was on," he said sheepishly before letting her go. Then he glanced down at Nhym, watching silently from beside Uhura. "I hope that didn't make any sense translated into Kitka."

"Don't worry," Uhura assured him. "It didn't make very much sense in English." She heard a chorus of excited Kitka wails, and looked up to see several natives peering down into the tunnel at them. She recognized Nhym's grandparents by the damp streaks of oil on their face masks, and touched Chekov's arm gently. "Can you lift Nhym up?"

"If she'll let me." He glanced down at the little girl, then surprised Uhura by pushing up his goggles before he bent to pick her up. The girl went into his arms willingly, lifting her mittened hands for her grandmother to catch as Chekov hoisted her to the tunnel's lip.

"Your turn next." The security chief turned back toward Uhura, his gloved hands already laced and lowered to form a boosting stirrup. His eyelashes were white with frost. Uhura smiled and reached up to lower his goggles for him, then put her foot into his interlocked hands and let him toss her up to Howard. The taller guard caught her wrists and swung her onto the ice sheet, then leaned down to haul the other men out.

"Good lord." Even through the narrow eye slits of her Kitka mask, Uhura could see the devastation the icequake had wreaked upon the native village. Alcoves stood open to the bitter cold along crumbled tunnels, their furred skin hangings torn away to reveal scattered belongings. The Kitka were already combing through the ruins, gathering what could be salvaged and packing it onto tables that—turned upside down —had suddenly metamorphosed into long, gleaming bone sleds.

"Is anyone else missing?" Uhura demanded, turning back to the little cluster of Chinit still standing beside her. Nhym's grandfather whistled a negative reply.

"All Kitka asleep in furs when ice shakes." He gave Nhym an affectionate swat on the shoulder. "Except for bad children out in halls."

Nhym ducked her head, then glanced up at Uhura in concern. "Time now to pack and move, Kraken Eyes. You come with Chinit?"

"No," Chekov said, before Uhura could answer. He pivoted to scan the scarred ice surface, shoulders tense beneath his snow-streaked insulation suit. "We're still missing personnel."

"Steno's people!" Uhura's eyes widened when she realized that neither the planetary officer nor his men were anywhere in sight. She reached up to dial her communicator to maximum output. "Mr. Steno, can you hear me? Are you trapped under the ice?"

A faint hiss of static answered her, followed by an equally faint voice. "He's not, sir, but I am."

"Jimenez!" Chekov identified the barely audible voice without hesitation. "Where are you?"

"At the communications console. I think I managed to save most of it—" His voice broke into a hiss of pain.

"If the console's working, I should be able to get a fix on its signal." Uhura toggled the directional receiver on her suit communicator, then swung around in a slow circle. "There." She stopped, facing sunward. Past the dazzle off the ice, she could see a large crumpled dent several hundred meters away. "I think that's where he is."

Chekov grunted, swinging his shovel up to his shoulder. "Publicker, I want you to get our supplies loaded onto the gravsled while we dig Jimenez out. Meet us there."

"Yessir." The guard hurried back to the collapsed puddle of their tent, careful to skirt the milling groups of natives as he went. Uhura followed Chekov and Howard across the ice sheet, listening to the console's signal grow steadily stronger in her ears. She stumbled once over a jagged ridge of ice, and felt Chekov catch her arm to steady her.

"You should be wearing goggles," he said sharply. "Publicker." He motioned sharply, and the guard ran an extra pair up to her, the strap already shortened.

"Oh. Thanks." Uhura pulled down Nhym's Kitka mask to dangle around her neck, and fitted the goggles over her eyes. The welcome blue screen of the polarizer slid down over the ice glare, bringing the windscoured arctic landscape into sharp focus. "I forgot I wasn't wearing them."

Chekov grunted again as they reached the side of the collapsed area. Here, the thinner arch of roof had broken like an eggshell, raining chunks down across a straggle of Nordstral gear. Uhura could see the tilted edge of a gravsled buried near one wall, a scrap of ice-pale green showing behind it. She opened her mouth, but Chekov was already moving, skidding down a slab of fallen ice toward the sled. Howard jumped down after him while Uhura picked her way more cautiously across the snow-crusted debris.

"Jimenez?" Chekov crouched beside the over-turned sled, careful not to touch it or the slab of ice it supported. As Uhura came closer, she could see the young Nordstral guard curled in the sheltered space beneath, the silver gleam of the console visible beside him. "Where are you caught?"

"Left ankle," said Jimenez, his voice barely louder over his mike than it had been on the communicator. "Between the gravsled and the wall. I think it's broken."

Uhura quickly unsealed the emergency medikit strapped onto her insulation suit belt while Chekov and Howard hauled blocks of ice off the gravsled. "Here." She pulled out a thin hypo and dropped to her knees beside the young man. "This should help."

"Thanks, sir." He showed her where to open the shoulder seam of his insulation suit, then sighed when she pushed back his body slip and pressed the hypo to his pale brown skin. It hissed as it discharged its dose of painkiller. "That feels better already."

"Good." Uhura fastened his suit shut against the cold, then reached down to pat his hand reassuringly. "Lieutenant Chekov will have you out soon, then we'll get your ankle splinted."

"That's great." Under the dull gleam of the guard's

plastic visor, Uhura saw the clenched muscles of his jaw relax. "I'm glad you're here. You're a lot better at this rescue stuff than we are."

"It's our job to be better at it." Ice crunched as Chekov came around the edge of the overturned sled and squatted down to search for a handhold along its base.

The young man sighed. "I know that, sir. I tried to tell Mr. Steno—"

"But he didn't listen to you," Chekov finished for him. "Small wonder." He rocked slightly on the balls of his feet, securing his grip on the sled. "Ready to lift, Mr. Howard?"

"Aye, sir."

"All right. On my count of three—"

"Where *is* Mr. Steno?" Uhura asked, more to distract Jimenez from the sled-lifting than from any real wish to know the answer. "Did he leave you here when the quake started?"

The young guard shook his head. "No, sir. He left a lot earlier than that . . ."

"One," said Chekov between clenched teeth. His shoulders knotted with effort as he hefted the sled. "Two . . ."

". . . with Alion," finished Jimenez.

The heavy sled rose without warning, then went crashing down into the ice a meter away.

McCoy knew there was no way he could outrun the cascading flood, particularly with the unconscious first mate limp in his arms. He turned, Nuie protected by the curve of his body, and met the onslaught of inrushing sea with the broad of his back. The biting, rotten-fish odor of brine stung his nose. Water colder than imaginable washed around his hips, making his

143

legs as unresponsive as logs. The sodden weight of his clothing dragged at him, making it hard to stand. His injured hand screamed a throbbing litany of pain as saltwater scoured it like old-fashioned steel wool.

The water surged past and ran down the corridor to meet the panicked rush of crew erupting from their quarters and elsewhere aboard the ship. Their shouted cries and queries flew about like erratic ammunition.

Someone grabbed his arm. "Dr. McCoy! What happened?"

"I don't know." He shook his head, shoulders sagging under the combined weight of Nuie and their water-soaked clothing. "There was a call to the bridge. Nuie . . ." He shifted the Kitka's heavy form. He needed to get him to sickbay and check his vital signs, if he wasn't dead already. "Then everything— Somebody said something about an icequake . . ."

A wealth of profanity greeted that information. "Where's Captain Mandeville?" someone else asked.

"I don't know." Captain Mandeville? Where was *Kirk?* For the first time, McCoy noticed the water had subsided from around his legs, sloshing about his ankles as though he were a child wading in the Chattahoochee. He turned as best he could, Nuie dragging at his arms. The door to the bridge was closed and Kirk wasn't in sight. That meant . . .

"Oh, dear God!" McCoy slammed to his knees on the hard decking, cradling Nuie, forgotten, in his arms. He stared at the door like it was the final epitaph on the headstone of a friend wrongfully taken, and felt a cold deeper than Nordstral's sea take hold of him.

"Dr. McCoy?"

Dammit! It was just like Kirk to make certain everyone was safe, then stay behind to face the danger by himself. McCoy knew it would get Kirk killed one day, but not yet, dear Lord, please not yet . . .

"Dr. McCoy!"

Someone tugged McCoy's sleeve. He felt an irrational urge to bite them for their trouble. "There was water coming in." He struggled to get up, and finally managed with the helpful aid of a hand under his arm. "I don't know why. I think we hit something. Captain Mandeville went to take care of it. Captain Kirk got us off the bridge . . ." He felt more exhausted than he ever had, as though the fighting spirit had just been sucked out of his bones like the winning kraken sucking down the loser's vitals. How could he go back to the *Enterprise* and tell everyone that Kirk was dead?

"They're still in there? Flooded bridge!" The *Soroya* crewman looked grim as she turned and started issuing orders. McCoy stared at the closed-up bridge.

"Dr. McCoy?"

He suspected the query had been repeated several times before he heard it. He caught himself staring at the iron barrier of the bridge door, his heart cold with dread, and shook his head hard. His eyes met the crewman's. "Yes?"

"Do you need help getting Nuie to sickbay, sir? I don't think you should be here, in case . . ." The sentence died off.

McCoy felt a surge of annoyance. Here was exactly where he *should* be, in case. But there was also Nuie to consider. Nuie who, for more time than was excusable, he hadn't even really been thinking about. Kirk would have McCoy's head on a platter if the Kitka crewman died because he chose to needlessly hang around a rescue operation when he could be putting his talents to better use elsewhere. He could practically hear Kirk berating him, and was amused by the man's ability to lead even when he wasn't in the same room.

"I can handle him," he replied, and wondered just exactly to *whom* he was referring. "Do—Do you think they might actually be *alive?*"

The crewman positioned herself a little more noticeably between McCoy and the working crew, giving him an intangible nudge toward sickbay. "If they got to the life units in time, sure. If they didn't, there's nothing you're going to want to see."

He appreciated her bluntness. Now was not a time for delicately skirting around the issue. "How long?"

"Depends on how long it takes you to get out of here and let us do our work."

A tiny smile curved McCoy's lips for just an instant and he nodded. Stooping, he shouldered Nuie into a fireman's carry and continued down the corridor to sickbay. He never once looked back to watch the crew at their industry. He didn't want to jinx their efforts.

Chekov squinted up toward the sun, trying to gauge their distance from the Kitka encampment by the star's slow procession across the arctic sky. He caught himself wishing he'd spent more time before planetfall studying the Nordstral star system, but discarded that thought with a steamy sigh: skirling curtains of snow corkscrewed across the land and sky—he could barely see the sun, much less glean any useful information from it.

"Damn him," he muttered for what felt like the hundredth time since they'd set out after Steno and his men. He was meaning the invective more and more every time he uttered it.

"Chekov, you're starting to sound like you take this personally."

He looked back at Uhura, a few lengthy strides behind him, and reminded himself again that she'd never be able to match their pace if he didn't force himself to walk slowly. Stopping to let her catch up, he noted with approval that Publicker and Howard— nearly treading on the lieutenant commander's heels —halted, also, to make sure their loaded gravsled didn't overtake her. As far as Chekov was concerned, thinking to put six-foot-three-inch Howard in the rear and himself in the lead had done wonders at forcing their little group to stick together.

"Are we still on course?" he asked Publicker.

Bent over a tricorder, his goggles granting him a false expression of manic, iridescent attention, Publicker nodded. "Yessir. There's a lot of interference, though."

That didn't surprise Chekov—he'd noticed the returning static on their suit communicators. "We'll see how far we can get before we lose it."

"Yessir."

Uhura stayed beside him when they started walking again. "Are you planning to leave Steno to freeze when we find him? Or merely walk him to death?" Her breath billowed and steamed in rapid rhythm beyond her filter, laying a furry rim of frost along the top of the Kitka mask hanging around her neck. Chekov eased his pace again, feeling guilty.

"No." He scanned the broken ice horizon, saw nothing of use or interest. "We'll render whatever assistance Mr. Steno requires, collect what survivors we can find, and escort them all back to Curie."

Uhura nodded, making the bone mask bob. "Uh-huh. Just checking."

147

Chekov frowned down at her, unsure whether or not she was joking. He sometimes couldn't tell, and it bothered him that she might think him capable of something so unprofessional as throwing Steno out an open airlock—much as he might want to.

"This isn't personal, Uhura, it's . . . professional. I don't care that Steno seems to trust Alion more than his own people do. I don't even care how certain Steno was that Alion's people had actually located the shuttle crash site. Steno jeopardized the safety of any survivors he might find by sneaking away without informing anyone else."

"He left Jimenez with the communication equipment," Uhura pointed out. "Jimenez would have told us—he *did* tell us."

"Whether or not Steno *left* someone isn't the point!" He brought his hands up in front of him, frustrated at having nothing nearby to fidget with. "You don't try to outperform your reinforcements on a rescue mission. We're here to do a job *together*— dammit, we're the only chance those people have to survive! If anyone suffers because of Steno's arrogance . . ." No appropriate English idiom suggested itself, and Chekov still wasn't sure he liked what Uhura's translator had done to his Russian before, so he left the sentence hanging.

"You'll pin his ears back?" the communications officer suggested.

Chekov glanced down at her, decided she was smiling from the tilt of her head, and snorted. "I'll pin something back," he grumbled, "that's for certain."

"Lieutenant!" Publicker's voice interrupted them, dragging everyone to a stop again. He shook his head when Chekov turned. "I've lost the signal."

It was Howard who swore this time.

"What was your last reading?" Chekov asked, coming back to stand with him.

Publicker handed over the tricorder with a shrug. "Faint and barely recognizable as human, but only about a half kilometer from here." He pointed over Chekov's right shoulder. "North, and a couple degrees west of our position."

"All right." Chekov turned to take Uhura's arm and pull her closer into their huddle. "Contact Jimenez," he told her. "See if the Kitka have set up in their new village yet. If Steno really has found our shuttle survivors, we'll be sending up a flare soon for an escort." He wasn't sure he liked the idea of letting Alion's men try to lead them back, even on the off chance the shaman knew to what new location the Kitka had gone. The thought of being alone and unprotected on the ice sheets with Alion set his teeth on edge. "Howard—set the gravsled for automatic follow. I'll want everyone's hands free in case—"

"Chekov!" The cry, thin with pain and terror, drifted to them across the tumbled ice sheet, jerking everyone around to search for the source of the call. "Lieutenant Chekov! Oh, thank God!"

Uhura spotted him and pointed with a silent gasp.

Steno's ice-green insulation suit nearly hid him from view as he clambered toward them over a sweep of broken ice. He was too far away to make out any details, but Chekov guessed from the roils of steam obscuring Steno's face that his plastic mask was either broken or gone. There was no mistaking his long, bony frame, though, or the frantic impatience of his gestures. "He's gone mad! It's a trap for all of us! We've got to—"

An eruption of snow and glittering crystal drowned out the rest of Steno's cry. Two men—short and square like natives, and bedecked with white feathers and rattling bones—burst over the tilted ice pack and swarmed over Steno like frost on glass. One flashed a bone knife across the station manager's midsection, and a curtain of blood splashed over the snowfield to instantly burn its way below the crust and out of sight. Steno went down without a scream.

"Hold it!" Chekov didn't know what he hoped to accomplish, standing on an open ice sheet in solid black insulation suits that wouldn't do a thing to stop those native blades. Instinct demanded he try something, though, even when his hand reaching for a phaser brushed only empty hip instead.

The second native pointed up that loss by raising one of the stolen weapons and opening fire. Phaser light cut a bubbling line of water into the ice barely a meter in front of them. Chekov knew what that setting would do to human flesh.

"Come on!" Grabbing Uhura by one arm, he shoved Publicker into a run ahead of him. Howard needed no such urging; he'd already broken into a run, the gravsled purring along obediently at his heels.

"They'll just come after us!" Publicker objected even as he followed Chekov's lead.

"Then run faster," Chekov growled, keeping one hand on Uhura. "We already know what they'll do when they catch us." Kitka wails rent the air behind them, and Chekov sprinted forward to shove his underling again. *"Go!"*

The sound of unseen phaser fire had never seemed so shrill and deadly.

Chapter Nine

"I THINK we're gaining ground."

Uhura glanced up from the windblown swirl of snow across her feet, trying to decide which of the black-suited figures near her had said that. Cascading wails of interference on the communicator channel made it hard for her to identify voices. Nordstral's auroras had grown so strong that they were visible even in daylight, iridescent streaks across the ice-white sky.

"Are you sure, Mr. Howard?" There was no doubt whose voice that was: the tense snap in the words would have identified it even without the Russian accent. Uhura wondered how Chekov could still be so keyed up. In the hours since they started running, she'd lost track of everything but cold and exhaustion. Her right side had gone numb from the constant battering of wind, and her left side felt like someone had stapled it to her ribs. The Kitka mask around her neck occasionally jerked in the wind like a top-heavy kite.

"Not really, Chief." Uhura turned her head and saw the tall security guard standing off to one side, leaning into the wind as he scanned their smudge of trail. "But there's no one back there firing at us anymore."

"Maybe they used up—all their charge." Publicker sounded as breathless as Uhura felt. For the past half hour he'd been fighting to keep the gravsled from skating past them as they descended a long, irregular slope on the ice sheet.

"Either that, or the magnetic field's gotten bad enough to take out the phasers." As if to emphasize Chekov's point, a particularly vicious howl of static erupted on their communicator channel. Uhura winced and dialed the volume down.

"Whatever." Publicker sounded plaintive as he yanked at the sled, battling a sudden gust of snow-laden wind. "Do you think we could take a minute to rest?"

"That depends." Chekov glanced around at the blowing curtains of snow. The afternoon sun was slowly dimming behind their frost-white veil. "Uhura, do you remember what time those boreal winds hit us yesterday?"

"I think—" Uhura's side stitched with pain and she doubled over, gasping. Chekov moved to stand beside her, one hand cupped under her elbow to support her until she could catch her breath and straighten again. "I think they hit about 1400 hours, planet time. Do you think they're coming back again?"

"It sounds like it." The air around them glittered with snow as the wind rose to a howl. "Is there any chance you can make contact with Jimenez in this mess?"

"I can try." Uhura tilted her head, listening past the wind's shriek to the fading wails of auroral static. "The interference seems to be dying down a little."

"All right." Chekov caught the gravsled's tow bar as it floated past and angled it down into the snow, to keep the sled anchored against the pull of the slope. He turned the servomotors off to conserve their charge. "Then let's give Publicker his rest break."

"Not a moment too soon." Publicker collapsed beside the silent sled, his breath puffing out through his filter. "Boy, if there's one thing I hate, it's sweating inside an insulation suit."

Judging from the sound of his snort, Uhura guessed that Chekov didn't find that funny. "It's better than getting caught by Kitka, Mr. Publicker."

"Or trying to dry off in this tropical breeze." Howard shouldered through the snow toward them. He reached out to yank Publicker to his feet despite the other man's reluctant groan. "You want a perimeter guard, Chief?"

"Three corners watch." Chekov took his place at the head of the gravsled, face turned outward toward the snow-shrouded horizon. "This weather didn't take long to clear last time it hit. Let's hope that's the standard pattern."

Uhura adjusted her communicator for a narrowbeam scan, then programmed the output to rotate in a slow, searching circle. "Uhura calling Jimenez. Repeat, Uhura calling Jimenez."

"He's probably asleep." Publicker was rubbing his gloved hands up and down his arms, although there was no way the frictional heat could have penetrated his insulation suit. "Or passed out from that broken ankle of his."

"We left him extra medical supplies," Howard

reminded him. "And he knows we need him on the console, to relay our location to the *Enterprise.*"

"Uhura calling Jimenez," Uhura said, biting her words off as crisply as she could to keep them from fading into the background hiss of static. The falling wails of interference had vanished for the moment. "Uhura calling Jimenez, do you read me? Uhura calling Jimenez—"

". . . read you . . ." The words barely crackled past the communicator's internal hum. ". . . tune . . ."

Uhura hurriedly focused on that scrap of response, patching Chekov's communicator into her stronger output signal as she did so. "Uhura calling Jimenez. Can you read me now?"

"Much better, sir." Despite the static, the young man's voice sounded steadier than it had that morning. "Have you found the shuttle crew?"

"Not yet," Chekov said grimly. "Jimenez, are you alone?"

"Yessir." The urgency in Chekov's voice brought a reply as crisp as a Starfleet cadet's. "The Chinit brought me to one of their private alcoves. They're out hunting now."

"Good," said Chekov. "This is a Starfleet Priority command. Get in touch with the *Enterprise.* Tell them that a group of Kitka headed by the shaman Alion have been observed slaughtering Nordstral personnel and are now pursuing us across the ice. We need transport *immediately.*"

"Yessir." Uhura could almost hear Jimenez swallow down his shock. A distant howl of interference shivered through his signal. "When do you want me to contact you with their reply, sir?"

Chekov glanced over his shoulder at Uhura and she shook her head. "We'll contact you, Jimenez, when we can," she told the wailing communicator. "You'll have to keep alert for times of low auroral interference."

". . . sir." The transmission began to fade again, as the howls grew louder. ". . . luck . . ."

"We've lost him." Uhura closed her eyes, her head aching from the combined shriek of wind and static. She dialed the volume on her communicator all the way down to give herself a moment of relative silence, then jerked upright with fear clawing at her throat. Even with the communicator off, she could still hear howling.

"Chekov!" she gasped, then cursed and spun the volume back up on her suit channel when he didn't reply. "Chekov, listen to your outside mike! This noise isn't just coming from the auroras—there are Kitka near us!"

"Damn!" The security chief swung around and yanked her to her feet. "Howard, give me tricorder readings. Number of aliens, estimated direction and distance from us. Publicker, get that sled turned on."

The tricorder whirred and spat its readings out as the gravsled hummed to life. "At least five Kitka, sir, but the magnetic flux won't let it calculate distance or directions," Howard reported.

"All right." Chekov kicked the tow bar out of the snow and shoved it into Publicker's hands. "I want you to head downhill."

"Downhill?" The guard sounded baffled.

"We've been traveling downhill all morning. It's the only direction we can be sure the Kitka aren't coming from. We need you to show us the way."

Publicker still didn't move. "But, sir—how am I supposed to know which way is downhill?"

Chekov said something short and pungent in Russian. "Give me that sled!" He yanked the tow bar out of the other man's hands, then deliberately let it go. The gravsled skated past them, gathering speed as it headed down the slope of the ice. Chekov strode after it, pulling Uhura with him at a near run. Around them the snow had whirled itself into a solid white wall that blocked out sight and muffled sound. Uhura turned up the volume on her outside mike and winced as the wind's scream became a roar. Beyond it, the Kitka howling sounded closer. Her side tried to knot itself as she ran.

The boreal winds fell suddenly into silence, dropping their veil of snow to reveal a landscape of cracked and shattered ice. Uhura shouted a warning as she saw what lay directly ahead of them: the dark blue emptiness of a crevasse, slashed canyon-deep across the ice sheet.

She flailed her arms and skidded to a stop a bare meter from the edge, dimly aware of the gravsled sliding past her. In the flurry of startled yells and triumphant howling from behind, it took Uhura a long moment to realize that Chekov hadn't stopped when she did. Instead, dragged by his stubborn grip on the gravsled, he was slowly toppling over the dark rim of the ice.

McCoy eased Nuie off his shoulders and onto one of the beds in sickbay. What he wouldn't give for one of his good old diagnostic beds from the *Enterprise!* He needed something with a readout screen showing simultaneous vitals and other necessary information, not this star scout's cot! Oh, well. He didn't call himself an old-fashioned country doctor for nothing. Be that as it may, he wasn't going to examine Nuie until he'd taken care of his hand. It was bad medical practice to bleed on your patients.

He still didn't have his familiar medikit, but didn't want to take any further time by retrieving it from his and Kirk's makeshift quarters. He'd spent enough time cleaning Muhanti's lab to have a good idea where everything was that he'd need. And what he didn't know where to find, he'd look for.

Muhanti. Thought of his attacker made him pause. The last he'd seen of the ship's doctor, Muhanti had disappeared behind a curtain of greenish seawater. Was he dead, too?

"What do you mean, 'too'?" McCoy growled to himself. "Jim's not dead. It takes more than a slug of cold water to kill Kirk." Anyway, he hoped that was the case, and would try not to dwell on possibilities. If he did that, he couldn't uphold his end of the job, and Kirk would never forgive him for that.

He found the necessary materials to clean, suture, and bind his hand. Then he brought a portable sphygmomanometer, a stethoscope, and a tiny penlight from one cabinet. Nuie's heart beat strongly and his eyes reacted to the light. McCoy noted his blood pressure and hoped it was within normal limits for a Kitka. He stepped away from the bed, considering, and the communicator on his belt beeped for attention.

Hope swelling inside him, McCoy snatched the small device into one hand and flipped it open. "Jim? Jim, is that you?"

The deep, impassive voice that answered did not belong to Jim Kirk. "Dr. McCoy, can you hear me?"

"Yes." Even Spock's voice was a welcome familiarity right now. "And much as I hate to admit it, you've never sounded so good."

"Indeed." He could almost imagine the Vulcan lifting one saturnine eyebrow. "The planet is currently experiencing a period of magnetic calm, no doubt accounting for the clarity of your reception."

The doctor rubbed his eyes, almost laughing. "That's not what I meant."

"Dr. McCoy," Spock cut in, "we have little time. Nordstral has just experienced a pole reversal."

"*Pole* reversal?" He searched his memory for some clue to what this entailed, but came up with nothing that made any sense. "Are you telling me this goddammed planet turned itself upside down?"

"No, Doctor." For a Vulcan, Spock's tone was almost a sigh. "The planet's magnetic field has reversed its polarity such that the north pole has now become the south pole."

"Is that what made our ship crash into the ice?"

Spock paused. "The *Soroya* has crashed?"

McCoy opted not to mention Kirk's absence or his own worries about their captain's safety. "Some kind of icequake, they said. Knocked us around a little."

"Tectonic disturbances are often linked to magnetic reversals," Spock admitted. "As are volcanic eruptions."

McCoy snorted. "Volcanic eruptions—oh, that's just what we need. What's the prognosis, Spock? Is Nordstral all done having its magnetic fit?"

"Standard theory states that dipole magnetic fields generated in a planet's liquid core suffer reversal only once every few million years. However—"

"Dammit, Spock, I hate your howevers."

"My apologies, Doctor, but scientific reality cannot be altered to suit your preferences." A flash of static cut across Spock's voice, then dashed away just as quickly. ". . . computer analysis of Nordstral's magnetic field indicates that it is far more complex than a simple dipole. There appear to be other magnetic components controlling the field from closer to the planet's surface. Increasing fluctuation of these secondary components gradually destablized the main . . ." Another burst of static drowned him out again, for longer this time. ". . . predict that the poles will continue to reverse on an extremely short time scale, possibly as often as every thirty hours."

"Good lord!" Interference screeched from the small communicator, and McCoy winced away from that as much as from Spock's news. "You mean we're going to get banged around like that once every day?"

"I'm afraid so, Doctor." His voice sounded like overheard whispers from a distant room, although smothered in static and auroral wails. ". . . not certain . . . the cause of secondary fluctuations . . . ship's sensors indicate . . . extremely unusual fashion . . . still analyzing . . ."

McCoy waited until the white noise nearly gave him a headache, then snapped his communicator shut with a curse. Just like Spock to leave before getting to the good parts.

A groan from the prostrate man swung McCoy around and brought him striding back to the bed. He bent down, one hand firm in the center of Nuie's chest, holding him in place. "Take it easy, Nuie. It's McCoy. You're in sickbay."

Weirdly colored eyes opened and stared up at him in confusion. "Dr. McCoy?"

"It's all right, Nuie. You're fine. At least, I *think* you're fine. How do you feel?"

The Kitka paused, as though taking internal inventory. For all McCoy knew, he might be. "I feel okay. A little dizzy, maybe. What happened?"

"You had a little bump on the head." McCoy helped the first mate to slowly sit up. "I'd like to take more time to examine you, but—"

"Dr. McCoy?"

"Yes, Nuie?"

"Why are we wet?"

The question shot an abrupt, unhappy bark of laughter out of McCoy. "We're wet because the bridge began to flood." Quickly as he could, he recounted what occurred.

Nuie clutched his hand. "Dr. McCoy, do you remember hearing anything?"

"Hearing? No. I—" His eyes narrowed. "Wait a minute. There was something." He remembered when, too, but didn't feel he needed to get into a discussion about Muhanti trying to carve him up for Thanksgiving dinner. "A groaning kind of sound. I thought it was a kraken again."

Nuie shook his head. "It was the ice. Oh, this is bad." The first mate looked at McCoy worriedly. "I have to get up to the bridge. They've probably cleared it by now, and I need to know what's happened. I need to find out how bad off we are, and get in touch with the company. If Captain Mandeville is lost . . ." Nuie shrugged and hopped off the bed. His eyes widened with surprise when his feet splashed down into several inches of water.

McCoy stared at their feet. His had been wet and chilled since the deluge on the bridge. He'd never noticed the gathering flood.

A quick glance around showed the leak where several rivets had been strained by the accident. Water poured in a steady tide, unnoticed until now.

McCoy grabbed Nuie's arm and pulled him toward

the door. "We have to get out of here! Is there a way to seal this room off so we don't flood the ship?"

"The door itself should do it, but we'll need to compensate for the intake, or the drag will keep us under."

McCoy didn't want to think about that. It was only one more worry in a string of worries he didn't have time to consider. He reached the door and stopped, staring at it. The door had been chocked open when he arrived with Nuie. He'd left it that way, in case anyone called, needing him. Now the door was shut, flush with the ugly wall around it.

Suddenly afraid, McCoy reached for the wheel in the center of the door and gave it a tug. The door didn't budge. He tried to turn the wheel first one way, then the other, but it clunked to a halt barely a quarter of the way around. He turned and looked at Nuie. "I don't think I want to know what this means."

The Kitka nodded, eyes hooded. "You already know, Doctor. It means we're locked in."

Teetering on the edge of the deep ice crevasse, Chekov's first thought was that they couldn't afford to lose their gravsled and—with it—their only sources of food and shelter. He clapped both hands to the gravsled's tow bar as it lumbered away and down, hauling back with all his strength and praying the sled's straining servos wouldn't insist on equalizing with the crevasse floor a hundred meters below them.

Howard shouted in alarm, and Chekov had no time to order him away before the ensign had flung both arms around his chief's middle and added his own weight to the pull. Relenting, the gravsled bobbed over the lip of the crevasse and glided back toward

Publicker and Uhura as if that had always been its goal. Howard and Chekov tumbled into the snow still locked together, scrambling back from the dropoff's edge even as they fell.

Not pretty, Chekov allowed, disentangling himself from Howard and getting to his feet, but effective. "Thank you, Mr. Howard."

The taller man brushed a dusting of snow off his insulation suit, still breathing raggedly. "Jeeze, Chief, you scared me."

Turning to edge back toward the crevasse, Chekov kept his hands carefully behind him, as if that would somehow prevent his accidental dislodgement. The rift went deeper than he could see, its bottommost reaches obscured by slabs of dancing light, blown snow, and awkward knobs and ledges of broken ice. Everything was so clear—like a mountainside carved in glass—that light glared brilliant aqua through a crusting of pockmarked snow. Only the faintest smudge of darkness a few hundred meters to his left hinted that something must span the crevasse to cast that brittle shadow. Chekov peered down the length of the crevasse, and was soon rewarded with a dim glimpse of something long and ragged jutting out across that abyss.

He caught Uhura's wrist and started off in that direction. "Publicker! Bring the gravsled—find the repelling cable."

Uhura trotted beside him, her attention still half behind them as the Kitka whistles grew closer and more dense. "What are you going to do?"

Chekov's heart soared as the narrow ice bridge solidified with nearness. Taking the cable Howard ran up to him, he pulled Uhura to a stop and turned her to face away from him so he could loop the cable snugly around her trim waist. "We're going over that bridge."

"Oh . . ." Uhura stood very still, eyeing the bridge. One hand played nervously with the blank Kitka mask still hanging around her neck. "Oh, Pavel, I don't know . . ."

"We haven't any choice." Cinching her tight, Chekov estimated the length of the bridge and played out a length of rope to hold between himself and Uhura before passing the remainder back to Howard. "Tie me, then Publicker, then yourself." Taking Uhura's shoulders so he could rotate her to face him, Chekov went on to explain, "We can't run very much longer. This way, we can knock out the bridge behind us so Alion and his people can't follow."

"If the bridge doesn't knock us out first." Publicker squirmed unhappily, twisting the excess rope between his black-gloved hands while staring at the slim tongue of ice. "That earthquake must have cracked it all to pieces, sir."

It wasn't as though Chekov hadn't already considered that. "That will just make knocking it down easier. Come on." He led them toward the foot of the bridge at an anxious trot. The only certainty he knew right now was that Alion's men would kill them if they caught them. God only knew why. If Chekov could start his people across the bridge—smallest to largest —the ice just might hold long enough to get three of them across. Then, when it collapsed, Chekov, Uhura, and Publicker would have a better than even chance of hanging onto Howard's line when he fell. If the ice bridge didn't hold . . .

Then they were all dead, just like they would be if they didn't try, so dwelling on that thought wasn't worth it.

At the foot of the bridge, Chekov twisted around to wave the gravsled forward. Howard shoved it up to Publicker, who jumped a little with surprise at being distracted from his singular study of the ice bridge. Reaching back to guide it around Publicker, Chekov passed it forward to Uhura and pressed the tow bar into her hand. "Take this with you. It won't add any weight to the bridge, and we need to make sure it gets across." *And you're the only one I'm certain can make it.*

She nodded, small hands tense on the bar. Turning, she squared her shoulders with a sigh and tried to laugh. "Hold tight, you guys."

Chekov nervously wrapped one hand in the cable. "Always."

She set her feet gingerly on the irregular expanse, toe first, heel to follow. The shrieking auroral static drowned his ability to hear individual footsteps, making it seem as though she picked her way across the crevasse in miraculous silence. To Chekov that silence only made her feel even farther away—that much more unreachable and unsalvageable should anything go wrong. Puffs of snow whitened the ankles of her black suit, roiling in a milky cloud beneath the slow gravsled; glitters of ice rained from the belly of the bridge down into the crevasse below. When Uhura leapt the last meter to stumble onto glacier sheet at the other side, Chekov released a pent breath so explosive he almost didn't hear Uhura's voice squeak over the communicator, "I'm across! It's all right—I'm over!"

He raised both hands, thumbs up, and smiled when she returned the salute. The gravsled drifted lazily behind her, seeking some level point on the rippling reach of ice.

Tapping his suit comm to a private channel, Chekov

glanced back at Publicker and Howard. "Are you ready?"

They nodded.

"Be careful." He hated to have to say it. "If I fall, she's not going to be able to hold me."

"We've got you, sir," Howard assured him. Publicker only nodded again, stiffly, and said, "Don't fall, please."

"I'll try not to." Then, insides twisting and knotting with vertigo, he eased up to the bridge and stepped out onto the expanse.

He felt the crunch beneath his feet more than heard it, felt the fractional layer of frozen snow shatter beneath each step and sink down into the hard ice beneath. He'd never considered himself afraid of heights, but something like this was entirely different —not fear, but deadly mistrust of his own beleaguered senses. Wind and sound and light tried to fool him into illusions of pendulumlike motion. Peripheral vision showed him nothing but down, down, and more down for as far as he could see to either side, but looking at his feet made his whole body feel impossibly tall and disconnected. Water, as black as obsidian with foamy flecks of waves chopping across the surface, wound a sluggish ribbon through the bottom of the crevasse. Chekov forced his eyes ahead, concentrating instead on Uhura's stark black figure at the foot of the bridge. So long as she stayed before him, he was all right—so long as she drew closer, he was all right. He was almost nose to nose with her when his footing finally slid from bridge ice to glacier ice and stumbled him into Uhura on his way to more solid ground.

"Not a lot of fun, is it?" she commented quietly, her tone of voice amused.

Chekov laughed a little, but otherwise opted not to answer. Opening his comm channel, he stepped aside to wave the next man over. "All right, Publicker, come on."

Hands still worrying with the knot tied at his waist, the figure poised at the bridge's lip shook his head with slow resolve. "No . . ." Publicker's voice sounded young and shaken over the crackling channel. "I . . . I don't think I want to do this, sir."

Chekov's stomach clenched with dread. "We all have to do things we don't want to, Mr. Publicker." It hadn't occurred to him that Publicker's reticence was anything more profound than his own. "I don't intend to come back over there," he went on, trying to sound stern, "so you'd better start moving."

Howard's lean figure moved up close behind Publicker's shoulder. "It's okay, Mark, we've got you."

Chekov lifted his eyes to scan the icescape behind the two for signs of the approaching Kitka. "There's no turning back, Mr. Publicker. You've got to come on." *And hurry!*

Whether Publicker took the first shaky steps on his own or Howard nudged him forward, Chekov couldn't tell. Either way, Publicker inched onto the spar of ice with his elbows tucked close to his sides, his knees nearly riveted together with terror. Chekov caught himself digging his feet into the ice, afraid Publicker even had his eyes closed as he shuffled across, but restraining himself from calling out for fear of startling him into a panic.

At not quite halfway across the younger man suddenly froze, his chin jerking as though he'd heard a frightening noise.

Howard fidgeted at the foot of the bridge. "Mark . . . ?"

"It moved!" Publicker gasped, and Chekov felt his heart leap into his throat.

"Keep moving!" he shouted, running backward to extend the cable between them and keep himself as far as he could from the crevasse's edge.

"It moved, sir!" Publicker staggered back the way he'd just come, hands gripping his arms. "I felt the ice move under me!"

"Publicker, *come here!*"

A thundercrack of sound underscored Chekov's order, and Publicker spun to face the tumult just as the bridge behind him shattered and tore loose a segment of glacier wall. Howard, arms flailing, did his best to backpedal while the ground crumbled beneath his feet. He toppled headlong into the crevasse, grabbing instinctively for the cable that bound him only to Publicker and—through him—to Chekov and Uhura on the other side of the rift.

Chekov knew what was coming only moments before the cable snapped taut and yanked Publicker backwards off the disintegrating trestle. He spread his legs wide, jamming his heels into the brittle snow, bracing himself for the dual weight of his plummeting guards and praying that Uhura had the sense to cut him loose if he couldn't save her from being hauled into the abyss.

When both men slammed against the end of their belay, Chekov had only long enough to see the cable slice a deep wedge into the remnants of the bridge before the force of their combined weight jerked him off his feet and dragged him, and Uhura, toward the lip of the crevasse.

Chapter Ten

McCoy LEVELED A FINGER under the stocky Kitka's nose. "Now, wait just a damned minute!" He worked hard to keep his voice at a normal level when panic wanted to send it shrieking, and him along with it. "That door was wide open when I brought you in. *I* didn't close it, I know for damned sure *you* didn't, and there's no vagrant breeze to help it along! So how—"

"Only two doors lock from the outside aboard the *Soroya*—the door to Captain Mandeville's quarters and the door to the wardroom. Even then, you can't lock somebody *in,* as they're easily opened from the other side." Nuie reached out and ran a callused hand ruminatively around the door's center wheel. His fingers tightened briefly, checking the spin in either direction. The wheel barely budged. "This has been jammed from the outside."

"But that means—" McCoy stopped, realized his

168

finger was still thrust oratorically into the air. He swore and jammed it into a pocket. Staring at the heavy door, he worried the inside of his lip. He didn't like what this meant any more than he liked the chill sweat coating his body under the wet Starfleet uniform. "Who would lock us in?" he asked quietly, his voice almost calmly speculative while his mind gibbered and capered around the inside of his skull.

"How should I know?" Nuie replied with an honesty that made McCoy want to knock his head against the wall. "I was unconscious."

McCoy hazarded a look over his shoulder at the leak. Was it his imagination, or had it grown in strength during the few moments he'd taken his eyes away? "Do you think whoever locked us in knew about that?" He thrust a chin toward the spill of water.

"If you're asking me do I think someone locked us in here to kill us, I'd say there's a good chance."

Ire momentarily put fear to bay and the Starfleet officer glared sourly. "Don't Kitka ever *lie?*"

Nuie blinked impassive silver eyes. "This Kitka doesn't."

The man's frank honesty elicited a short laugh from McCoy, when he felt about as far from happy as he'd ever been. There was a flutter in his chest, as of a million frantic birds beating their wings against his ribs. "Well, I don't know about the Kitka, Nuie, but the McCoys never go down without a fight. Just ask the Hatfields."

"The *who?*"

"Never mind." Hands on his hips, McCoy turned to watch the steady fall of water. "Can we plug that, or at least slow it down?"

Nuie gave the wall brief, careful consideration before answering. "Maybe . . . if we were outside. Look closely, Doctor. The break isn't just there. That's just an opening. The seams have been strained here, but somewhere else, too." He reached out and let the water cascade gently over his fingers. "All of the equipment is up in the turret, anyway."

"Forget I asked." McCoy crossed the room and began randomly but quickly opening doors and drawers.

"What are you doing?" Nuie splashed over to stand at the doctor's elbow and watch.

McCoy tried not to think about how much the water had risen while they talked; tried not to recall what it felt like to drown. He knew once he let the fear get hold of him, he was lost, and Nuie with him. "I'm looking for something to whale the tar out of that door." When that only made the first mate look confused, McCoy sighed and rolled his eyes. "I mean something to hit it with, Nuie. To see if we can break through." He lifted free a contraption made of weirdly jointed metal parts. "Something like this." The crude instrument hadn't been used in modern hospitals since before McCoy was an intern. For the first time, he was glad to find Muhanti's sickbay behind the times.

He grabbed another piece of equipment and thrust it into Nuie's hands. "Here. Let's give it a try." He led the way back to the door. The water was above his ankles and his feet were numb with cold. Salty brine odor tainted the air like iodine or the taste of copper.

He hefted the implement back over one shoulder and swung. It made a satisfying racket against the wall. Nuie immediately joined in, powerful shoulder muscles rippling the damp material of his shirt. Their blows swung and fell together, developing a kind of cadence. After several moments McCoy held up a hand. "Is it any looser?" he puffed, winded. He promised himself that if he got out of this alive, he'd start taking Kirk up on his offers of working out together in the gym.

Wet hair straggled across Nuie's eyes as he bent and shoved a hand against the door. It didn't budge. "No."

"Then we do it again."

And again. And again. By that time the water had risen to calf height. The bottoms of McCoy's uniform pants fluttered like underwater weeds. His feet felt like unwieldy blocks of wood tied to his ankles. He stamped when he walked, trying to restore a sense of circulation because he couldn't feel his individual toes.

"Where the hell's the crew?" he groused, pacing back and forth. "They can't *all* be up by the bridge." He faced Nuie. "What are the intercom capabilities aboard ship?"

The first mate shrugged from atop one of the sickbay beds, legs crossed and clear of the rising water. "Standard Nordstral communications network. There are speakers throughout the ship."

"Can we transmit from the lab?" McCoy asked eagerly.

"I don't know. It wasn't something I ever had to worry about, but I expect so. Standard operating procedure for Nordstral, even on a vessel as old and rundown as *Soroya,* is to have everyone easily accessible to the captain. The doctor is next in command after me."

McCoy nodded grimly, his thoughts of Muhanti warring with his desperate desire to be just about anywhere but here. "Let's give it a try."

McCoy hated slogging through the chill water to Muhanti's cramped corner desk, stuck in a tiny area between the last bed and the lab's outer wall. Water trickled around his knees. His joints felt tight from the cold. The intercom unit was a push-button wall affair not unlike those intermittently spread through the vast corridors of the *Enterprise*. Thoughts of the great ship gave McCoy an odd admixture of feelings. Would he ever see her again?

His thumb stabbed the button and held it down. "McCoy to bridge. This is Dr. Leonard McCoy calling the bridge or anyone else who can read me. Over." Nothing. "This is Dr. Leonard McCoy. If you can hear us, First Mate Nuie and I are trapped in the lab. There's a hull breech and water is coming in." He licked his lips, needing to stop and calm the tremble in his chest. All that water. All that water, just waiting to rush in and fill his lungs . . .

"Dr. McCoy!" The sharp urgency in Nuie's voice, and his hard hands, warm on McCoy's arms even through the cold, wet parka, brought the doctor's eyes up. The Kitka's face was pinched with worry. "You got very gray for a minute. I thought you might pass out."

"The thought crossed my mind," McCoy rasped, chest tight. "Nuie—I can't take this. We've got to get out of here." McCoy hated the way his voice shook; hated that he couldn't stop it from shaking. "I—I'm afraid of water. Can you understand that? I don't know what I'll do if—"

Nuie's hands tightened on his arms and shook him

gently. "Dr. McCoy, relax! It's just the brain sickness. You're being affected like the rest of the crew."

McCoy drew himself up straight and shook off Nuie's supportive hands. "Bull! I know the difference between brain sickness and being scared out of my ever-loving mind!"

The ship abruptly slewed to one side. Equipment flew off counters and something crashed in the lab. McCoy would have fallen but for Nuie's quick reflexes. They froze, arms tight around one another, waiting to see what the *Soroya* would do next. She shifted sideways, sighed, and was silent.

"What the hell was that all about?" McCoy's voice was a thready whisper. His throat was dry and he was too scared to work up spit.

Nuie shook his head, nostrils working the air. "Dr. McCoy . . . do you smell smoke?"

The fierce yank of the cable slammed Uhura back toward the edge of the crevasse, boots skidding uselessly across the wind-blasted surface of the ice. She struggled to unknot the loop around her waist, her gloved fingers stiff and slow with fear. Her breath jammed in her throat, already anticipating the fall into freezing-cold water—

Then Chekov grunted, and the tension on the rope suddenly went slack. Now that she was no longer fighting the pull of two guards dangling below, Uhura caught her balance and managed to loosen the loop of rope. As it dropped, she swung around to see Chekov on his back at the edge of the crevasse, legs rammed into its upthrown rim and shoulders straining to hold the humming rope. His boot heels ground against the snow-crusted ice, slowly losing their fragile purchase.

Years of Starfleet training broke through Uhura's shock with memories of climbing exercises run on walls of slick, wet granite. *"Pitons!"* She spun and scrambled across the snow for the loaded gravsled. "Chekov, do we have pitons?"

"In—equipment—case." His voice came in painful gasps, as if he could barely spare the effort of making words. "Red—bag."

Uhura yanked the case out without bothering to undo any straps, then tore it open with frantic haste. A canvas bag of climbing pins spilled out at her feet when she shook it. She grabbed up a handful and ran.

"I've got them." She scrambled to a stop just behind Chekov and smacked a piton into the ice as hard as she could. Its sharp steel point barely made a dent, but a quick twist detonated its internal charge, blasting a hard plastic extension down into the ice. Uhura grabbed the cable and anchored it with a swift loop and turn around the pin, then knotted it as hard as she could.

Chekov grunted again, even more breathlessly. "Set?"

"Let me get one more in . . ." Uhura tugged the rope taut between him and the first pin, in case Howard and Publicker were dangling just above water level. Despite the ominous silence from their communicators, she refused to think about the chance that they might have fallen in already. Surely the weight on Chekov wouldn't be so great if either man was floating. A second piton exploded down into the ice sheet. She snagged the rope around it, then caught up the free end and knotted it there, too, for good measure. "All right, I've got it. You can let go."

Chekov did so, rolling sideways with a sharp gasp of relief as the rope thrummed and snapped tight around the pins. The gasp became a cry of pain when he tried to scramble to his feet. Uhura looked over in concern, seeing the security chief bent double on the ice.

"Chekov! Are you hurt?"

He shook his head vehemently as she dropped to her knees beside him. "Just cramped from holding the rope." He sounded as though he were talking through gritted teeth. "Give me a minute, then I'll haul Howard and Publicker up—"

"Don't worry." Uhura patted his pain-knotted shoulder gently. "I can do that."

"You?" Chekov tilted his head to stare at her in what looked like amazement. "How?"

She grinned, although she knew he couldn't see it, and rose to her feet. "With the solar-powered winch you put in the equipment case."

A spate of caustic Russian followed her as she headed back toward the gently drifting gravsled. Uhura's grin faded when she saw how far the sled had traveled from the spilled bag of climbing pins. She snagged the tow bar and pulled it back with her, using the dangling end of the cable to fasten the sled to her embedded pitons. Then she dug the bright yellow winch out of the equipment box and turned back toward Chekov.

He had levered himself up to a painful crouch by then, peering intently down the side of the crevasse. "I can see them." He tapped impatiently at the transmitter inside his insulation suit collar, as if that would make it work better. "Howard, can you hear me? Publicker?"

"They may not be"—Uhura swallowed at the sudden fierce turn of Chekov's goggles toward her—"conscious," she finished lamely. She knelt on the ice near where the rope disappeared over the edge, digging in the snow crust with her hands to make enough space for the winch. "They must have hit the side of the ice pretty hard."

"True." The security officer fell silent. Uhura finished threading the rope into the winch, then switched it on. The heavy metal drums growled and began to turn, hauling the rope in despite its icy hiss of protest. Uhura sighed and sat back, looking at Chekov.

He was staring at the far side of the crevasse, shoulders tense under his snow-splattered insulation suit. "I can't see the Kitka," he muttered, so softly he must have been talking to himself. "Dammit, where are they?"

Uhura dared a glance into the blue-edged depths below them. Gray slabs of ice floated in the foam-dark water, the shattered remnants of the bridge they'd crossed. On either side, the break in the ice sheet stretched into the distance, widening to their left into a black arc of open sea. "Chekov, there's no way they can reach us now. They've probably gone back to their village."

"Maybe." He fidgeted with his communicator—dialing the radio down to listen to the outside mike, Uhura guessed. The growl of the winch deepened as it reeled in more rope. She kept a careful eye on the slithering cable, ready to reach out at the first glimpse of an insulation suit. After a moment Chekov came to join her. "Any sign of them yet?"

"Not yet." Even as the words left her mouth, though, something scraped heavily against the ice ledge they leaned over. As smoothly as if they'd practiced the maneuver, Chekov reached out to haul the black-suited figure up over the edge while Uhura spun to switch off the winch. When she turned back, it was with a cry of horror.

"Publicker!" His insulation suit was so badly shredded it hung loose across his chest and neck, his breath filter held in place only by his own desperate grip on it. He'd somehow lost his goggles, leaving his face white with frost. Blood had frozen in a thin trickle below one ear, where the ice had slashed too deep for his insulation suit to protect him.

"His communicator's gone." Chekov unknotted the rope from around the young man's waist, then shook it free. Uhura switched the winch on again, and the security chief lowered Publicker to the ground. "Publicker, can you hear me through the mike?"

Publicker nodded, squinting his eyes painfully open. He took a deep breath, then erupted into coughing. The moisture from his unfiltered breath glittered in the air around them. "Can't breathe," he gasped, his voice hoarse and weak in the arctic air. "Can't—"

Chekov cursed and leaned down to wrap the remnants of Publicker's tattered insulation suit as closely around him as he could. "There should be a spare filter in the sled," he told Uhura grimly. "And a set of goggles, too."

"I'm going." The gravsled bobbed beneath her frantic fingers while she searched. "I can't find them. Where—" The deepening growl of the winch warned her an instant before she heard the scrape of something against ice. She and Chekov lunged forward at the same time, catching at the limp, misshapen figure that bumped its way over the lip of the crevasse. Uhura bit at her lip hard when she saw the awful way Howard's arm dangled in front of him.

"Oh, God—what happened to him?"

"Steady." Chekov gripped her arm briefly. "I think he's dislocated a shoulder, that's all." He bent to lift the tall guard's other arm, then let it go. It fell back limply, and Chekov grunted. "He's still out. I'll try to put his shoulder back before he wakes up. Go find Publicker's breath filter, or his lungs will burn on this air. There should be one in the emergency box, up in front near the medikit."

"All right." Uhura scrambled around the tangle of rope and winch, heading for the front of the sled while Chekov knelt over Howard's sprawled figure. She dialed her outside mike up as she went, listening to Publicker's gasping cough. "Hang on, Publicker!" she called back to him. "We'll have you fixed up in no time."

His reply was a cry of hoarse, wordless panic. Uhura swung around, startled. The guard had risen to his knees, swaying on the very edge of the ice sheet as he stared across it. Her gaze followed his as a shiver of distant howling split the air again.

On the far side of the crevasse, a flicker of white on white was all that showed her the feather-clad Kitka running directly toward the gaping chasm. Uhura watched in horror as they flung themselves toward the edge, wondering what on Earth they were trying to do. Then she noticed the slender flash of bone-white poles they carried, and realized with a sickening catch of breath what they intended. Chekov must have looked up and seen it, too—his warning shout rose with hers as two of the natives planted their long spears into the icy edge of the crevasse and vaulted themselves across.

The leap began in deadly silence, a long, glittering white arc through the snow-frosted air. It ended in a crash as the natives landed on their side of the ice, bare meters from their sled. Uhura cried out as the ice shook with the impact, hard enough to throw her to her knees. For some reason, though, the crashing didn't end when the natives hit. It got louder, joined after a moment by a familiar groan of shattering ice. Uhura felt a jolt of separation, and suddenly realized that the entire ice sheet had fallen away beneath them.

She screamed once as they fell toward the water below.

McCoy's nostrils flared, catching a whiff of acrid odor. His eyes darted around the sickbay's close confines and his fingers twisted in the material of Nuie's shirt. "There!"

A thread of smoke drifted out the lab door, riding low on the air currents, delicately touching the water like early morning fog burning off the surface of a mountain lake. It grew as they watched, darkening, and they heard the crackle of flames.

The men hurried toward the lab, legs laboring against the cold wash of water caressing their thighs. McCoy spared the leak a brief glance as he passed, and his heart fell, seeing it fountain ever faster.

His outthrust arm stopped Nuie in the doorway. Beyond them, flames rode the rising water like proud flagships of an ancient, conquering race. Fire licked the walls and blackened the edges of the lab furnishings. Smoke billowed and thickened.

McCoy cursed luridly, coupling Muhanti's name several times with physical feats one could only do if they were ten feet tall and possessed a double-jointed spine. At that moment McCoy would have been only too happy to donate the time and energy into making the necessary adjustments to Muhanti . . . and perhaps a few more besides.

"It's his stupid experiments," he explained to Nuie,

raising his voice to be heard over the rising crackle of flame. "When the ship shifted, it must have sent everything flying." His brows drew together. "Something must have been oil-based." The flames slicked and slid across the water's surface like ice skaters with weak ankles.

An errant flag of smoke made Nuie cough. He tugged McCoy back out of the doorway. "We've got to put it out, Doctor. It'll use up our oxygen before the water reaches ceiling level."

Frankly, McCoy wasn't thrilled with either prospect. Both involved death by suffocation, and that was never his first choice when it came to picking a way to die. In bed, surrounded by loved ones and admirers, was more his style, but he didn't bother telling that to the Kitka.

"I don't know where Muhanti kept his extinguishers. They're probably underwater, anyway," McCoy added sourly.

"We'll close the door," Nuie responded simply, "and the fire will burn off its oxygen."

McCoy stared at him in admiration, feeling patently stupid. "Nuie, I stand in awe."

"Don't bother." Nuie gestured unhappily and McCoy turned around. The back wall of the lab was bent and twisted like that in sickbay. Water poured silently down the wall, deadly as any stealthy killer. "Oh, damn . . ."

A klaxon suddenly went off over their heads, and McCoy nearly leapt out of his skin. Water sprayed in every direction from a ceiling conduit as the sprinkler system came into play.

"Just what we need," the doctor groused, wincing as his heavy jacket settled soggily around him. "More water."

Nuie's expression was sardonic. "Come on, Dr. McCoy. Help me close the door."

It took both of them to drag the door shut against the pressure of water. By the time they finished, the water was to their chests. The alarm inexplicably quit as abruptly as it began. McCoy listened with feverish hope, but there were no sounds of impending rescue. "If that didn't get their attention, nothing will."

"I'm afraid you may be right, Doctor."

A sad little laugh escaped McCoy. He wasn't sure whether to hug Nuie or hit him for sounding so much like Spock. Looked like it would be the Vulcan delivering the eulogies, after all.

The press of frigid water against his chest made it hard to breathe. "Nuie, I—"

With a scream of outraged protest, the ship rolled. Both men went flying. McCoy landed hard and submerged. All of the air shot out of his lungs in a panicked rush, leaving him bruised and sore and abruptly breathing water. His eyes flashed open to the sting of saltwater and a murky, greenish hue. With a bellow of utter terror, he burst to the surface clawing for purchase, feet slipping unfeelingly along the deck.

Hands grabbed for him and he batted them away in his fright. Eyes wide and staring, he didn't see much at all until Nuie bodily lifted him onto one of the submerged bunks and held him there. The first mate's soothing litany finally calmed McCoy enough to blink and bring their surroundings into focus. His chest spasmed, rising and falling rapidly with the terrified cadence of his breathing. He took a deep breath and ordered himself to slow down, relax. McCoy's head sagged between his shoulders, and it was several moments before he could bring himself to release the stranglehold on Nuie's sleeve. "I'm sorry . . ."

"There's nothing wrong with being afraid," Nuie said firmly. "It's stupid to apologize for it."

"Then I'm stupid and sorry. It's just . . ." McCoy ran a wet hand through his dripping hair and shook his head, unable to find words.

"Stay on the bed." Nuie's hand rested briefly on his shoulder. "It'll keep you farther out of the water a little longer."

McCoy raised his head and stared bleakly into the other man's odd eyes, eyes he suddenly knew he would remember for the rest of his life. "We're going to die, aren't we?"

Nuie's gaze never wavered. "Yes, Doctor. I think we are. I guess it's a little too late for this Kitka to learn to lie."

The small joke elicited a weak chuckle from McCoy. "Yes, I guess it is." His gaze wavered, wandering into the middle distance. "I always thought I'd die with Kirk, or maybe with Spock. At least, with a friend."

"You are dying with a friend, McCoy."

That brought his attention back. The serious expression on the Kitka's face only confirmed his words.

McCoy held out his hand. "Thank you, Nuie. And the name's Leonard."

The worn hand gripped his tightly for a moment, and released it. "Nuie of Ulu Clan. The ulu is the special knife of the Kitka. You can do many things with the ulu." Nuie reached for the back of his belt and pulled forth a blade shaped like a one-third cut of pie. What would be the inner point was capped by a protruding handle made of bone and decorated with a kraken cut in relief. "I am knife bearer for Clan Ulu."

McCoy blinked at the sharp device, not sure he

liked even more dangerous objects inserted into this situation. "I thought you were a city kid, Nuie."

"Some things go beyond city or icebound, Doctor." The Kitka looked down at the blade, pensive. "The ulu stands for a lot of things to the Kitka, most of which wouldn't mean anything to you. Mostly, though, it stands for my people's need to meet with the god when the time comes for us to die."

Before McCoy knew what was happening, Nuie bared his forearm and slashed it deeply with the ulu.

A roaring wall of water geysered up all around their iceberg as it plunged into the green-black ocean. Chekov scrambled away from the surging whitecaps, trying to regain his footing on an ice shelf now bucking and heaving in rhythm with the churned-up waves. Water like a cold, firm hand shoved against the back of his legs, hissed past him over dissolving snow, froze to a glassy glare before the edge could peel back on itself and slip away. Chekov scrabbled, on hands and knees, beyond its reach and beat at the frosty glaze already adhering to his insulation suit. The ice broke and scattered with a crackling loud enough to challenge the static over his communicator.

Still unsteady with the iceberg's movement, hands outstretched to either side, he stumbled in a circle to take stock of their situation. The gravsled bobbed at the end of its tether, bumping ruts in the ice at what was now the highest point of their sloping raft. Howard lay tangled in the ropes and pitons near the sled; Uhura's frantic anchors had saved him from watery death yet again today. Near the top of a sharp incline, Uhura's slight figure picked its way across frozen snow and broken ice, fixated on something below and ahead of her—and not the stout, white-feathered man clambering up the slope behind her.

His heart spasming with fear, Chekov broke into a run even as he pushed up the suit's external volume. *"Uhura!"*

The native spun to face him, but Uhura only waved impatiently, her attention elsewhere. "It's all right," her voice crackled over the communicator channel. "I see him."

She couldn't have been talking about the native, but Chekov had no time to ask her to elaborate. The Kitka abandoned Uhura without even a pause, springing downslope at Chekov to tackle him into the water-slicked snow.

Ice, hard and ridged, knocked his breath away upon impact. Chekov rolled, trying to dislodge his attacker, only to have the Kitka clamp strong legs about his middle and pin him. Glossy feathers afforded no hold for insulation-suited hands, and Chekov found himself gripping nothing but air when the Kitka swiveled to jerk a broad-bladed knife from one boot top.

Oh, God, please no! Chekov recoiled instinctively from the blade's downward swipe. One hand flew up between them—a desperate attempt to keep the Kitka from his throat—and pain as bright as the Nordstral auroras shot through his forearm.

He felt the gritty scrape of ivory blade against human bone, felt the Kitka's weight rock forward with the blow, and heaved his legs upward to slam the native in the back. Overbalanced, the Kitka whistled in surprise and faltered. Chekov wrenched his injured arm away from the knife, swung a right-handed punch at the native's shoulder. The blow separated them again, tumbling the Kitka down the ice toward the open water and leaving Chekov to curl up on his side, gasping.

The splash of the Kitka hitting water was an oddly comforting sound—it let Chekov know exactly how far away the native was, assured him that the native was busy with something else now besides attacking him. Let the Kitka worry about his own survival for a while.

Rolling to his knees, Chekov caught himself with his good hand when nausea surged up through him and turned his vision gray. Even so, there was no mistaking the spattered pattern of scarlet in the snow all around him. He moaned softly through his teeth. Oh, please God, don't let this be happening. He couldn't afford to bleed to death—not out here, not right now. Taking a few deep, shuddering breaths to steady himself, he clenched his jaw for strength and looked down to access the damage.

Blood dribbled in a slow, dark patter between the fingers he'd clasped over the wound. Not bright enough to be arterial flow, not thick enough to be venous. Good—that meant no imminent death, although his breath still came tight and his heart still labored. He could flex his left fist, too. It rifled pain clear up to his temple, but it told him the knife had passed between muscle and bone, not between the two arm bones where severed nerves would have rendered the hand useless. All in all, much better than he had a right to hope for, considering the circumstances.

He staggered to his feet, still hugging his wounded arm to his stomach. Shock had almost numbed his senses, but he could feel a buzz of dizziness behind his eyes, a slow, maddening clench of muscles in his chest that fought his breathing. Best to find Uhura, make sure she was all right before adrenaline deserted him and left him to pass out face first in the snow. He'd probably follow the Kitka down into the water then. Given his current condition, that wouldn't be a good idea. "Uhura?"

Her voice came to him clearly, both over the communicator channel and through the air: "Chekov! Come help me!"

It took nearly all his concentration to crest the brief incline between them—hands, knees, remember to breathe. Even so, he was panting as though he'd just climbed Mount Everest when he slid down the other side. Uhura labored at the water's edge, her back to him and her hands nearly elbow deep in the frigid sea. When Chekov saw what she struggled with, horror startled a wordless cry from him and he lunged forward to grab at her hands.

In the water at Uhura's feet, Publicker bobbed barely even with the rocking iceberg. His eyes, closed and sunken, looked bruised against his ice-white face, and his lips were already the damning purple-black Chekov had learned to associate with people stranded out too long in the snow. Publicker's missing respirator meant his lungs were unprotected; the gashes in his insulation suit meant water had splashed against his skin since the moment their ice slab first broke free. Prying at Uhura's fingers with his own blood-slicked hands, Chekov ignored her frantic protests and dragged her mercilessly away from the water's edge. No longer supported by someone else's efforts, Publicker sank out of sight without a struggle.

"What are you *doing*?" Uhura jerked as hard as she was able, panic and frustration sharp in her voice when she discovered all her strength wasn't enough to loosen Chekov's grip. "Chekov, he's unconscious! He could die!"

His own head spinning, his heart sick with shock and despair, Chekov pushed her hands firmly against her sides and held them there. "You're wrong," he said, his voice very hoarse and tired. "He's dead already."

Chapter Eleven

UHURA CLOSED HER EYES, unable to watch as Publicker's frozen face sank below the dark and silent water. She reached out blindly for Chekov, wanting the touch of another person to erase the lingering feel of icy hands sliding out of hers. Her fingers met the security officer's rigid arm, then jerked back from his flinch and gasp of pain.

"You're hurt!" She spun around, eyes flying open to stare stupidly at Chekov's face, as if she could read any expression past the shimmer of his goggles. Then she saw the way he held his left arm, hugged tight to his chest with his other hand clamped below the elbow. The sleeve of his insulation suit glistened with icy streaks in the arctic glare, but it wasn't until Uhura saw the red stains on the ice behind him that she realized it was blood.

"Oh, my God!" She scrambled up the steep icy

slope, pushing him back toward more stable footing. "What happened?"

Lacking a free hand, Chekov jerked his chin toward the dark water of the crevasse. Their slab of ice rocked gently as some current stirred beneath it, tugging it away from the jagged blue walls. "Sub-zero water. With an insulation suit intact, it wouldn't matter. Once it got inside his suit, though, he never had a chance."

"No, I mean what happened to *you?*" Uhura reached out to catch at his good shoulder when he swayed.

"A native came at me with—a knife." Chekov's voice, which had been merely strained before, thinned into breathless gasps as he spoke. "I fought—him off—oh, God!"

He shocked her by lifting his good hand and tearing at his breath filter. It snapped open, letting out an explosion of frost-white air. Glittering ice crystals swirled and vanished in the arctic wind.

"Chekov, what's wrong?"

"Can't breathe—" His words echoed Publicker's so eerily that Uhura felt a shiver scrape up her spine. "Can't—" Chekov staggered down to his knees, the smooth surface of his insulation suit sliding out of her small hands.

"No!" Uhura grabbed at the security officer, suddenly terrified that he would slide down the icy slope into the water. One last shred of frost-white breath choked out from his open insulation suit, then he toppled facedown onto the ice. Uhura's quick lunge barely kept him from landing on his injured arm. He ended up in a twisted sprawl, half across her lap and half across the ice. Through the opened breath filter frost sparkled on his cheeks and chin, white as the bloodless skin beneath it.

"Oh, no." Uhura fumbled at his belt for his medikit. No simple knife wound could have caused this kind of reaction in the security chief—unless the knife blade had been poisoned.

She snapped the hypodermic of universal antitoxin out of his kit, then peeled Chekov's body slip away from his face to expose the muscles of his throat. She had the hypo almost in position when his limp body suddenly wrenched against her, convulsing into a rigid arc of pain. Uhura gasped as his head slammed backward into her arm, hard enough to send the slim hypodermic flying. She watched in horror as it landed meters away, then skittered down the sloping ice into the sea.

"No!" Panic made the communications officer ruthless. Shoving Chekov's stiffened body off her lap, she grabbed across her waist, clawed her medikit open and yanked out her own antitoxin shot. This time she didn't bother looking for muscle—she slammed the hypodermic down onto the nearest bare skin she could find and shot it home.

And nothing happened.

"Chekov, damn you, don't you dare die on me!" Uhura jammed both hands down onto his chest, forcing out whatever air remained in his lungs. Below the yielding foam of the insulation suit, the muscles of his torso felt like solid metal. She yanked her own breath filter off, gasping as the cold air seared her lungs, then leaned over to push what air she could into his frozen lungs. One breath, two breaths, three—and the tension ran out of him like melting ice.

Uhura sat back, breathing so hard her lungs felt burned. She couldn't see any difference in Chekov—

190

no rush of color into his ice-pale face, no sudden flutter of closed eyelids. If he was breathing, he was doing it so slowly she couldn't tell. Oh, God, was he dead?

She leaned down, not even sure what she hoped to do. Something thin and hard bumped against her chin as she did, and she lifted a hand to feel Nhym's Kitka mask, hanging loose and forgotten around her neck. An idea struck her suddenly. She dragged the bone mask over her head, almost tearing off her breath filter in her haste. The shining bone surface gleamed warm as milk as she held it over Chekov's ice-rimmed lips. The shine stayed in place for a long, excruciating moment, then faintly clouded with a film of mist.

"Thank God." Uhura dropped the mask from shaking fingers, then swung Chekov's breath filter back over his face to protect him from the cold. Her own cheeks were burning with frost. She began to snap her filter closed, then stopped abruptly.

From somewhere behind her, her outside mike had picked up the unmistakable crunch of a footstep.

The physician that was the heart and soul of Leonard McCoy galvanized into action. He vaulted off the bed into the stinking, frigid water and grabbed Nuie. "What the hell are you *doing?*"

The shaman thrust him away like a bothersome child. "You must not stop me in this, Leonard. This is a part of my life that needs to be completed. You cannot interfere."

"The hell I can't!" He attempted to grab the Kitka's bare arm and failed, hands sliding free across the flow of blood. "Dammit, Nuie!"

Someone pounded on the outer door. *"Bones! Are you in there?"*

The muffled cry stopped McCoy dead, freezing him for an instant before he spun and clawed his way to the door, water spraying in all directions. He hammered the thick metal with a fist made of cold-stiffened appendages that only barely resembled fingers. *"Jim!"* Relief so profound he almost wept flooded through him and made his legs flutter, threatening to send him under again. Just hearing his friend's voice drove the terror to bay.

"Bones, open the door!"

"I can't! It's been jammed from the outside! Jim, it's flooding in here! We're almost under!"

He watched the door wheel tock back and forth a minuscule distance, then heard Kirk swear loudly. "I'll get you out! I promise! Who's in there with you?"

"Just Nuie."

"How high is the water?"

McCoy swallowed hard. "Almost to my neck. We can get up on the beds and counters, but that won't make much difference in a few minutes."

"Do it! It'll give you extra breathing time. I— What the hell is that?!"

Behind McCoy rose an eerie, ululating wail. He whipped around and a cry tore from his throat. Nuie stood with his arm stretched high and straight above his head like a mountain's summit. Blood tracked down the corded muscle, staining his uniform and blushing the water with rosy tendrils. Head thrown back and eyes closed, his voice rose again in the weirdly pitched Kitka song. "Get in here, Jim, before we have a ritual suicide!"

"I'm coming as fast as I can!" Kirk cried.

McCoy licked his lips nervously and stepped toward Nuie. "Put away your knife, Nuie. It's not time for us to die." *Liar,* a portion of his mind singsonged. He reached up and clamped his fingers firmly around Nuie's slashed forearm, one eye on the ulu in the Kitka's other hand. Blood welled under his palm from the cut, warm to the touch, and he pressed more firmly against the hard flesh. The first mate flinched and the song cut off.

McCoy felt drawn into the silver eyes. "Nuie, we're *not* going to die. Not today," he stressed. "Kirk's alive, and he'll get us out if anyone can. I've known him a long time and there's no stubborner man in the galaxy. He's cheated death more times than anyone I know."

"You can only cheat death as long as she lets you," Nuie replied pragmatically.

McCoy felt like beating a head against the wall, uncertain if it was his or Nuie's he felt most like bashing. *I don't need this conversation.* "Then death must like Jim Kirk a lot, because she keeps letting him beat her at her own game." His numb fingers tightened, sticky against Nuie's skin. "Dammit, Nuie, you're my *friend!* I won't let you die!"

"It's not your choice, Leonard, it's mine. If I die without speaking with the god, if I don't offer myself, I'm nothing as a Kitka, my world's afterlife will reject me. My soul will be trapped forever inside a shell at the bottom of the sea. I won't go on to join the cycle . . ."

McCoy looked into Nuie's eyes and finally understood what he saw there. The Kitka was not afraid of death, but he was terrified of leaving this world without performing this ritual. His dying was intrinsically woven with his living, warp and weft of the same material. Nuie had accepted McCoy's fear with understanding. The doctor could do no less, although it galled him to admit that he had no right to deny the man his culture.

"Okay! I agree! But we're *not* going to die!"

"Can you promise me that?"

McCoy couldn't lie when faced with that frank, patient gaze. "I can't promise you anything, Nuie." He sighed and released him. "I know what I believe, but I can't expect you to believe it, too. If we *are* going to die, though, when the time comes, I'd like to speak with the god, too. I'd like my death to mean something."

Deep emotion touched Nuie's eyes and was gone. "You do me a great honor, Leonard, but I'm sorry. I cannot accept. You're not Kitka. The god wouldn't take you."

Annoyance rankled McCoy. "What's the matter, do I smell bad?"

"I don't know how you smell to the god. All I know is that it wouldn't accept you, and your body would float around uneaten."

"Well, it's a damn sorry world when a man can't slit his wrists or offer himself up to Heaven in lieu of drowning." He glowered at the faint smile that touched Nuie's mouth, and gestured at his arm. "Have you bled enough for one day?"

"For now." Nuie's swished the gash in the water, apparently unbothered by the sting of salt.

"For now," McCoy mimicked, and spat saltwater. Fear shot him clawing for the submerged bunk. He hauled himself atop it with arms that would barely hold his weight and stood, putting his mouth as far out of the water as he could. "*Jim!*"

"I'm here, Bones!" Kirk's response seemed to come

from every angle and the quality of his voice had changed.

"Where?"

"There!" Nuie pointed to a grillwork along the ceiling juncture of one wall. "The ventilation shaft."

"That's right," Kirk called. "You need to climb up in here, Bones. I've got some of the crew with me and they guarantee we can get you out this way and dog a makeshift hatch to keep out the flooding."

"What about the rest of the system? Won't that flood, too?"

"We're taking care of it. Stop arguing and get in here!"

McCoy peered through the murky depths. "There's nothing to stand on."

"Then you'll have to tread water." Kirk was beginning to sound impatient.

McCoy couldn't blame him, but . . . "Dammit, Jim, I'm a doctor, not a synchronous swimmer! I can't tread water!"

"Then you'd better learn."

"I'll help you, Leonard," Nuie offered, arms moving rhythmically, feet already several inches off the floor.

McCoy eyed the dark hollow of the shaft. "I'll never fit."

An explosive sigh resounded through the ventilation system. "Would you rather just drown?! Get in the shaft, McCoy. That's an order."

"I hate when you play hardball," McCoy muttered. Arms held rigidly before him, he slid forward off the bunk, eyes fixed intently on the dark, square, hopelessly small ventilation grill.

* * *

"Is the chief all right?"

The anxious, husky voice on the comm channel made Uhura's breath hiss out in relief. "Howard!" She snapped her filter closed and scrambled to her feet, turning toward the sound of footsteps. The security guard's tall figure circled the gravsled, then began climbing the tilted ramp of ice toward her. He moved a little stiffly, but his arm hung normally at his side. She assumed that Chekov must have had enough time to reset it before their ice slab fell.

"Thank God you're still here." Uhura skidded down the white slope to meet him, impatient with his slow progress. "Give me the antitoxin from your medikit."

Howard's shimmering goggles focused on her for a moment, then swung back up toward Chekov's still figure. "He's poisoned?" His left hand moved awkwardly to his belt pouch. "How did he get poisoned?"

"In a fight. The Kitka must put some kind of paralyzing venom on their weapons." Uhura took the capsule of antitoxin he handed her, then turned to hurry back up the slope. "I gave him one dose, but it took a long time to work. I want to give him another, just to be sure."

"Shouldn't one dose have been enough?"

Uhura shook her head, trying not to fumble the antitoxin in her hurry. "I don't know. These are supposed to be broad-base detoxifiers—if they can't neutralize the poison, they should keep a victim alive long enough to get him to a sickbay. That's where a real doctor could take blood samples and manufacture some more specific antidote." It frightened her to know they didn't have that option.

Howard crouched down to watch as she snapped Chekov's breath filter open and gave him a second shot. The security officer was still as pale as the ice around him.

"He looks bad, sir," said Howard worriedly. "Has he lost a lot of blood?"

"I don't know." Dull red ice crystals splintered off Chekov's wounded arm as Uhura unsealed the foam of his insulation suit. Beneath the torn body slip a narrow gash in his forearm oozed a crimson glaze of blood. Uhura bit her lip and fumbled in her medikit for the canister of sterilizing bandage. The white spray hissed through the frigid air, forming a film across the wound. Uhura sealed the insulation suit over it, then stripped off her glove so she could touch Chekov's bare cheek. It felt cold as clay against her hand. "He's losing heat."

"How can he be, with an insulation suit on?" Howard sounded puzzled.

Uhura shrugged as she pressed Chekov's breath filter closed again. He never stirred. "If his body isn't generating any heat, the insulation suit can't trap it. We need to warm him up from the outside." She put the canister of bandage away, then got to her feet with sudden decision. "The first thing we need to do is set up the tent. Do you think you can carry Lieutenant Chekov down to the gravsled?"

"Sir?" Howard glanced up at her, clearly startled. "The lieutenant's not *that* heavy."

"I know," said Uhura gently. "But you dislocated your shoulder when you hit the crevasse wall."

"I did?" The security guard rotated his left arm gingerly. "So *that's* why it feels so sore. I wondered why I was out cold for so long. The last thing I remembered was falling off that ice bridge, and the next thing I know we're in the middle of the ocean."

"In the middle of the *ocean?*" Uhura looked

around, eyes widening in amazement. In her single-minded struggle to keep Chekov alive, she hadn't even noticed their ice floe moving. Yet now they rocked gently in the midst of a black expanse of water, with the smudged gray cliffs of the ice sheet far behind them. She could barely make out the dim blue shadow of the crevasse they'd floated out from. "Good Lord!"

"Aye, sir. Looks like we'll be camping here for a while." Howard heaved Chekov up over his good shoulder, then stood up with a grunt. "What do we do after we set up the tent? Put the lieutenant next to the heater?"

"No." Uhura glanced over at him, smiling. "I've got a better idea than that."

"We're not going to tell the chief about this, are we?"

Uhura finished closing Howard and Chekov into the doubled sleeping bag. The dimming arctic sunset lit the interior of the tent faintly, just enough to show her the embarrassed expression on the younger guard's face. She chuckled and patted his shoulder.

"It's for his own good, Mr. Howard. He'd understand."

"No, he wouldn't." Howard glanced down at Chekov's dark head, pillowed against his shoulder. Both men wore only their thin white body slips, to let body heat pass between them. "I just hope he gives me time to explain when he wakes up." He glanced up as Uhura rose. "Where are you going, sir?"

"Out to get some food from the gravsled. We haven't eaten since last night." Uhura pulled on her goggles, then unsealed the edge of the tent. "Give me a yell if the lieutenant wakes up."

"Don't worry," Howard said wryly. "If *I* don't, *he* probably will."

Uhura smiled and slipped outside, hearing the tent hiss shut behind her. A last gleam of rose-quartz sunset lingered on the far edge of the sky, casting a faint shimmer across the dark water. The reflection continued behind them for another hundred meters before it vanished at an indigo wall of ice. Uhura felt fear clutch at her briefly, a hollow feeling under her ribs that had nothing to do with her empty stomach. Their floe seemed to be drifting parallel to the icy shore, carried along by some current in the water. What if it never got any closer?

". . . Commander . . ."

The faint rasp of voice spun Uhura back to the tent before she realized it hadn't sounded like Howard and it hadn't come through her outside mike. She gasped and dialed up the volume on her insulation suit communicator. As she did, she noticed that the usual howl of auroral interference had faded to a distant whistle.

". . . Jimenez calling . . ." Static sizzled through the words, the unavoidable static of long-distance contact. Uhura tuned on the scrap of signal with frantic haste, catching it just as it began to fade. "Jimenez calling Lieutenant Commander Uhura. Jimenez calling—"

"This is Uhura." She dialed her transmitter up to maximum output, praying it would carry. Insulation-suit communicators weren't designed for planetary distances. "Can you hear me?"

"I hear you, sir!" Jimenez's hoarse voice cracked with relief. "Thank God you're still alive—wait a minute . . ."

Uhura opened her mouth to ask what she was waiting for, but Spock's calm voice in her ear answered the question before she could ask it. "Update your status, Lieutenant Commander."

"Aye, sir." As usual, the Vulcan first officer wasted no time on useless questions. Uhura took a deep breath, marshaling the events of the past day into some sort of order. "We're out of danger from hostile natives, but are now stranded on an iceberg, drifting in a stretch of open sea. Ensign Howard has a bruised shoulder and Lieutenant Chekov collapsed after being wounded by a Kitka knife. We've treated him with universal antitoxin, but he's still unconscious. Ensign Publicker—" Her voice shook, but she steadied it again. "Ensign Publicker drowned when the ice collapsed beneath us during a Kitka attack."

"A regrettable loss," Spock said. "Have you lost much of your equipment?"

"No, sir. We still have the gravsled and the survival gear. I think we also have enough food for several days."

"Excellent. I hope to be able to send a rescue party down to the planet sooner than that, but I cannot promise it. Commander Scott has not yet managed to completely shield the shuttle stabilizers from Nordstral's magnetic fields. He estimates at least another day of work will be required." A distant wail of interference from the auroras nibbled at the edge of Spock's transmission. "I have managed to triangulate your current position from your communicator signal. Can you estimate the direction and rate of drift of your iceberg?"

Uhura glanced at the faint smolder of sunset on the horizon and did a quick mental calculation. "Approximately sixty degrees west of north, sir. We appear to be moving at a rate of several meters per minute."

"Acknowledged. If we fail to make contact again, I shall attempt to extrapolate your future location from that data." Spock paused as a second wail shivered through their fragile contact. "I must warn you, Lieutenant Commander, that our ship's sensors indicate significant changes occurring in Nordstral's magnetic field. It appears that the planet's secondary magnetic components, which previously kept the main dipole field from destabilizing, have begun to erode. The recent reversal of the magnetic poles—"

"What?" Uhura hadn't meant to interrupt, but the concept left her dazed. "The entire magnetic field reversed itself?"

"Yes, and it may continue to do so as destabilization increases. Auroral intensity has increased at all latitudes, with violent magnetic storms raging in the upper . . ." His voice faded under a snarl of louder interference. ". . . magnetic reversal is likely to be accompanied by further tectonic disturbances . . ." Another, longer wail drowned him out again. ". . . take appropriate precautions . . ."

A final shriek of auroral static broke their contact and left Uhura's ears ringing. She winced and tapped down the volume on her insulation suit comm unit, then glanced up at the night sky.

Auroras rippled across the velvet darkness, dropping long curtains of cold white fire down to the sea. The colors shifted as she watched, shimmering from icy blue to violet to a fiery cascade of deep midnight-red. It seemed to Uhura as if Nordstral, locked in the endless gray-white of glacial ice, had been forced to concentrate all its colors in its glowing night sky. Her sigh misted the air around her as she looked away. It was hard to believe something so beautiful could also be so potentially deadly.

She turned back toward the gravsled, picking her way through the tangle of pitons and ropes that still lashed it to the ice. Their equipment lay scattered around it, half unpacked in their frantic rush to put up the tent. Uhura rummaged in one of the unpacked boxes for a flashlight, then started looking through the marked cartons of food. Maybe they could get Chekov to swallow some nutrient broth—

A sound brought her upright suddenly. Somewhere, far out in the immense darkness of the polar sea, someone—or something—had just taken a deep whuffling breath. It didn't seem possible that anything could be alive in that freezing cold water, but now that Uhura was listening, she could hear a whalelike whistle fluttering at the edges of her mike's sound range. It seemed to be coming from the same direction as the breathing noise. Uhura turned and gasped.

Several meters beyond the edge of the ice floe, something glowed under the water. The glow grew brighter as Uhura watched, coalescing into two indistinct spots. Then, with a sudden rush of splashing water, the glow surfaced and became two huge phosphorescent eyes, staring down at Uhura from a massive shadow-pale head. Breath whooshed out in a storm cloud of frost from two neck openings, making an odd clattering sound as it did. For some reason the noise reminded Uhura of Alion.

"Oh, no." She took a step backward as the beast blinked its eyes and lowered its dripping head toward her. After the accumulated terrors of the past day— waking up to an icequake, being chased by Kitka, and then falling off the edge of the ice—an encounter with a sea monster was more than Uhura could bear. She tilted her head back to meet its shimmering eyes, unable to focus on anything except that phosphorescent gaze . . .

And then remembered what her own gaze must look like to it. With a curse, Uhura reached up to slide her goggles off, blinking involuntarily as the cold night air slapped her face. By the time she managed to slit her eyes open past a rim of icy tears, the glow in the night had vanished. Only a gurgle of parted water marked the kraken's quiet passage.

Uhura didn't wait to see where it was going. She grabbed the nearest box of food and dove for the tent.

McCoy floundered in the cold water for a moment, panic catching sharply under his skin like barbs on a hook, then felt the warm security of Nuie's strong arm around him.

"Just relax." The Kitka's voice was gentle in the doctor's ear. "Let me do all the work."

Easier said than done, in McCoy's opinion, but he tried to do as he was bidden. He rolled onto his back at Nuie's urging, although relaxing was out of the question. Nuie secured an arm around him and with two strokes had them both across the room and treading water under the ventilation shaft.

It appeared the ulu was good for something other than slashing open one's arm; Nuie manipulated the weapon to serve as a screwdriver and release the brackets holding the screen over the shaft. He tucked the curved knife out of sight and snugged an arm around McCoy's waist. "In you go." He hefted him up.

McCoy clenched frozen fingers on the edge of the

shaft and hauled himself upward. Water cascaded off his clothing, running in rivulets back down the shaft. The sight didn't particularly please McCoy as it only lent proof-positive that the ship was listing. "Jim?" His voice echoed oddly in the tiny space, and for an instant he was a precocious child again, scaring himself in the forbidden crawl space under his grandparents' house.

"Bones! This way! Straight ahead!" A faint flashlight beam shone down the dark tunnel. Like a moth drawn to flame, McCoy forced his numbed limbs to move toward it and tried to ignore the closeness of the walls around him. He heard Nuie lever himself out of the water and start down the shaft.

Reaching hands grasped McCoy and pulled him clear. He slithered to the ground, legs unable to support his weight, all the heat leached from his body. Someone threw a blanket around his shoulders and hugged him soundly. He looked up into Kirk's eyes and managed a smile. "I haven't been so glad to see you since the last time you hauled my butt out of the fire."

Kirk grinned with relief and briskly rubbed his friend's arms. "It's good to see you, too, Doctor."

McCoy gave Kirk the once-over. One eyebrow cocked speculatively at the captain's attire. The pants fit decently enough, but the thick sweater was a size too small. "I like your outfit."

"Good. You're getting one just like it." Kirk looked up as Nuie pushed free of the air shaft. "Nice to have you in one piece, Nuie."

The Kitka shed his shirt in one fluid movement and accepted a worn towel from one of his crewmates. He rubbed it hard over his wet hair and across the raised flesh of his arms and chest. "You have Leonard

McCoy to thank for that, Captain. Is there dry clothing?"

"Right here." Another crewman handed them each a bundle, and the next few moments were spent struggling out of wet clothes that adhered like a second skin and into the general-issue wool worn by every seaman aboard.

McCoy rubbed a towel across his hair and watched two of the crew secure the makeshift hatch over the shaft opening. It didn't strike a chord of confidence in him. "You sure that thing's going to work?"

"It better," Kirk said gravely, his voice low. Serious hazel eyes flicked over McCoy as he turned and faced Nuie. "This isn't the place or time I'd choose to deliver this information, but I don't have any choice. Captain Mandeville and Dr. Muhanti are dead, killed when we collided with the ice sheet, along with the rest of the bridge crew. I'm sorry."

Nuie accepted the news without comment, although McCoy thought he detected a flash of sorrow in the stoic Kitka's eyes, and wondered how long he and Captain Mandeville had been crewmates. Had their relationship been like his with Jim? Had Nuie been willing to die for his captain, to follow her into any sort of danger the way he would for Kirk? He supposed at some point he could ask . . . but it wasn't his business to know.

"You're senior personnel aboard *Soroya*," Kirk continued. "As such—"

"Begging your pardon, sir," Nuie interjected smoothly. "But *you're* senior personnel. Federation officers take precedence when they've been called into a Priority situation. I have no doubts about my ability to captain the *Soroya*," Nuie added. "But I'd appreciate it if you'd take command, sir."

Kirk studied the older man for a moment, then nodded once. "All right. I accept. You'll remain as first mate. The backup bridge is functional. I want you to take the conn. The others can fill you in on what happened. Start work crews to get us under way and to search out any other leaks we might have. Doctor, you'll come with me."

"Aye, aye, Captain." Nuie led the crew out of the room at a brisk pace, turning in one direction while Kirk, trailed by McCoy, headed in another.

"And just where are we going?" queried the doctor, rolling his too-long sleeves as he hurried to catch up.

"To the oxygen generator." Kirk's eyes speared him. "It's inoperable. If we don't figure out a way to start it working again, getting this ship under way will be a moot point."

"Wonderful," McCoy remarked sourly. "Any other charming points I should be made aware of?"

"Not at the moment, but I'll keep you posted."

"Thank you." McCoy tugged at his sleeve again. "Jim, just what exactly *did* happen to us?"

"An icequake and tsunami, the crew tells me." Kirk's expression was grave. "And aftershocks. As near as we can figure, the force of the quake threw us against the ice sheet. Mandeville tried to cut through, but the laser was inoperable, so she tried to do it manually. She was in the turret when it was sheered off against the ice."

McCoy felt the color drain out of his face. He had to remind himself to keep moving, to keep following Kirk along the sub's wet passages. "The turret's gone?"

"All three levels, including the laser and the main drive for the oxygenation system. The bridge began to flood."

"I remember. That's when you ordered everyone out. Would have been nice if you'd come along."

"Believe me, Bones, I had every intention of following you, but the door shut and I couldn't get it open." For the first time, McCoy saw in Kirk's face more than moral support for his fear of drowning. Now he saw *understanding,* and was heartily sorry his friend had gone through it.

"I don't remember much but the water coming in." Kirk shook his head. "I don't think I'll ever forget that," he mused. "I got onto an oxygen tank before the bridge started coming apart. The rest of the crew just wasn't fast enough for the surge of water."

"How did you get out?"

The question made Kirk smile faintly. "Through an escape hatch, believe it or not." His expression grew distant.

"Jim . . ." McCoy halted him with a hand on his arm, outside the room that housed the remainder of the oxygen generating system. *"Is* Muhanti dead?"

Kirk frowned. "The last time I saw him, he went in after Mandeville and disappeared. No one's seen him since. Why?"

"Well . . ." McCoy pursed his lips, afraid of how he would sound. "Muhanti was a screwball . . ."

"Is that your professional diagnosis?"

"It's not funny, Jim. He was being affected by whatever put those people into *Curie*'s psych ward. I'm certain of it. And he seemed to have developed a personal grudge against me. If he's dead . . . then who locked Nuie and me in the lab?"

"You think some other of the crew are being affected?"

"We can't discount the possibility, especially since we don't know what's causing the illness. And we've got to watch ourselves as well." He ran a hand over his face. "If I get any more irritated, I'm going to jump out of my skin."

"Take it easy, Bones. I think you're having a normal reaction."

"I only hope that's what it is." McCoy straightened his shoulders and tried on a brave smile for his captain.

Kirk clapped him soundly on the shoulder in mute thanks. "Let's take a look inside." He eased open the unlatched door.

Except for several inches of water on the floor, the room and its machinery seemed at first examination to be undamaged. No motion or hum broke the stillness, and the air already tasted stale, mute evidence of something being very wrong, despite appearances.

McCoy slouched against the wall and hung his head. "Where's Scotty when you need him?"

Kirk paced back and forth, eyes pensive. "Up on the *Enterprise,* preparing a shuttle. We've got to do it without him."

"In case you haven't noticed, neither of us is Scotty. I flunked engineering, and, as I recall, you—"

"Come on, Bones," Kirk cut him off. "Ready to walk in the steps of the miracle worker?"

McCoy grimaced. "Do I have a choice?"

Chapter Twelve

"I DON'T THINK we're getting any closer, sir."

Uhura peered through the icy mist shrouding Nordstral's polar sea, trying to make out the dim blue line of ice cliffs in the distance. "Is the shore curving toward us, Mr. Howard?"

"No, sir. It's straight as a phaser shot." By balancing at the sharp ridge of the ice floe, the tall security guard could just see over the sea-hugging mist. His voice sounded grim. "No chance of hitting it by accident."

"Then we'll just have to hit it by design." Uhura turned back toward the red splash of their tent, barely visible through the glittering arctic fog. The gravsled was a dim gleam of ice-coated metal beside it. "Can you think of some way we can maneuver this floe through the water?"

Howard followed her down the slope, boots crunching on the mist-glazed ice. "Not really, sir," he admitted. "I didn't do too well in my engineering classes at the Academy."

"Well, I did." Uhura gnawed on her lip, trying to decide what Scotty would do if he were there. Actually, she knew what he'd do—he'd tell everyone what an impossible job it was and then he'd proceed to do it anyway. The question was, how? "The gravsled hasn't got internal propulsion, so it wouldn't do us any good. We don't have any other large motors with us, do we?"

"No, sir." Howard skidded to a stop in front of the tent and bent to unseal it. Looking in on Chekov had become a standard half-hour ritual between them since they'd gotten up that morning. By now, several long hours later, they'd done it so often that they only needed to exchange a few words.

"Still unconscious?" Uhura asked from outside the tent.

"Aye, sir." She heard the sleeping bag rustle as Howard zipped it closed again. "He seems to be breathing a little easier, but his color's still not too good."

"At least he's staying warm." Uhura stamped her feet to loosen the crystalline rind of ice that the fog kept depositing on her boots. "Mr. Howard, could you get me a canister of soup while you're in there? I think it's getting colder."

"Here you go, sir." Howard emerged with the self-warmed container already steaming in his hand. Uhura took it from him gratefully, snapping her breath filter off to drink it. The hot broth tasted more like vitamin supplements than the vegetables it was supposed to be made from, but it spread a pleasant warmth through her once it was down. Uhura crumpled the empty carton, then tossed it toward one of the gravsled's waste holders. It missed by half a meter.

"Wind!" She spun around, stretching her hands out to either side. Misty air poured over them, a flowing stream too slow to be felt through her insulation suit. "The wind is blowing!" She scraped away the glaze of ice over the watch embedded in her insulation suit sleeve. "And it's not even 1400 hours yet. Come on, we need to get ready."

Howard followed obediently as she motioned him toward the gravsled, but his voice sounded puzzled. "Get ready for what, sir?"

"The boreal winds." Uhura began stacking equipment back on the sled, forcing herself to be careful despite the urgency sizzling through her. "Try to keep the sled packed as flat as you can, even if it means leaving something off. We'll have to put Chekov on top when we take down the tent. If we put him back in his insulation suit and bundle him in a sleeping bag, he should stay warm enough."

"Sir, wait." Howard caught her hands as she reached for another carton of food. "I don't understand. Why are we taking down the tent? Once the winds come, won't we want to be inside it?"

"Not if we want to get this iceberg to shore." Uhura lifted her trapped hands and thumped him on the chest impatiently. *Think,* Ensign. We'll have a steady wind overhead and a floating raft underfoot. Haven't you ever gone sailing?"

The young security guard ducked his head and let her go. "I grew up in Calgary, sir," he said apologetically. "We didn't see many sailboats up there."

"Well, you'll get a close-up view of one now." Uhura pulled a coil of rope out from their climbing gear and handed it to him. "If I can't find anything taller, Mr. Howard, you're going to be the mast."

* * *

Wind blasted over the polar sea, embroidering its dark surface with a rippling lace of foam. Uhura glanced across the whitecapped water to the icy shore, much nearer and clearly visible now that the morning's mist had blown away. She frowned as she saw the looming wall of blue-green cliffs, shot through with glitters of reflected sunlight.

"Mr. Howard!" She bent her head, trying to see her companion past the bulge of their tent-turned-sail. "Have you found us a place to land?"

"I think so, sir—bear a little more to the right!" The security guard had a better view of their forward progress than she did, stationed as he was beside the makeshift mast they'd fashioned out of tent supports.

"Acknowledged." Uhura knelt beside the crude block and tackle she'd made from their climbing winch, bracing herself against the tug of the wind. The winch whirred into motion with reassuring quickness, reeling in the mainstay and hauling the sail several points to starboard. The tough nylon tent fabric shivered as the wind caught it at a new angle, then pulled taut again with a startlingly loud crack. The mast swayed, straining at the rope rigging she'd pitoned into the ice around it, but nothing broke or fell over.

Uhura sighed in relief, feeling the ice floe rock uneasily beneath her as it shifted direction in the water. Caught between the drag of ocean current and the driving force of the boreal winds, the crude raft steered a wavering and uncertain path toward the shore. Uhura only hoped the wind would last long enough to get it there.

She fastened the rope mainstay to its piton again, then glanced up at the gravsled, floating just beyond the edge of the sail. Bundled inside his sleeping bag,

Chekov's limp body made a barely visible mound at the top of the equipment. Uhura regretted having to abandon so much of their bulky medical equipment, but knew bringing Chekov mattered more.

"Almost there, Commander!" Howard's voice sounded suddenly eager. "Just a little bit more to the right . . ."

Uhura reached out for the winch, but never touched it. The ice floe shuddered to a plowing stop beneath her, slamming her forward into the sail just as the overstrained mast snapped and toppled over. She struggled to free herself from the settling fabric, terrified that it would take her with it into the ocean when it fell.

"Commander!" Hands yanked at the sail, unraveling its tangled folds enough for Uhura to see sunlight glinting between them. She dove through the opening and was hauled to her feet just as the sail splashed down into the sea.

"What happened?" Uhura stepped out of Howard's grip and turned to glance at the shore, baffled by their abrupt stop. The iceberg had jammed into a jutting pinnacle of ice with its blunt end firmly lodged against the shore. The waterlogged sail trailed in the water behind it, like the tail on a tree-caught kite. Uhura glanced down at Howard, biting her lip to keep from laughing. "So much for our careful navigating."

"Yes, sir." The security guard sounded as if he were smiling. "We're not going to tell the chief about this, either, right?"

"Right," Uhura said firmly. She glanced up, gauging the short, snow-covered slope that led to the ice sheet above them. "We'd better start climbing. Now that we've lost the tent, we're going to have to make some kind of shelter by nightfall."

"Aye, sir." Howard picked up the tow bar of the gravsled and started up the hill, punching footprints into the snow with each step. Uhura followed him, stretching her legs to use the same set of tracks. "What kind of shelter did you have in mind, sir?"

"I don't know," Uhura admitted. The snow crust got deeper as they made their way upward, making her breath puff out around her mask as she struggled through it. "I don't suppose that Nordstral manual you read told you how to make igloos?"

"Afraid not." Howard leaned into the steepening slope, his own breath shortening with effort. "We could try to dig under the ice like the Kitka."

Uhura shook her head vehemently. "Not a good plan. Spock said there might be more tectonic disturbances as Nordstral's magnetic field got worse. I think that means more icequakes."

"Well, at least they didn't happen while we were floating out on our iceberg," Howard said cheerfully. He gave the gravsled a final heave that pushed it up over the icy crest of the hill ahead of him. "Maybe our luck's finally starting to turn, sir."

"Maybe." Uhura hauled herself up over the lip of the ice sheet, eyes widening as she looked around. Only a few meters away from them the ice was split by an unexpected vertical slash of rock, its black crystalline surface shattered with frost cracks. It wasn't the stone island that startled Uhura, though—it was the unmistakable shadow of a Kitka-small doorway, carved into its ice-scraped side. "And then again, Mr. Howard, maybe not."

McCoy sat back and pressed the heels of his hands against his tired eyes, uncertain of just when—and by whom—the heavy-grit sandpaper under his eyelids had been replaced by gravel and shards of glass. A headache thumped insistently across the bridge of his nose and behind his left eye. His wounded hand kept time beneath its soiled coil of bandage. He couldn't remember if he'd taken any antibiotics, and couldn't recall the last time he'd eaten or slept.

Wearily, but proudly, he watched Kirk prowl the room like a watchful, hunting cat—checking and rechecking linkages, running the process through in his mind, and no doubt bestowing a beneficent prayer wherever he deemed appropriate.

That mind. McCoy hadn't been kidding when he said he was no match for Montgomery Scott, but Kirk . . . Tenacious as a terrier, the *Enterprise* captain stuck to their task, approaching the problem from every angle, until it began to release its secrets to him. McCoy was surprised to find that, after all these years, there were still depths he'd yet to discover in James Kirk.

"Windisch showed me the ship's plans," Kirk had said when he and McCoy first began to survey the damage. He pointed at a machine squatting in several inches of water in the center of the room. "That's the oxygen generator. Saltwater infiltration has left it inoperable, not to mention that the ventiliation drive unit was located in the turret, and that's long gone. We've got to come up with another way to run the system."

"That's a tall order, Jim." McCoy pursed his lips. "I know it sounds primitive, but . . ."

"Any suggestion is better than no suggestion at all. What's on your mind, Bones?"

"Well, we've got a lot of manpower here. How about a treadmill system? That shouldn't be too awfully difficult to rig up."

"You're not thinking like an engineer, Bones," Kirk prodded. "Whoever's on the treadmill will use more oxygen than they produce. We have to come up with something better than that."

McCoy knew that tone in Kirk's voice from long experience. Not only did they *have* to come up with something better, they *would* come up with something better. Kirk would accept nothing less, not from McCoy, and particularly not from himself.

The doctor stared around the room. Machinery was not his forte. He was more comfortable with the workings of a living organism than he was with the alloyed flesh and bone of the *Soroya*. He'd never quite been able to understand someone like Scotty or Spock —especially Spock—who could sit for hours tinkering with some busted piece of equipment, happy as a pig in . . .

He made his mind veer away, and instead watched Kirk out of the corner of his eye. The captain scowled at the oxygen generator as though it was a misbehaved intern. The mass of machinery was little more than a metal lung, once it was under way. And what did it take to power a lung?

Kirk stamped his feet, splashing. "Stinks in here, doesn't it, Bones? I wonder if this is what the plankton holds smell like? No wonder they have a good ventilation system . . ." His voice trailed off and he stared down, swishing at something in the water with the toe of one boot. His head slowly came up and he turned toward McCoy. "Plankton . . ."

"What about it, Jim?"

Kirk gestured sharply with one hand, eyes focused into the middle distance as he fought to grasp whatever thought had flitted through his mind. He spoke slowly, measuring his words. "Spock said the biota on

216

Nordstral acts just like earth plankton, except that it uses energy from the planet's magnetic field. That means it takes in carbon dioxide and water, manufactures carbohydrates, and discharges . . ." His eyebrows rose and he stared at McCoy.

"Oxygen! Do you think we can do it, Jim?"

"We have to, Bones! It's our only chance. *Soroya* cleared her tanks when she picked us up, but she's collected more plankton since then. We should have enough to use."

"Providing the tsunami didn't rupture the tanks."

"You always look on the bright side of things," Kirk complained. "Nuie will be able to find out. That only leaves us with two problems."

"Which are?" McCoy slid off the pipe he'd been sitting on and splashed down beside Kirk.

"How to extract the oxygen from the plankton holds, and once we do, how to ventilate it through the ship."

"Well, I haven't got the faintest clue for the first, but I know a way we might be able to do the second. When Nuie took me on tour of the ship, he showed me the drive unit. If that's still functional—and we'd better hope to the kraken it is or we're not going anywhere fast—there must be a way we can patch into it to jerry-rig a drive for the ventilation system."

Kirk's smile was pure appreciation. "Bones, that's amazing! Sometimes you remind me of Spock."

"There's no need to get insulting, Jim."

The captain's smile widened into a toothy grin. "It's a great idea. Let's get to it."

Nuie was left in control of the bridge, with a warning that every crewman not doing mandatory work should return to their bunk and try to relax, thereby using as little oxygen as possible. Kirk and

McCoy commandeered a Kitka crewman and presented him with the problem.

Watching the Kitka work, glad to take a backseat to his engineering expertise, McCoy was reminded unwillingly of Spock. The Kitka was coolly logical, his tools spread around him on the floor, his hand reaching unerringly for whatever he needed without his having to look up from his task. McCoy and Kirk lent a hand wherever necessary, be it hauling pipe from cannibalized sections of the ship, securing fixtures, or passing tools.

The scariest part for McCoy was hooking it all together, drive unit to filtration system, and waiting to see if it worked. The ship listed even more dangerously when the engines were shut down to allow the linkup; McCoy, left with Kirk near the plankton tanks, was afraid they'd roll. They heard the Kitka over the repaired intercom, working in a near-silent fever. Still, he shouted with relief when the last bolt tightened. "Fire her up!"

"Now, Nuie." Kirk spoke quietly into the intercom, voice laced with tension. They edged closer to the door in case the entire makeshift workings split.

The initial hum of the engines at the other end of the ship built slowly, under command of Nuie's voice coming gently over the intercom, and McCoy held his breath.

"Captain Kirk?" Nuie's voice over the comlink. "Hold your hand over the vent."

Kirk raised a hand above his head and in front of the screening. A delicate breeze moved the hair on his wrist, and he smiled with such relief, McCoy finally relaxed. "Well done," Kirk said. "Nuie, you've got quite a crew here."

"I know this, Captain," the Kitka replied from the

bridge, his voice counterpointed by a ragged cheer from the rest of the crew.

"I'm certain you do. Oxygen room—how's it look from your end?"

"We've got a few tiny leaks we're pinning down, Captain, but other than that, I think we've got a go-ahead." The Kitka engineer sounded very satisfied, and with good reason.

"All right. Keep monitoring. I want someone by the drive unit at all times."

"Aye-aye, sir."

And no rest for the weary at their end, either. Here it was, better than an hour later, and Kirk still roamed the tiny room outside the storage tanks, checking and rechecking their handiwork.

McCoy realized he'd almost been asleep. He forced his eyes open and shrugged away from the wall, hunching deeper in the warmth of the seaman's sweater. He was about to suggest that one of them catch some shut-eye when Nuie's voice came over the intercom. "Captain, would you come to the bridge, please."

Kirk exchanged looks with McCoy, his arched brows over weary eyes more than clearly conveying *Now what?* "What's the problem, Nuie?"

"I'd rather speak to you here, sir."

The captain sighed and ran a hand through his hair. "I'm on my way." He winked tiredly at McCoy. "It's your baby, Bones."

"I've never been that fond of kids, Jim. Besides, I'm not the babysitter Scotty is."

Kirk nodded in understanding. His hand on McCoy's arm stopped the doctor from following him. "I have utmost faith in you."

McCoy glowered. "I hate emotional blackmail."

With a disgruntled sigh, he straddled a length of piping. "Don't be long."

"Depends on the nature of the latest catastrophe." With a sardonic wave, Kirk was gone.

McCoy swung his legs on either side of the pipe, swishing the water that covered the floor. He stuffed his gloved hands into his armpits and hunched his shoulders. When he got back aboard the *Enterprise,* the first thing he was going to do was take a hot shower. A *long,* hot shower. Maybe one that would last until they reached a starbase. And after that . . .

He had drifted into a slight doze, happy with his daydreams, when he heard a sound behind him. He shifted slightly, turning. "Jim?" His head exploded with sudden pain and everything went dark.

Consciousness didn't steal up on Chekov so much as crash over him, driven forward by a swell of panic so sharp it made him gasp and fight to sit upright.

"Sir?"

He couldn't truly see—only glittering darkness, slashed by bands of twitching yellow—and his muscles knotted, stiff as twisted leather, at the first hint of independent movement. He kicked at the blankets covering him, suddenly too hot to stand their weight.

"It's all right . . ." Strong, male hands pushed him back to the uneven pallet. "Sir, it's all right! We're safe for now—we've found someplace to stay." The voice flitted across his sick awareness just beyond what he could identify. He knew that it spoke out of loyalty, though, and loyalty he could trust. That calmed him and let him relax, even if only a little.

"Where are we?" Chekov wasn't sure at first if he'd asked that in the right language. The translators might not be trustworthy, might take too long to make his words understood. So he asked again, more carefully, and was rewarded this time with a change of lighting and a small hand on his arm.

"Chekov? I'm right here." From somewhere nearby he heard quiet, deliberate movement, then a ration canister's whispered *pop-hisss*. Uhura's brown face appeared on the fringe of his vision. Hopeful concern moved in her eyes, but her breath didn't steam when she breathed—the steam came from something she held out of sight in her hands.

It occurred to him that perhaps he'd only just opened his eyes.

Rock—rough and glittering black—formed the sides and roof of their shelter. Yellowed furs lined the uneven walls, and flat, smokeless oil lamps skipped shadows across every surface. Uhura knelt by Chekov's shoulder, her insulation suit peeled away to leave her face and head uncovered. "I don't suppose I can get you to eat something?"

He didn't know whether or not he answered, but she coaxed him into drinking half the warm soup mixture anyway. He didn't have enough strength to fight her, so was glad that it tasted recognizable and good and not like her usual offerings. "That tastes wonderful."

Uhura laughed, her voice hoarse with strain and exhaustion. "You must be in worse shape than I thought." Then, just as quickly, her face folded into a frown of quiet worry and she added, "It's good to talk to you again. I don't know when I've been so worried."

With those few words, she woke what memories Chekov possessed—their flight across the ice, the attack by Alion's men, the loss of Publicker into the churning water. That last memory sliced him with cold all the way to the bone. To try and drive it away, he asked, "Where's Howard?"

"Outside. He sat with you all last night—it's my turn now."

I woke up for a while, then, Chekov thought, but didn't say it. But he couldn't remember what else had happened. "Where are we?"

Uhura glanced around as though only just noticing the place herself. "A native shelter." Reaching behind her, she drew a stooped, older woman into his sight. Something about the arrangement of her blunt native features looked familiar to Chekov, although he couldn't recognize her face. "This is Ghyl," Uhura explained, "a friend I made back at the village. She came here several days ago to pray." Her smile flashed, nervous and grateful, against the darkness of her skin. "It's lucky for us she did."

Chekov struggled into a sitting position, his mind already whirling around three words from the middle of her answer: *several days ago.* Dizziness swelled over him and nearly knocked him flat again. "How long have I been out?" he asked, fighting back the weakness.

Both women reached out to steady him as he swung his legs over the pallet's edge and propped his forehead against one hand. "About fifty hours," Uhura admitted, shaking out a nearby wad of fur until it was recognizably a parka.

Fifty hours! Chekov waved aside the lieutenant commander's attempt to settle the parka over his shoulders, trying to make both his stomach and vision settle enough to register the actual layout of his surroundings. Predictably, Uhura ignored him; when the fur slid away from the smooth surface of his insulation suit, she simply held onto the front of it herself to keep it from falling again. Chekov looked around at the cluttered native hovel, rubbed at a bone-deep ache in his left arm and asked, "What happened?"

The frown that skated across Uhura's face warned him the answer would be unpleasant. "I think one of Alion's men accidentally poisoned you."

That figured. "Accidentally?"

The old woman spat a harsh hiss that sounded deep with displeasure and disgust. "God's kiss," Chekov's insulation suit translator supplied, echoed rapidly by, "Kraken venom." Not sure how else to interpret this contradiction, Chekov decided Ghyl's words must mean both things at once.

Ghyl fussed with the blankets around him, smoothing down the furs, straightening the wrinkles while Kitka sentences squeaked out of her almost too quickly for the translator to track. "On harpoons," the English words came slowly, "god's kiss helps the Kitka in our hunting. It causes sleep for Kitka and animals, only pleasant sleep. For humans, it seems the kiss causes much more." She fixed him with a cold, white stare, her hands moving angrily along her thighs, as though rubbing for warmth. "But no accident," she assured him. "Alion knows this kills humans. He has bragged to us of this. He takes his Feathered Men to hunt god from the water—he doesn't wait for god to bring himself onto the ice to die. He wants the kiss, but for his own bad things. He wants to kill all humans."

Chekov lifted his head long enough to take the canister of soup from Uhura's hands. His mouth still liked tasting the soup better than his stomach liked taking it, but he forced himself to drink it anyway. He needed something nutritious inside him. His brain knew that, even if his body didn't agree at the moment. After all, fifty hours down after being shot full of native poison—McCoy wouldn't let him out of sickbay for a week once the doctor found out.

"Your people are obviously frightened of Alion and his men," Uhura said, reaching across to touch Ghyl's arm. When the old Kitka woman shook her head sternly, Uhura asked, "Why don't you do something to stop him?"

Ghyl whistled her distress. "Fear makes the people weak. He came from the south with strong young men and strange, southern weapons and ways, and began telling everyone what to do. This is not the Kitka way."

Chekov looked up sharply, having to wait through more translation even after Ghyl fell silent with surprise. "Not the Kitka way?" he asked her, putting the empty soup canister on the ground between his feet. "Then Alion isn't your leader? He isn't your shaman?"

Chekov guessed from the length of the Kitka translation that something in his words hadn't gone across easily. Ghyl's expression of anxious confusion only verified this.

"Your . . . magic man." He shrugged off Uhura's parka in unconscious irritation, feeling like he ought to be using his hands to make things clear, but not having the faintest idea what he wanted to do with them. "The one among you who talks to your gods."

Ghyl surprised him by turning her face away and spitting violently. "Each person speaks to god in whatever way god finds most fitting. Alion wishes to make himself god for all the Kitka people, that's why he uses young men to scare the old." She pulled her lips into a severe frown, eyes flashing. "Someday, god will make Alion pay for his arrogance, and only god will be god then."

If we're lucky, Chekov thought, god will come get him before he catches up and kills us all.

"Lieutenant Commander Uhura?" Howard's voice floated into the small chamber from somewhere distant below them, effectively ending the discussion before any further speculations on Alion's spiritual future could be offered. "Commander," he called again, youth and uncertainty clear in the lilt of his words, "I think you'd better come look at this, sir."

Guided by the direction of both women's gazes, Chekov looked toward a corner to his right and behind him, and spotted the irregular oval of a carved doorway among the stone and leaping shadows. Catching Uhura's arm with one hand, he whispered simply, "Help me," and pushed unsteadily to his feet.

The room only swayed a little as he lurched upright, but even that steadied when Ghyl moved in on his other side to take his elbow. He resisted leaning against her, sure he'd topple her slight frame if he so much as breathed against it.

Uhura bore his weight easily enough, though. Perhaps too easily, he thought, if the effort still left her free to tug the ever-present parka over his shoulders again. "I have the insulation suit." He nearly lost his balance trying to move away from the garment. "I don't need a parka."

Uhura countered by sliding his arm down one sleeve and gesturing Ghyl to do the same. "You're shivering." She reached up to fit a pair of goggles over his head.

Not shivering, he could have told her, *trembling.* He felt so weak, he could barely hold his head up, much

225

less stand. Explaining that would probably get him shoved back into bed, though, and he didn't want to be flat on his back right now. Walking around a little would help. At least he hoped so. "All right," he sighed, pulling down her own goggles for her. "Let's go find Howard."

The oval doorway led down into a rough tunnel of stairs, marching through lustrous rock toward the moan and salty sigh of ocean. Ghyl led the way, Uhura behind her so that Chekov could steady himself with a hand on the lieutenant commander's shoulder as they navigated the humid half-dark. They broke into sunlight on the side of an ice-streaked incline, alternating black rock and blue ice delineating where steps had been cut into the surface to carry a person close to the ice-choked expanse of plankton-green water.

At the foot of those stairs Howard stood with rigid impatience, fists at his sides while he studied something in the water below his feet, then glanced upward to verify the others were coming. He jerked his head in silent surprise when he finally caught sight of the approaching trio, but by way of greeting said only, "Chief, I'm glad you're here," when they finally stepped down even with him.

"What's going on?" Chekov asked. Out here now in the wind and salt spray, Chekov was glad for the parka, despite its heavy weight. By pressing a handful of fur across his mouth, he could almost breathe comfortably enough to forget he hadn't bothered to reinstall his breath filter before coming outside. "What did you find?"

In answer, Howard only pointed and stepped away from the spar of cloudy ice to let the others see. Chekov went down on all fours to study the blurred image, but couldn't make sense of the abstract patterns of scarlet, black, and green beneath his hands. "What is it?"

Uhura leaned over his shoulder, then gasped, her hands flying to her mouth. "Blood," she said. When Chekov frowned back at her, she pointed at a cloud of bright color just below the surface. "That's blood."

"And a face, I think." Howard leaned down as well to sketch the outline of a pale oval just above Uhura's frozen blossom. "It's somebody, sir. I'm just not sure who."

Somebody. The images made sense, then, quite suddenly. A cap of dark hair, obscure smudges of black where eyes would sit, all positioned above a man-sized column of Nordstral green. Over it all, blood like dye cast into angry water, discoloring everything from neckline to crotch.

Choosing a spot above the dead man's left breast, Chekov scrubbed at the ice to heat it, trying to force it clear enough to see. Just before the wind skated over to frost his new-made viewport, he glimpsed a scrawl of black, human lettering in the shape of a name: VERNON STEHLE, M.D.

"It's the shuttle crew." He felt suddenly sick and shivering all over again. "My God—we've found our rescuees."

Chapter Thirteen

McCoy wasn't unconscious for long. He came to, stiffly upright against a pipe, arms bound behind him. He blinked several times against the pain at the back of his head and tried to orient himself. Raising his head, he gaped at the man standing against the opposite wall, his shoulder leaning indolently against the pressure gauge for the tank. "Muhanti! You're supposed to be dead!"

The ship's medical officer was soaked to the skin, his dark hair plastered to his skull like a shiny, black cap. His shoes were missing. His entire body shook, but McCoy couldn't tell if it was from cold or something else.

Muhanti smiled in an oily fashion, and McCoy saw that he was quite insane. His eyes reminded McCoy of Baker's, from the tape Dr. Kane showed them all those years ago aboard *Curie*—someone lucid

228

trapped behind a wall of thoughts they cannot understand or breach. "That's what the Federation would like, isn't it, McCoy? It's what you were hoping. Unfortunately for you, it takes a lot more than the Federation to kill Pushkali Muhanti!" He proudly thumped himself on the chest, and his shirt stuck to his skin.

"No one wants to see you dead, Muhanti."

"Liar," the doctor replied easily, obviously amused. "The Federation learned about my hypotheses and my discussions with Captain Mandeville regarding the debilitation of our crew, and decided to get rid of us." One finger rose to lazily trace the contours of the pressure gauge and the release lever beside it. "Your psychologists must have had a field day studying her personality. It isn't too awfully difficult to come up with a way for an obsessive-compulsive to kill themselves." He chuckled, but it wasn't a happy sound. "They practically do it for you, any number of times. Always putting themselves first, playing the martyr." His fingers tightened around the dial, palm flat against the face. His knuckles whitened with strain, but Muhanti didn't seem to notice. "Your captain has some of the same traits, I've observed," he remarked conversationally, then winked broadly as though he and McCoy had just shared a delightful joke.

"What are you talking about?" McCoy struggled in his bonds. "Untie me, Muhanti, and we'll discuss it."

"We can talk about it just fine as we are, my dear colleague. I'm not stupid enough to believe Federation lies." He strolled toward McCoy, and the Starfleet officer pressed back against the piping behind him. "Do you know what the natives think is happening? *They* say the gods are angry with them. Glaciers calve and the Kitka say it's the ice crying in despair for what they've done in letting Nordstral come here and take the plankton." He leaned conspiratorially close, and McCoy swallowed hard. "Personally, I think they've realized what they have here and are trying to get out of the contract so they can sell to the highest bidder." Muhanti laughed; it was a sound with no soul behind it. "Good luck to them! I *know* Nordstral Pharmaceuticals. Now that they're making money from that plankton, there's nothing the Kitka can do about it!" He twirled in a slow circle, voice dreamy. "The Kitka say the ice never cried before we came. That there were no quakes, no mental illness, and no magnetic storms. They say the winds are worse now, since our coming. And all because we take a little plankton for ourselves." He snorted in disgust.

McCoy barely heard him. Something Muhanti had said made a resounding *ping* in McCoy's brain.

"But I know the truth. I know what you're trying to do here, and it won't work." Muhanti grasped the release lever and slammed it home. The *Soroya* groaned as her entire harvest of millions of tons of plankton washed back into the Nordstral depths.

McCoy fought his bonds. "Muhanti, *don't!*"

The Indian doctor snarled and stepped close enough that McCoy could feel the heat of his body even through the wet clothing. "The Federation is the pirate king of the galaxy. I know you want what we have here."

"You *idiot!*" McCoy railed. "We'll suffocate without that plankton!"

"You're the idiot." Muhanti reached out and snaked his fingers deep into McCoy's hair. "You still think you have me fooled." He drew McCoy's forehead against his damp chest and held it there despite the other man's struggles.

The intercom crackled to life. "Bones! What's happened? Bones!"

"Ah, your captain's voice. Too bad you can't warn him that the game is over and I'm in command now." Muhanti's fingers traversed McCoy's skull, probing like blind moles in dark tunnels. "I see . . ." he murmured. "Oh, yes, it's all right here for anyone to read." He bracketed McCoy's head with his hands and tilted his face up almost lovingly. "A shame to waste such a brilliant mind."

"What the hell are you talking about?" McCoy wished he could snap his head around and bite Muhanti, but the other doctor held him too firmly.

"I can tell by the bumps on your head that not only is this a Federation plot, but one contrived by none other than yourself, Dr. McCoy. It really is quite brilliant. What a shame that I'm smarter than you are, and that you put your mind to such a wasteful scheme." He tsked-tsked in feigned pity. "You realize, of course, that you'll have to die."

"Now, wait just a minute, Muhanti—"

The ship's doctor drew forth an ulu from his back pocket. "The Kitka have been useful in some ways," he murmured, almost dreamily considering the light-catching upward curve of the blade. His eyes flicked to McCoy's. "Don't be alarmed or worried, dear friend. I'm quite a skillful surgeon. You won't feel anything too long." He grasped McCoy's chin in one hand and lay the knife against his cheek.

"Muhanti!"

Kirk's cry came from the door, but too late, too damned late. McCoy felt the blade taste his skin—

—and the *Soroya* bucked under them as though it were her metal flesh violated by the ulu. Muhanti staggered sideways, catching himself against the bulkhead and spinning to meet Kirk's advance.

Kirk stepped into the room, hands open and away from his sides. "Put the knife away, Muhanti. No one wants to get hurt here."

"If I'd the time, I'd sit down and laugh at your stupid jokes, Captain Kirk. Your being here only points up the Federation's deficiencies. Imagine you achieving a captaincy when they could have had me." He slithered behind McCoy and grasped his chin from behind. "Your friend and I were just discussing the best way to end this game, Captain. Perhaps you'd care to watch to see what's in store for you?"

Soroya shivered again, shimmying and gonging like a bell, and throwing Muhanti aside. Kirk flung himself forward and tackled him around the knees. They crashed to the ground, water flying in all directions. Muhanti eeled out of Kirk's grasp and thrashed to his feet, kicking out to keep the Starfleet officer at bay. Kirk rolled out of reach, watching Muhanti's knife hand, and got to his knees, poised to move in any direction. His eyes darted, seeking an opening or a weapon of some kind, but there was nothing to be found.

Muhanti thrust forward, raking the ulu before him. Kirk's sweater parted with a sigh and hung in unraveling tatters. At the moment Kirk pulled back, sucking in his gut from the cruel blade, he reached out and grabbed Muhanti's arm, slamming it twice against his upraised knee. There was the sound of something breaking and Muhanti cried out. The ulu dropped from his fingers and Kirk kicked it aside. One hand burrowed into the front of Muhanti's shirt, pulling him up, and Kirk punched him hard, once, across the chin. Muhanti's head snapped back and he staggered. His feet slipped on the wet flooring. He fought for balance and fell, striking his head against one of the pipes. He landed limp at Kirk's feet and didn't move.

Kirk swallowed, breathing hard, his eyes flicking toward McCoy as he knelt beside Muhanti. He felt along the man's jaw, then grasped a wrist and waited. After a few moments he looked up. "He's dead, Bones."

McCoy's eyes closed briefly. "Damn." He looked across at Kirk, seeing the same disappointment in his captain's face. "You might as well untie me."

The ulu sawed easily through the ropes binding him. He rubbed his wrists free of the sensation of bondage and tried to ignore Muhanti's slumped corpse. "What the hell's going on here, Jim?"

"We've been visited by our friendly neighborhood kraken." Kirk didn't smile. "That's why Nuie called me to the bridge. It appears she's taken a real interest in us since the accident."

"You mean that big ugly thing saved my life?" McCoy looked at the wall as though he could see beyond to the seabound leviathan. "I think I'm in love."

"According to Nuie, she's following us because of the bodies of the dead bridge crew."

McCoy made a face. "She's eating them?"

Kirk didn't reply. "Evidently, she thinks we're another kraken, giving birth in her territory. She's not particularly pleased." Another, lesser blow rocked the ship and they stood their ground. Kirk's eyes sought the wall gauge. "He jettisoned the whole lot?"

"Every last little green particle."

"Bones, we *need* that plankton. We can't survive without it."

"We can't be that far from open water," McCoy half-asked, hopefully. "Can we?"

"I don't know, Bones." Kirk sighed quietly and turned to face his friend squarely. "Maybe not. There's just no way to tell."

Uhura's throat ached with shock and disbelief, although she didn't know why she felt so stunned. After watching Alion's white-feathered men kill Nicholai Steno—after being chased and attacked by Kitka themselves—it should have come as no surprise that Nordstral's lost shuttle crew had suffered the same fate. But somehow, in all the rush of digging out from the icequake and then escaping from the shaman's men, it had never occurred to Uhura that their rescue mission might be fruitless. She glanced over at Chekov and Howard, still kneeling grimly over the frozen body of the Nordstral medic, and wondered if they'd expected this. Something in the focused tension of Chekov's stance told her he had, at least.

Motion caught at the edge of her vision, and Uhura turned to see Ghyl shoulder past Howard, then lower herself in painfully stiff stages until she lay facedown across the discolored patch of ice where Stehle was buried. Chekov grunted in surprise, hauling himself upright with a grab at Howard's arm. Ghyl ignored him. She lay motionless for a moment, then rose to hands and knees and scanned the area where she had lain. After a moment, her dark mask lifted and turned in Uhura's direction.

"Chinit Kitka not do this." The elderly woman sat back on her heels and pointed at the discolored patch of ice, cleared of frost by the brief contact with her body. Uhura bit her lip, glimpsing the single horrible slash across the Nordstral medic's midsection. "Chinit Kitka cut three times, left to right." Ghyl's mittened hand lifted to trace three diagonal slashes across her dark fur parka.

Uhura's breath caught in sudden horror. She took an involuntary step backward, although she knew how small and frail the native was. "The Chinit Kitka kill like this?"

Ghyl's wail sounded slow and troubled. "Not kill," said the translator after a pause. "Kitka not call kill, what you do to yourself."

Uhura gasped, then choked as cold air bit through her filter at her lungs. She could hear Chekov cursing across the comm channel in soft, vehement Russian. "You cut yourself open with knives?" he demanded of Ghyl.

The elderly woman touched both mittened hands to her mask in what looked like a ritual gesture. "It is forbidden for Kitka to speak of these things," she said, then glanced down at Stehle's body. Gathering frost had clouded it to a merciful blur again. "But when such evil touches god, who can be silent?" She looked back up at Chekov, pale eyes steady behind her mask. "We open ourselves with knives, yes. That is how we speak to god."

"You said you came here to talk to god." Uhura finally understood Nhym's horrified reaction to Ghyl's departure. She tried hard to keep her own shock out of her voice. "Why does god ask you to do this?"

Ghyl shrugged, a surprisingly human gesture. "When god's time is done, he gives himself to us. When our time is done, or when we need god's council, we give ourselves back in the same way. As the ocean feeds us, so we must feed the ocean."

"And do you also feed others to the ocean?" Chekov swept a hand out toward the dark green expanse beside them, his borrowed parka ruffling in the wind. White-crested waves rode the heaving surface in to smash against the lip of the long icy ledge they stood on. A hiss of spray splashed up from each impact, then froze to glittering mist and drifted skyward. "Is that what happened to this man?"

"I think perhaps," Ghyl admitted. Her wail sounded grim. "This is not how Chinit talk to god, but I have heard that other tribes speak differently. Some in the south cut only once."

Uhura winced, remembering the single vicious slash that had brought down Nicholai Steno. "And Alion and his men are from the south."

Chekov's shimmering goggles turned toward her briefly. "I hadn't forgotten that, believe me." He looked back at Ghyl. "Do the southern tribes usually send people to talk to god even if they don't want to go?"

"No!" The elderly woman's reply hissed with disgust. "God would know, and spit upon the one who did the sending. No sane Kitka would do such a thing."

"But an insane Kitka might," Uhura murmured.

Ghyl listened to the translation, then let out an ice-sharp keen. "One whose wits were wind-scattered, yes." She slapped a mittened hand against the ice. "Anyone with eyes can see that god refuses to talk to men from above the aurora. Otherwise, why would this one be here where we can see him? Alion believes god's anger is because of humans, and so humans must explain their works to god. Chinit Kitka believe god cares not for humans, only for god's own."

"Um—" Uhura was saved from answering by the faint crackle of radio signal in her ear. She gasped and hurriedly tuned the communicator. "Jimenez! Jimenez, can you read me?"

". . . read you . . ." The contact wavered, disturbed by the background howl of auroral interference. Uhura glanced up and saw the crystal-pale shimmer of magnetic disturbance still crawling across the sky. Either Jimenez hadn't waited for the auroras to subside, or the lull wasn't as complete this time as it had been before. ". . . urgent message . . . *Enterprise* . . ."

"Awaiting link." Uhura dialed down her outside mike and translator so its noise wouldn't distract her, then glanced at Chekov and made the palm-to-ear signal that meant communicator silence. The security chief waved back at her to show he understood, then relayed the message to Howard. Uhura's comm channel cleared slightly as both men tapped their units off, just enough for her to hear the distant murmur of Spock's voice. She dialed up the volume, forcing herself to ignore the descending wail of the auroras.

". . . has completed shielding modifications. The shuttle will . . ." A drowning wail of static interrupted. ". . . attempt to locate Admiral Kirk and Dr. McCoy first, then come for you. Update on your position, Commander?"

Uhura spoke in crisp bursts designed to pierce the static. "We're in a native shelter, carved into a large outcropping of black rock, along the shore of the polar ocean."

"Acknowledged and triangulated." Spock's voice strengthened briefly. "Your position appears to be quite close to the last known fix on the missing Nordstral shuttle. Have you seen any sign of the missing scientists?"

"We found one of them, sir. Dead."

"Ah. Due to hostile native actions?"

"Yes, sir." Uhura swallowed hard. "We think the shaman's group is killing them and feeding them to the ocean. It's the traditional way that Kitka die, but Alion seems to think subjecting humans to it will fix the planet's problems."

"Fascinating." Spock's voice broke off as another howl sounded, but this time it wasn't auroral interference. Uhura's eyes widened as she recognized the familiar sound of the *Enterprise* going on yellow-alert. "Commander, I would advise you to move to safe ground at once. Nordstral's magnetic field . . ." Interference snarled through his voice. ". . . a second complete reversal. The probability of resulting earthquakes . . ."

A screaming wail of static tore through the communicator and drove the *Enterprise* signal into complete disruption. Uhura winced, looking around frantically for Chekov and Howard.

They stood near the edge of the Kitka's ice-carved ledge, hands clapped to their ears in surprise. Uhura opened her mouth to call to them, but was thrown back against the hard rock cliff by a sudden shudder of the ground beneath her feet. A sun-washed explosion of auroras washed across the sky as the ground shook again, more gently, then was still.

Uhura steadied herself carefully, listening to Chekov sigh with relief. "That wasn't as bad as last time," he commented.

"No." Uhura scrambled to her feet, then glanced out at the polar ocean. It was sinking in ominous silence, its waves damping oddly flat as the water level dropped. Uhura recognized the signs and felt her throat contract with terror. She slammed her voice-mike volume as high as it would go.

"Chekov, Howard—get back up the stairs *now!*" Her voice rang urgently off the cliff behind them, spinning both men around to face her. "There's a tsunami coming!"

"Tsunami?" Chekov looked back over his shoulder at the still-withdrawing ocean. "But it's falling."

"Because it's still drawing water up." Uhura whirled and caught at Ghyl, still standing guard over Stehle's body. "Come on, we have to climb."

The native resisted briefly, her frail fingers plucking at Uhura's hold. "Let me stay! It is time to speak to god—"

"Here, let me get her." Howard picked the old woman bodily out of Uhura's clasp and headed for the stairs. "Help the chief, will you, sir?"

"I'm all right," Chekov growled as Uhura slipped an arm under his shoulder and hurried him toward the first of the rock and ice steps. Despite his firm words, she could feel the security officer's wiry body shake with weakness as he scrambled up the steep grade of the dark stone cliff. In the distance she could hear a gathering roar, as deep and bone-rattling as a starship's impulse drive. Stubbornly, Uhura refused to turn her head and look at the dark wall of water she knew must be racing across the polar sea toward them. If it was going to be higher than their flight of stairs could take them, she didn't want to know.

"How did you know it was coming?" Chekov demanded between painful gasps as they hurried upward. The opening to the enclosed part of the Kitka dwelling lay only a few flights up.

"Mr. Spock said the magnetic field had reversed again and there might be earthquakes. On Earth, that makes tsunamis." Uhura fought for breath as they rounded the last landing. "He also said there's a shuttle coming for us."

"Thank God." Chekov's unfiltered breath rasped through the mike. More daring than Uhura, he spared a moment to glance over his shoulder. "I think we're going to make it."

Too winded to speak, Uhura only nodded and took a better grip of his fur-clad parka, although by now she wasn't entirely sure who was supporting whom. The roar of approaching water echoed fiercely off the rock around them, along with the pounding of their frantic footsteps. Uhura concentrated on watching her footing, one icy step at a time. A shadow of rock passed overhead as they came up the last of the outside stairs, then Chekov yanked Uhura to an unexpected skidding stop.

"Chekov!" She turned to look at him in dismay, seeing the grim twist of his mouth below his opened breath filter. "What is it? What's wrong?"

"What *isn't* wrong?" It was a new voice, one Uhura knew although she'd never heard it speaking English. She gasped and jerked her head back to look up the rock-cut tunnel of stairs. Howard stood frozen a few meters above them, Ghyl a darker shadow at his side. Beyond him, a pale figure shimmered in the dimness. The familiar sound of metallic feathers chattered off the rock walls as he moved. A second white-clad figure loomed behind him, harpoon gleaming in his hands.

"What isn't wrong?" Alion repeated, his Kitka voice snarling out the English words. A blast of wind tore through the tunnel, nearly drowning out his voice. "What isn't wrong since you outsiders—"

His voice cut off as the tunnel darkened abruptly. With a roar that shook the rock below their feet, a wall of ice and foam and churning arctic water crashed against the unprotected cliff.

"What do you mean our navigation is *shot?*"

"Just what I said, Bones." Kirk briefly glanced at him as they strode toward the bridge. "The magnetic reversal and the accident played hell with our navigation equipment. We've got power, but we don't have any way of knowing where we are on the ice maps, and since the tsunami, there's no way of telling how far we've been thrown off course. We need to surface as soon as possible, but we don't know where the ice sheet ends and open water begins. Without a way of finding direction, we could bump along under the ice—"

"Forever," McCoy finished glumly. "And forever isn't an option we have. Damn Muhanti!"

"Muhanti's no longer our concern," Kirk said sternly. "The lives of these people depend on us, Bones. We have to figure out a way to navigate into clear water so we can surface, and we have to repair our makeshift oxygen generator to supply us until then."

"With what?" McCoy demanded testily. "Muhanti dumped the entire load of plankton!"

Kirk's irritation showed in the way the muscles bunched along his jawline like a clenched fist. "I don't know with what, Doctor, but we'd better think of something or none of us will be around to tell this tale!" He hastened his pace, and McCoy broke into a run to keep up.

All heads came up when they entered the bridge. Every eye fastened instantly not on him, McCoy

241

noted wryly, but on Kirk. There didn't seem to be a person alive in the universe who didn't, on some level, recognize Jim Kirk's innate talent for command. McCoy felt a faint renewal of confidence. They weren't dead yet.

Nuie's eyes widened as he took in Kirk's torn sweater and the shallow gash along McCoy's cheek. "What happened?" he asked, vacating his chair and gesturing for the captain to sit.

"Muhanti happened." Kirk punched a button on the console. "Crew, shut everything down and get up here."

"Muhanti?" The remaining navigator's eyes were round. "I thought he was dead."

"We weren't that fortunate," Kirk replied. He glanced toward the door as two of the missing crewmen skidded into the room. "He jettisoned the plankton."

Stunned silence met his announcement. One of the crewmen ran a hand through her short hair. "What do we do now?"

"We're working on it." Kirk's voice was crisp with command. "Any luck in contacting your land station?"

"For all the good it does," the navigator replied unhappily. "They know we're still alive and damaged, but they're dealing with their own problems. Part of the station caved in and there are people trapped. The other ships are scattered. We can't tell them where we are, so no one can come after us."

"Is our visitor still out there?"

Nuie blinked away the shock of the plankton loss and nodded. "Yes. She's maintaining a peripheral, like she's calculating the next place to attack. Sometimes she cruises downcurrent to investigate the bodies."

Kirk studied the murky screen. It was nowhere near as good as the one on the ship's true bridge, but it was their only link to the ocean around them. "Is she eating them?"

Many of the crew looked away at the question. Nuie's face remained expressionless. When he replied, his voice was very matter-of-fact. "She's eaten several Kitka bodies. She seems to be . . . tasting . . . the others."

McCoy cleared his throat into the uncomfortable silence that followed. "One good thing's come from all this, Jim."

Kirk's voice sounded very tired to his friend's ears. He doubted if the crew had picked up on it. "I could use some good news, Bones."

"I think I know what's caused the sickness." McCoy kind of liked the way all their eyes tracked to him. He leaned back, resting his butt on the edge of a console, and crossed his arms over his chest, tucking his sore hand into the crook of his elbow. "It's Nordstral's magnetic field."

Kirk's eyebrows rose. "I beg your pardon?"

"The magnetic field, Jim. Something Muhanti said while he was preparing to dice me up clued me into it. I'll need some corroboration from Spock just to make certain, of course." McCoy was pleased to catch himself talking as though they were going to be rescued. Maybe someplace deep down inside, he believed it. "Muhanti said there used to be no magnetic storms here, and that the boreal winds have gotten worse. Back in the late twentieth century, studies were done on the effect of magnetic fields on people's health. There was a lot of evidence to support the notion that not only were human beings affected physically, but mentally as well. Those findings led to new rulings in housing materials, the laying of tele-communication lines . . ." One shoulder lifted. "A lot of things changed, but not before a lot of people were harmed. As I recall, the symptoms for overexposure to strong magnetic fields were pretty similar to what's been going on around here."

Kirk sat back, shaking his head. "If you're right, and the magnetic field *is* causing the erratic behavior, why isn't everyone affected?"

The doctor shrugged. "My guess is differences in physiology. That, and whatever is causing Nordstral's planetary problems is probably exacerbating whatever magnetic properties are messing with people's brains."

"What can we do, Dr. McCoy?" the navigator asked.

He cocked an eyebrow at her. "At the moment, nothing. But if we could get our hands on *Enterprise*'s computer, I think I could come up with some courses of action."

A groan shivered through the iron hull, and they all fell silent, eyes wide.

"That's not the kraken's digestive tract, is it?" McCoy asked hopefully.

The navigator's hands slammed the console screen and she spun her chair around. "Hit the deck! It's another quake!"

McCoy flung himself to the floor and grabbed for the nearest purchase. This time he felt the sea drawing away from under the ship, the ship dropping into the undersea trough with a sickening lurch that left his stomach behind, the gathering of potent energy that was the tsunami. The ship groaned as the sea picked her up, and McCoy prayed that her seams would hold this second assault. Something crashed into them, or them into it, then the sea had them and they rolled completely over.

Chapter Fourteen

THE QUAKE-SPAWNED TSUNAMI slammed the cliff face with a sound like shattering glass. One blow, three blows, six—the ocean exhausted itself against the worn rock face, salt spray billowing across Chekov and the others in wild, breathy roars. What moisture surged up the steps around them froze to walls and floor with a hiss of brittle crackling—only enough to make footing treacherous, not enough to soak anyone or wash them down into the water. The ground beneath them bucked a single, half-hearted spasm before stilling again.

"Down the steps." Alion gestured impatiently, and the harpoon-wielding Kitka behind him supported the order with a sharp jab of warning. "I want your blood to spill into the water, not all over these stairs."

Chekov hesitated, mentally calculating the distance between himself and the shaman, the likelihood of

246

disarming either Kitka before they could turn on Ghyl or Uhura. The inside of his throat already ached from the cold, though, his lungs feeling tight and too small. Even a short fight without his breath filter could prove disastrous.

As if reading his thoughts, Uhura tugged at his parka hem in an effort to bring him down to her level. "No," she whispered over their private communicator channel. "He'll poison you, and we don't have any more antitoxin."

Alion leveled a chilling scowl on Chekov. "I'm impatient, Lieutenant Chekov. Start moving."

The oceanside ledge ran barely wide enough to hold them all, slick now with a new coating of ice, thanks to the tsunami and its resultant choppy waves. Chekov let Uhura drag him toward a corner far from Stehle's body, waving Howard to bring Ghyl close to them so they could keep both women between them. A futile effort, Chekov knew, but one he had to try nonetheless. There was nowhere to run on this wasted expanse —not with Alion and his man outside the steps, and water below every ledge and drop-off. Bracing his back to the rocky wall, Chekov hid his shaking hands inside parka pockets and tried to keep his breathing quiet. He could at least hide his unsteadiness from Alion, for all the good that would do them.

"You cannot kill them." Ghyl's wavering voice rose loud and shrill above the snarling waves. She stirred beside Uhura, fists clenched. "God will not take them, and the ice turns rotten with their bodies."

Alion laughed a very human laugh at her objection. "The kraken god will learn to eat them, if we spill their human blood enough. Maybe being prey of the god will finally convince them they should leave our planet. Failing that, I only want to make sure these few never report back to their Federation about what I've been doing here."

"We've already reported," Chekov told him, taking deep breaths to keep his voice firm and steady. "There's a shuttle on its way even now."

Turning his knife slowly in one hand, Alion shook his head. "Liar. The company had only two shuttles—both are now destroyed. I've paid plenty of men to sabotage Nordstral's equipment through the years. This latest crop were my best." He paced along the edge of the drop-off, occasionally glancing down at whatever lay below him. "So now you're stranded here, where only I and the kraken make the laws."

Chekov watched the ersatz shaman drift from one end of their lineup to the other, waiting for him to sheath his knife, or turn his back, or something. Of course, he didn't. Insanity, in Chekov's experience, tended to be more irritating than helpful. "What is it you gain by killing us?" he asked, hoping to keep the Kitka talking.

Alion shrugged. "Freedom."

"You've got that." He wondered if it was water beyond Alion's feet. That would be convenient.

"Not the kind of freedom I want," Alion said bitterly. "Not the freedom to grab and hold whatever power I can. No one at the equator would worship me, but among these primitive northern tribes, the knowledge and weapons I learned growing up in the cities give me power to make them believe anything I tell them to." He halted his pacing, knife clenched, trembling, in one hand. "I know god speaks to me. I know that I can rule the world, if only I can rid it of the humans who would teach Kitka to think for themselves. No matter what your Federation says, you're here to give Nordstral its independence, and that means you take power from me! I won't allow you to do that!"

Pushing away from the cliff face, Chekov gained his feet carefully to keep from alarming Alion or his army of one. One of the other unfortunate things about insanity was that you frequently couldn't reason with it. Especially when you were half sick and barely able to stand.

Switching off his external mike, Chekov pulled the parka's hood across his face as though to protect his breathing. Alion stayed where he'd last stopped pacing, loudly explaining his plans for ruling the northern Kitka.

"Uhura?" Chekov whispered. "Howard?"

"Sir?"

"Chekov, don't—if he hears you—"

Chekov cut her off, not wanting to take up time they might be running short of. "Listen to me. They're both smaller than we are, but armed. If I distract Alion, can you two take care of his man?"

Howard hesitated slightly, then nodded without voicing a reply. Uhura angled a goggled look up at Chekov, her hand still on Ghyl's arm while the elderly woman fingered her belt knife. "Distract him how?" she asked, unhappy.

Chekov didn't worry about a verbal reply. Dashing forward in the midst of Alion's speaking, he dove low for the shaman's middle, knowing he might not have the strength to tackle him otherwise. God, I hope it's water! he thought again as his shoulder plowed into Alion and overbalanced them both.

Then, driven onward by the force of both their

weights, they plunged over the drop-off into whatever waited below.

Soroya ended her travails upright and slowly oozing water. Emergency lighting bathed the interior a lurid orange-red and a klaxon shrieked.

"Turn off that damned thing!" Kirk ordered close by McCoy's ear, and the sound cut off. The doctor realized he was pinned under his captain and a female crewman. He shifted as Kirk got up, and the crewman rolled aside to free his legs.

"Sorry, Dr. McCoy."

"Under different circumstances, my dear, the pleasure would be all mine." McCoy slowly got to his knees, then stood. He felt battered over every inch of his body. "Jim?"

"Come here, Bones." Kirk was across the bridge, he and Nuie on their knees beside the navigator's sprawled form.

McCoy knew by the angle of her head, even before he touched her, that she was dead. For benefit of the others, he snaked a hand beneath her skull and felt along the neck. "Hangman's fracture," he muttered.

"What?"

"She must have hit her head. Her spine's severed at the second cervical vertebra. I'm sorry, Nuie."

The Kitka bowed deeply, touching his forehead to the cooling skin of the navigator's face. He remained that way a moment, then straightened. Tears dampened the sides of his nose.

God, I want to get out of here. McCoy looked around. "Jim?"

Kirk was busy with each of the crew, helping them to their feet, making certain they were all right, that there were no other deaths, no life-threatening injuries. He stood in the center of the bridge, hair awry, sweater hanging in tatters. Bathed in flashing color the shade of a desert sunset, he looked like nothing so much as a barbarian warrior out of history, bathed in the blood of his enemies. Only now his enemy was nothing he could touch, and McCoy knew from experience that Kirk didn't like those kinds of odds.

"Let's assess our damages." Kirk's voice was hoarse with strain. "Get someone out to check the rest of the ship. The rest of you, stop the flow in here if you can. Slow it down, at least." He staggered and dropped into a chair.

McCoy was instantly at his side, one hand stealing around his captain's wrist. Kirk shook him off irritably. "Don't mother me, Bones, I don't have time for it!" He shook his head, eyes clearing.

Only a fool or the inexperienced ever argued when that tone came into Jim Kirk's voice. McCoy subsided, eyes watchful, and wished he had his medikit on the bridge. Funny to think of it still back in the wardroom. For all he knew, it was underwater by now.

"Looks as though someone else sustained damages, Captain." One of the crew nodded toward the viewscreen and reached to twist a knob and fight the picture into better focus.

The kraken floated before them and off to starboard. She hung in the water like a bird suspended in flight, but this bird was wounded. A long rift had opened in her abdomen. Gouts of bright blood jetted out of the cut and stained the water like vermilion blooms.

A cry welled from Nuie and the kraken shifted as though she heard. His eyes were stark with pain, their iridescent color even odder in the red light. McCoy touched him, but the first mate didn't respond.

"Captain!" A crewman's cry tore everyone's eyes, except Nuie's, from the wounded animal. He straddled one chair, a comm link pressed tightly to his ear. "A call coming in! It's . . . it's the *Enterprise*!"

Uhura staggered back, sent sliding by the force of Chekov's lunge for the Kitka shaman. She watched in horror as the two men toppled over the rim of the ice-coated ledge, her breath catching as she waited for the fatal splash of water that would follow. It never came. Instead, she heard the painful thud of bodies hitting ice, then the yammer of a nearby Kitka wail.

"Howard!" With a start, Uhura recollected the second Kitka they were supposed to be taking care of. She spun around to see the security guard circling the armed native, arms lifted defensively as he tried to avoid the threatening harpoon. Ghyl crouched on the ice beyond them, looking down over the edge where Chekov had vanished.

An idea hit Uhura and she tapped at her communicator controls swiftly. "Tactical surprise, Mr. Howard," she warned across their insulation suit channel.

"Aye, sir." Howard paused briefly in his circling, and Uhura dialed the volume of her communicator up to feed the output directly to her external mike. With an intensity that startled even her, a shrieking wail of auroral interference shattered the arctic silence. It sounded like a cavalry troop of Kitka coming over the horizon. The white-feathered native yowled in shock, swinging around to see where the noise was coming from. His dark-tipped harpoon moved away from Howard for an instant, and the watchful security guard sprang. A moment later the Kitka lay sprawled and disarmed on the ice.

Howard straightened up with the harpoon in his

hand, breath puffing around his filter. "Sir!" He waved the harpoon, and Uhura skidded across to him to get it. "Go help the chief! I'll get this guy tied up."

"All right." Uhura took the bone-carved weapon in a careful grip, aware of the deadly stain of kraken venom glistening at its tip. She turned and ran for the place where Chekov and Alion had disappeared, passing Ghyl's small wind-ruffled figure as she went. The Kitka woman lifted her knife, but Uhura waved it aside as she rushed past. "It's all right—I've got a weapon." Instead, Ghyl took up a steady, keening ululation at Uhura's back.

Uhura skidded to a halt at the far edge of the ledge, dark rock dropping down to a wave-lapped platform of crystalline green ice. Two fur-clad bodies struggled on that treacherous surface, one dark and silent, one white and spitting Kitka curses. Their breath grunted out in white explosions as they heaved and staggered across the narrow rock shelf. With a gasp, Uhura saw that Chekov was doggedly pushing the shaman toward the sea, ignoring the battering of blows Alion rained against his bent head and shoulders. The security officer's strategy was clear: he meant to knock them both into the freezing ocean water.

"No!" Uhura flung herself recklessly down the sheer rock face, boots slipping on its solid glaze of ice. She hit the bottom hard. Her breath slammed out of her lungs and left her gasping, but Uhura tried to scramble to her feet anyway. Her left knee spasmed into fire-hot protest with the motion, and she fell back onto the ice with a cry of pain.

The sound of her arrival must have jarred the fighters apart. Uhura looked up, slitting her eyes against the dazzle of pain-sparked tears, just in time to see Alion's pale bulk looming over her. The shaman didn't waste any time with words. He pulled the harpoon out of her fingers with a savage yank, then turned and swung at Chekov.

"Spock!" Kirk's face was graced with the smile McCoy hadn't been certain he'd ever see again. "Patch him through."

McCoy cut Kirk off before he could speak: "Well, they say bad news comes in threes. First we have a kraken, then a tsunami, and now you, Spock."

"Greetings, Dr. McCoy." The Vulcan sounded as dry and droll as ever. If he'd been there, McCoy would have hugged him, past history be damned. "It is good to hear your voice, as well."

"Spock? This is Kirk."

"I'm gratified to learn you're still alive, Captain. Commander Scott has completed the shuttle modifications you have requested and can rendezvous with your party as soon as you bring the *Soroya* to dock. How long do you think that will take you?"

"I'm not sure, Spock. The *Soroya*'s been hit by two tsunamis, and we've sustained a lot of damage. We have partial power—" Kirk glanced at the pilot for her confirming nod—"and only about six hours of oxygen left. Right now, we don't even know where we are or how far we may have drifted off course. We're looking for open water, but if we don't find it, we're going to be trapped under the ice. There's no way we can break through."

"Unfortunately, the *Enterprise* cannot help with that. Her sensors will not penetrate Nordstral's magnetic field sufficiently to allow me to locate your position. We can only track you so long as we maintain radio contact."

"Which," Kirk sighed, glancing grimly at McCoy,

"we already know is sporadic. What about the rescue team? Any luck in contacting them?"

"Yes, sir. Lieutenant Chekov, Lieutenant Commander Uhura, and Ensign Howard have survived an attack by the Kitka. They report seeing Nordstral personnel murdered by one of the Kitka's shamans, and there is evidence that the crew of the initial shuttle were murdered as well. According to Lieutenant Commander Uhura, this Kitka shaman has been 'feeding' Nordstral staff to the ocean in some sort of native ritual."

The hiss of air drawn through clenched teeth drew McCoy's eyes to Nuie's face. The Kitka stood rigidly over the navigator's sprawled body, fists clenched at his sides and an expression in his eyes which McCoy could not divine.

Kirk scrubbed at his forehead, frowning thoughtfully. "Why the hell would the Kitka do that? All the reports I've seen indicate they're completely peaceable."

"I am not certain that the ritual itself is a warlike act, Captain. Dr. Stehle's files on the magnetic biota indicate that, given the strength of Nordstral's magnetic field, their growth potential is limited only by the presence of basic amino phosphatic nutrients." Spock's voice took on the faintly abstracted tone McCoy always associated with the Vulcan's most impressive deductions. "Due to the Kitka's protein-rich diet, these nutrients tend to become concentrated in their bodies. Were they all to die on the glacial ice and remain frozen there, the sea would become barren within a few thousand years. Apparently the Kitka have come to somehow understand that, and have evolved this system to keep the planet's ecosystem in balance."

McCoy's eyes widened as he glanced at Nuie. "So that's what you were trying to do when the lab flooded—"

"I was only trying to do what's right for a Kitka," Nuie said, smiling faintly. "I told you it wouldn't be good for you to feed the ocean, too."

Soft as the exchange was, Spock must have overheard it. "Indeed it would not, Doctor. The human nutrients in your body are entirely unsuitable for maintaining Nordstral's ecologic cycle."

"Then why are the Kitka murdering Nordstral personnel?" demanded Kirk.

"On that point, Captain, I do not have enough data to hazard a conjecture." Spock paused. "However, I can state that the Kitka's efforts to keep their planet in balance have been completely overwhelmed by the harvesting activities of Nordstral Pharmaceuticals."

"What's the harvesting got to do with it?" Kirk demanded.

"The secondary magnetic component!" McCoy pounded one fist into the other, mind racing ahead of his words. "My God, it's the plankton, isn't it, Spock?"

"No, Doctor. It is the magnetic biota."

"Dammit, Spock, you know what I mean!"

"Well, I don't," Kirk broke in. "Will somebody please explain this to me?"

McCoy swung around to face him. "The plankton on Nordstral are magnetic, Jim! Spock said there was a surface component to the planet's field that was causing the poles to reverse. It's the damned plankton!"

"Technically, Doctor, it is the absence of biota that has triggered the reversals," Spock corrected. "My computer models indicate that Nordstral's marine microorganisms exert a stabilizing effect on its internal magnetic dynamo—one that must have evolved through many milennia in order to keep the planet suitable for life. Much like the Gaia hypothesis developed for Earth—"

"Spock," Kirk interrupted. "You're telling me all the tectonic problems on Nordstral have been caused by too much plankton harvesting?"

"Indeed, Captain."

Kirk began to pace the deck. "How long will it take the planet to recover if we stop all harvesting immediately?"

"According to my projections, approximately three hundred Nordstral years."

McCoy snorted. "Fat lot of help that does us. We need that plankton in the sea now, not three centuries from now!"

"Can't we clone enough to replace what the harvesters have taken?" Kirk asked. "Kane said they had cloning facilities on their orbital platform."

"The *Curie* would not be able to clone the trillions of metric tons required, Captain."

"But the *Enterprise* should be able to," McCoy pointed out triumphantly. It wasn't often he was able to think of something before Spock. "Our botany lab can churn it out and you can fill the cargo holds with seawater and turn it lose in there to breed."

McCoy was delighted with Spock's overlong pause. "If we use the magnatomic decelerators to provide a source of magnetic energy, that proposal might actually have some merit," the science officer agreed at last. "We would, of course, have to physically deliver the biota to the planet's surface, since the transporters—"

Kirk's attention was drawn by movement on the

viewscreen. The wounded kraken was slowly turning away from them, laboriously plying her winglike flippers in slow, obviously painful, sweeps. Blood trailed behind her, clouding the image. "Where's she going?"

"Captain?" Spock sounded as close to confused as he ever came.

"To ground," Nuie replied, voice tight with emotion. "The god is dying and giving herself to the people, even as we go to her in death."

"You mean she beaches herself?" Kirk's head snapped around. "Pilot, we need all the power you can coax out of this hulk. Get us moving!"

"Aye-aye!" She began snapping orders at the rest of the crew and they fell to work with a willingness gratifying to behold, given their exhausted state.

"I beg your pardon, Captain?"

"Sorry, Spock. There's a wounded animal here that beaches itself when it's going to die. We're going to follow it to open water. Continue to monitor this channel for as long as you can. We'll let you know as soon as we reach surface. Meanwhile, get plankton samples from *Curie* and start cloning." He turned to the pilot and slapped the back of her chair. "All right, Mr. Windisch—follow that kraken!"

The harpoon shaft stung Chekov's palms when he flung his hands up to intercept Alion's swing. Uhura stumbled back, out of Chekov's sight, and he hauled back on the harpoon with all his strength in the hopes of throwing Alion off balance. Frost prickled his cheeks where the shimmering goggles ended, knifing down his throat to seize his lungs in icy claws.

The shaman countered by rocking his own weight forward and stumbling the lieutenant back several steps. Chekov clenched his teeth against a cough, but didn't loosen his grip on the harpoon.

"It's pointless," Alion told him. Kitka breath swarmed in curling billows around the edges of his mask. "I only need to scratch you—you and her both—and you're dead!"

Chekov opted not to risk his breath by answering.

Uhura arrowed into his line of sight again, a chunk of milky ice gripped in both hands. Blood singing with panic, Chekov jerked at Alion's weapon again, desperate to disarm him. He took a breath to shout at Uhura, and every muscle in his chest seized around a convulsive cough he couldn't choke away.

Alion needed only that break in Chekov's attention. With a powerful torque of shoulders and arms, the shaman whipped the harpoon shaft in a tight circle and snapped it from Chekov's hands. Chekov tried to jerk back, but only slid on the ice beneath him. The impact of the harpoon shaft against his face knocked him to the ground, facedown in the snow, with nausea and unconsciousness washing over him in alternating waves.

"See?" Alion's voice rose, high and triumphant, from somewhere impossibly distant above him. "This kind of power keeps us all from being equal. You should understand that now." Chekov felt the harpoon head dig against the neck of his parka and remembered, very vaguely, that he ought to be afraid. "Be in awe, Lieutenant—this is where you meet a god."

Waves, crashing and roaring anew, drowned Alion's voice in a frenzy of breaking ice and hissing snow. Still coughing, blood stinging the inside of his mouth with the taste of copper, Chekov steeled himself for the prick that meant Alion had delivered the last wound he was ever likely to feel. He curled his fingers into the frozen snow and closed his eyes.

The pressure at the nape of his neck lifted, then a harpoon clattered to the ice beside him, bloodless. He resisted an urge to look behind him, even when someone's labored breathing blew hot salt smell over him and someone else nudged him heavily with one foot.

"Chekov . . ." Uhura's voice tickled his ear over the inside channel, so faint as to be thought more than spoken. "Oh, God, Chekov, don't move—don't even breathe!"

Fear crept over him again, leaching into his bones like the cold from the ice sheet beneath him. The rough handling moved erratically up his legs, across his back, onto the hood of his parka. He could see a shadow then—long, thick, and decidedly nonhumanoid. When a cool, white nostril as broad across as his hand brushed his cheek in its snuffing, he looked without meaning to, pushing up on one elbow and turning such that their faces almost touched for that instant.

The kraken reared back in surprise, blowing a startled cloud of steam out either side of its sinuous neck. Jaw feathers clattering, ivory chest speckled with a mixture of Kitka blood and tattered parka, the Kitka's enigmatic god blinked orbs as wide and shimmering as reflective polar goggles, then pulled back into the ocean and sank silently away.

Chapter Fifteen

THE EMERGENCY HATCH clanged back, and a crisp, cold gust of wind whistled down into the *Soroya*. McCoy breathed deeply, relishing the fresh air against his face. He elbowed Kirk aside, only half-kiddingly. "Let me at the oxygen first."

"By all means, Doctor," Kirk said with an obliging grin. "After you."

McCoy navigated the short corridor in something just a little under light-speed, and emerged into Nordstral's blinding sunlight. Wincing, he slapped a hand over his eyes and reached back with the other, fingers waggling. "Give me the damned visor!" Someone tucked it into his hand, and he bent his head to snap it into place. He looked up, eyes protected behind the polarized material, and gaped at his surroundings.

The ice ran in an unbroken sheet to the horizon. Distance gave it the impression of absolute flatness

261

and utter uniformity. It was only up close to the ship that he could detect the fine whorls and hollows created by the ever-present wind. Several meters to their left lay the injured kraken. McCoy couldn't tell whether or not she was still alive. A large group of people he guessed were Kitka stood not far from her, strung in a tight semicircle and watching her in a very grave manner. Beyond them was a familiar white and red *Enterprise* shuttle, and lounging in the doorway—

Someone poked him from below. "Move it, Bones," Kirk griped good-naturedly. "No one wants to stay in here any longer than they have to."

McCoy's cheeks flushed. He hadn't meant to sightsee. He swung himself out of the hatch and stumbled upright onto the ice. In a moment, Kirk landed gracefully beside him. Nuie was right behind him, and the Kitka's appearance was greeted by a cacophony of whistles and trills from the assembled natives. He tugged up his hood and answered them in kind.

"What are they saying?" Kirk asked.

"They want to know if we killed the god. I told them no."

"How did they get here so fast? Is there a village nearby?"

"Probably. I'm not sure where we are." Nuie grinned broadly at the look Kirk gave him. "They've been expecting us, though."

"What?"

He shrugged his broad shoulders. "Well, not *us*, but the kraken." He whistled a few lines and waited for a reply. "One of the old women had a dream the god would beach itself here." He shoved his hands in his pockets and strolled toward the assembled Kitka.

Kirk lifted his eyebrows in interest, but turned

away, only then recognizing who approached from the shuttle. "Mr. Scott! Welcome to Nordstral. It's good to see someone besides McCoy for a change."

"Aye, and it's good to see you, too, Captain." The Scotsman's eyes twinkled, and McCoy could just imagine what a spectacle they must be in their borrowed clothing and battered condition. "You didn't think I'd be letting Sulu fly one of my shuttles all on his own, now, did you?"

"Of course not, Scotty." Kirk clapped him on the shoulder. "Not and pass up a chance to see what's been going on down here."

Scott grinned broadly. "It's also a chance to get away from all that work Spock's had me doing." He glanced over at McCoy. "You'll be glad to hear that every nook and cranny on the *Enterprise's* cargo bays is now filled with wee magnetic beasties. Mr. Spock's almost ready to start shooting the first batch into the oceans."

McCoy scowled. "Is he taking precautions to keep the plankton heavily shielded? The last thing we need is for the *Enterprise* to have an outbreak of Nordstral's magnetic insanity."

"Oh, aye. He had my engineers clad all the holds with demagnetized plating—"

"Can we debate the details of this plan later?" Kirk asked plaintively. "Right now, all I want is to get back to the *Enterprise.*"

McCoy smiled at the note of longing in the captain's voice. Too long away from his lady made him anxious. He was as bad as Scotty in that respect. "I'll be there in a minute, Jim." He glanced toward the assembled Kitka.

Kirk followed his gaze and nodded. "Scotty, power up. We'll be with you in a moment."

"Aye, sir." The burly engineer disappeared back inside the shuttle's open hatch.

Together, Kirk and McCoy walked toward the water. The Kitka parted to let them through, and they found themselves close beside the injured kraken. She sprawled across the bloodstained ice, her tail limp and trailing like weeds in the water, her neck outstretched to its full length, hard white feathers frozen to the ground. McCoy watched closely, but couldn't see any signs of respiration.

He marveled at the great creature, yet was struck by a sense of wonder lost, as though here, out of her element, she'd somehow been reduced to the ordinary. Her mottled shadings were gray and dull without the water, and her wide eyes, staring ahead of her at nothing, were no longer iridescent.

"She's dead," Nuie's sad voice confirmed behind them. McCoy looked around and back at him, but could find nothing to say by way of comfort.

Kirk, rightfully, didn't even attempt it. He held out his hand, "Thank you for everything, Nuie. You'll make the *Soroya* a fine captain."

"Thank you, Captain."

Kirk nodded and shook the man's hand a final time. "Bones, whenever you're ready." He turned and walked toward the shuttle.

McCoy watched him enter the ship, then turned and extended his own hand. "Well, I can't exactly say it's been a pleasure . . ."

The Kitka surprised him by laughing. "No, I guess you can't. Here." He dipped into one pocket and brought out the ulu. "Take this. Let it remind you of our adventure . . ."

"As though I could forget!"

". . . and your brother on Nordstral."

Emotion clogged McCoy's throat. He took the ceremonial knife and cradled it in his hand for several moments before he could trust himself to look at Nuie. "Thank you."

"You're welcome. Now, go back to your people. We'll take care of the kraken." Nuie squeezed his shoulder once, then turned away and led the other Kitka closer to the kraken. Several already had their knives out.

McCoy looked away, staring at the *Soroya* instead. He was amazed at how low she rode in the water, and how awful she looked with the gaping wounds in her sides. It was a miracle any of them had survived.

He looked across the expanse of black water, then at the surrounding ice field, dazzlingly brilliant in the sunshine. It was alien to him. It always would be. He ran the ball of his thumb gently along the ulu blade and was astounded to see a tiny line of red appear. "Damn." He pocketed the weapon and sucked momentarily at his thumb. It was time to go home.

Uhura watched in astonishment as the kraken's glowing eyes made descending bright streaks in the water, then vanished entirely. After seeing it devour the Kitka shaman with one snap of its sharp-toothed jaws, she still couldn't believe it had left Chekov untouched. She hobbled over to the security officer's sprawled body, forcing herself to ignore the pain in her left knee.

"Chekov, are you all right? Did Alion hit you?"

Chekov made a choking noise that froze Uhura's breath with fear until she realized it was breathless laughter. "He hit me several times. You didn't notice?"

Uhura gave him a gentle swat on the top of his

head—the only place she could be sure he wasn't injured. "I meant with the harpoon tip," she said severely, but a smile of sheer relief tugged at her lips beneath the breath filter. If Chekov had been poisoned, he would have been showing the signs of it by now. She reached out and helped him struggle to his feet. "That kraken got here just in time."

"Yes." The brief spurt of laughter faded from Chekov's voice and left it grim. "I don't think that was a coincidence."

"But what . . . ?" Uhura's eyes widened as she suddenly realized what he meant. A wash of horror swept through her. "Oh, no! You don't think Ghyl—"

"I don't know." Chekov's mouth tightened below the shimmer of his goggles, and they came to a halt at the rock cliff rimming the ledge. He raised his voice, tapping on his insulation suit's comm. "Mr. Howard? Are you up there?"

Footsteps crunched on ice and a tall figure appeared at the edge of the icy platform. "I tried to stop her, sir," Howard said, his voice breaking slightly. "But I had that Kitka to tie up, and she did it so fast . . ." He held out one hand to show them the scrap of bloody fur. "I almost caught her when she threw herself in the ocean. This was all I got."

Uhura swallowed tears, unable to reply. She turned her face into the ice-crusted fur of Chekov's parka, and felt his hand come up to clasp her shoulder gently. His voice was gruff.

"It's not your fault, Mr. Howard. There wasn't anything you could have done." He cleared his voice, speaking more to Uhura than to the security guard. "Ghyl knew what she was doing. She wanted her god to make things right, and she succeeded."

"I know." Uhura gave a last sniff and lifted her face

from the musty-smelling fur. "If she hadn't called the kraken to come here, you and I would both be dead."

"And Alion would be alive and armed with a poisoned harpoon to use against Howard. She saved all of us." Chekov bent before Uhura knew what he was doing and made a stirrup of his hands. "Come on. We need to get back to the shelter."

"I'm not going to let you lift me! Chekov, you're hurt worse than I am." She stepped back and tugged him to his feet. "I'll kneel down, and you can step on my shoulder—"

"I'm too heavy to—"

"Sir, if you would just—"

Their tangled voices broke off abruptly when a familiar hailing signal sang in their insulation suit comms. "Enterprise shuttle calling landing party," Sulu's crisp voice reported through the wail of auroral static. "Do you read me?"

"Loud and clear!" Uhura replied. The strength of the shuttle's signal meant it had to be approaching. "Have you got a fix on the native rock shelter?"

"Right where Mr. Spock said it would be." A low drone rolled over the horizon and grew louder. The helmsman's voice grew clearer through the static. "I can even see you guys now. Hey, what are you doing down on the beach? It's too cold to get a suntan today."

Chekov's laugh made a cloud of ice-white mist around his face. "Finally, these damn black insulation suits are good for something. Sulu, there's a wide rock ledge down here—it's probably the best place to land the shuttle."

"Acknowledged." The silver shine of the planetary craft caught the pale pink glow of arctic sunset as it circled the platform they stood on, then settled to a landing. "Hope you guys are ready to start talking. Captain Kirk wants to know why there's a Kitka tied up down the ledge from us."

"Oh, no." Uhura took a deep breath and saw Chekov doing the same thing. "He wants us to report right now?"

"We have a long ride back up to the orbital platform, gentlemen," said Kirk's unmistakably cheerful voice. "We might as well make good use of it."

"Yes, sir." Uhura looked over at Chekov and laughed. "Welcome back to Starfleet."

Chapter Sixteen

CHEKOV CAUGHT the turbolift door with one hand and stepped partway into the corridor. Balancing a covered food tray on his hip, he watched and listened carefully for signs of passing foot traffic while ignoring two polite, "Please do not block turbolift access," prompts from the computer. He wasn't blocking it, he reasoned—he was holding it to secure an escape route. Good security procedures. He didn't see or hear anyone, though, so stepped bravely into the corridor and let the lift hiss shut with a singsong, "Thank you."

He hadn't really expected to run into anyone on his way to Uhura's quarters. It was just late enough that the duty shift had changed, so the press of people coming and going through the corridors had eased. Anyone who wasn't at their duty stations was busy unwinding before heading off to bed. People tended to do such unwinding in their quarters or in the rec room, not in the open corridors. Waiting until shift change ended had been worth it, then, even if it had meant additional obstacles—like fresh personnel—to his getting out of sickbay.

Yesterday, when the shuttle came for them at the Kitka shelter, he'd thought he would sleep for at least a solid week. He'd stood outside the shuttle to make a verbal report to Kirk—limiting himself to bare bones for the sake of avoiding awkward explanations— helped Howard stow and log whatever remained of their gravsled and gear, then removed himself to the rear of the shuttle, where he could be alone on the trip back to the ship.

Threading his way between the narrow shuttle seats, Chekov had stripped off the hood of his insulation suit, aching from his teeth to his bones, and unsealed the front panel of his suit as he flopped into one of the empty seats. Just sitting in a warm, safe environment had felt like a delicious luxury; he almost tumbled into sleep the moment his head hit the back of the seat.

He had letters to draft, though, decisions to make. Tenzing's family would want to understand every- thing their daughter had been and done while she was away on board the *Enterprise;* Publicker's family would want his belongings shipped home, and they'd be disappointed to have no body. These were the duties Chekov hated most about his job, the ones he most wished he could delegate to some other officer. At the core of it, though, the people who worked under him were his responsibility. It was his responsibility, as well, to admit when he failed to take care of them.

A flash of pain exploded along his cheekbone, making him jerk away with a sharp curse. He hadn't realized how close he'd come to being asleep. It took him a moment to blink his surroundings back into familiarity.

Standing at his shoulder, McCoy frowned down at him in doctorly displeasure. "What happened to you?" he asked, gesturing at Chekov's face.

The lieutenant reached up to rub at his cheek, wincing at the feel of hot, tender skin beneath his fingers. "Nothing." He forgot that Alion's final blow would bruise so badly.

McCoy grunted. "Nothing?" Catching Chekov's jaw in one wiry hand, the doctor held his head steady while digging into the medikit on his belt. "Well, this 'nothing' looks like it's worth at least a hairline fracture. Hold still."

The whine of McCoy's medical scanner was sharp enough to make his ears ring. "Doctor, please, I'm fine—" He had work to do, letters to write, duty rosters to reassign . . .

"He was poisoned." Uhura climbed into the row of seats ahead of him, her own insulation suit shed, but her Kitka mask still dangling from around her neck. "Some native toxin that the Kitka get from kraken."

"What!"

Chekov dropped his head into his hands and sighed.

"When did this happen?" McCoy demanded of Uhura.

"About three days ago."

The doctor's scowl made Chekov wonder if he was going to get hit again. "For God's sake . . ."

"Mr. Chekov, you didn't mention anything like that in your report." Even Kirk had finally been attracted aft by the subject of their discussion.

Chekov felt himself blush hard enough to make his cheekbone throb. "Yes, Captain, I know, sir, but—"

McCoy interrupted by swatting Kirk on one shoulder. "I don't want to hear a *word* from you, Captain! If it weren't for the example *you* set for these boys, I wouldn't have to second-guess their bumps and bruises in the first place!"

"Now, Bones . . ."

After that, McCoy was too busy giving Kirk a piece of his mind to worry about further berating Chekov. Suspecting that his best defense would be camouflage, Chekov simply let himself drift off to sleep in the hopes McCoy would forget all about him by the time they got home.

Instead, he had awakened later on a stretcher already headed down to sickbay, when it was too late to do anything constructive. He'd slept off and on throughout McCoy's shipboard examination, then finally didn't awake again until sometime early the next morning. While he felt rested and healthy and ready to return to duty, McCoy insisted he stay in sickbay for further observation. Even Kirk wouldn't countermand that order.

As far as Chekov was concerned, the most boring thing he could imagine was spending an entire day confined to a bed in sickbay. Visitors stopped by throughout the course of the day—Sulu, Riley, various contingents from his security force—but they couldn't do much to cheer him; when he was already annoyed at being kept from constructive activity, it didn't help to see others interrupting their own work to come coddle him.

The only solution, then, seemed to be escape. At least temporary escape. An advantage of being chief of starship security was that he knew the ship's layout and duty schedules—and, consequently, the best time and way to absent himself from sickbay with the highest probability of success. He could always go back later and try to make McCoy's life so miserable that the doctor would release him and wish him good riddance. Other than that, the worst that could happen was they'd confine him to bed. He could always just leave again if things got too bad.

Uhura answered her door after only his second knock. She looked tired and distracted, but blinked at him in surprise when he smiled at her. "Chekov! I thought you were in sickbay."

"I am. Let me in before someone sees me."

She ushered him inside, sliding the door shut behind him. He tried not to notice the computer work on her desk, the bone mask hanging on her wall, or the bright, sunlit pictures of Kitka moving about on her small terminal screen.

"I didn't come down to see you," she said, her voice apologetic as she cleared off a chair for him to sit. "I meant to, I'm sorry—"

He waved her explanation aside, setting the food tray on the chair instead of himself. "It's all right. You've been busy."

Her gaze drifted toward the terminal and the Kitka moving there. "Yes . . . going over tapes, mostly. There's an awful lot to catalog."

He could imagine. Images of Ghyl giving some lengthy explanation in the whistling Kitka language shared the screen with views of Nhym pointing out bits of food, and Uhura—surprisingly enough— looking dubious about eating any of it. Noting Uhura in the picture reminded Chekov of where the films must have come from, and he surprised himself with a lurch of pain even McCoy and the *Enterprise*'s sickbay couldn't make go away.

"Tenzing took these, didn't she?"

Uhura touched his arm but didn't look up at him. "Yes."

So many things lost, he thought, watching Ghyl straighten Nhym's ivory mask and comb out her tangled silver hair. So many things gained. "She knew what she was doing," he said aloud to Uhura. "Her world and people needed saving, and she was willing to give everything to assure that. I think she would be happy with our solution."

Uhura nodded, wrapping her arms about her as if against a sudden chill. "She would be. I just wish she could have lived to see it."

Chekov found himself thinking those same words quite a lot lately.

Taking her hand, he turned her away from the terminal to face her toward the food tray he'd left sitting in her chair. "There's only one thing I know of that can distract you from anything."

Uhura grinned, looking embarrassed. "Food."

"Food." He rolled the chair between them and leaned against the back. "Remember before we left for Nordstral? I promised to bring you dinner."

"That's right, you did." She laughed, a little of the sadness leaving her face. "Did you fix this yourself?"

He made a face at her. "Are you kidding? I ordered it through the sickbay food system." Reaching over the chair back, he whisked aside the cover in a cloud of aromatic steam. "What do you think?"

Hands folded together, she bent at the waist to sniff at the plates. Her eyebrows crinkled slightly with concern. "It smells like cabbage."

"It's *halushki.*"

She angled a skeptical look up at him. "Which is?"

Chekov shrugged, tossing the cover onto the countertop behind him. "Cabbage." He grinned at her. "I ordered it especially for you."

She laughed again, a warm, welcome sound after all the cold unpleasantries of Nordstral. "Oh, Chekov— what would I do without you?"

He handed her a plate and slipped a fork under the contents. "If nothing else, probably eat a whole lot better."

McCoy peered around the doorway to the observation deck, trying not to sound too disappointed when he found only Kirk and Spock standing there. "Have either of you seen Chekov?"

Kirk glanced away from Nordstral's brilliant white globe, brows raised in curiosity. "What's the matter, Bones? Can't keep track of your own patients?"

"Apparently not." He crossed the deck, hands in pockets, to stand at Kirk's right. The stark black terminus of Nordstral's nightside silently crept across her surface as they orbited. "What's the point of trying to treat a patient when he's just going to override sickbay security and escape the minute I turn my back?"

Kirk shrugged with amused tolerance. "You guarantee he'll be in good health when he does it."

This from the man who would chew his own leg off to get out of a medical exam. McCoy decided to quit while he was ahead. "How's our bigger patient coming?" he asked, nodding toward the planet. Even at night, Nordstral's atmosphere sparkled with shreds of rainbow aurora, the equator cities ringing her like a diamond bracelet while the distant sun haloed her with a tiara of gold.

"So far, the prognosis is good." Kirk's eyes danced

across the nighttime features with a gentle pleasure that surprised McCoy. "They've got the remaining two harvesters seeding nutrients wherever they can reach in both hemispheres, and Spock's had torpedoes full of plankton launching all day."

"Marine biota," Spock corrected blandly.

Kirk grinned at him. "My apologies."

"I expect full recovery of Nordstral's magnetic field within fourteen days," the Vulcan went on, as though someone had asked him to elaborate. "The Kitka around the equator report observing biota reproductive blooms as far south as the thirtieth parallel, and the northern tribes say both the ice and the kraken have calmed remarkably in the last twenty-four hours."

"So have Maxine Kane's mental patients." McCoy hated agreeing with Spock, but he couldn't see any way around it. "She says Nordstral's planning to give the planet a couple months off while they redesign a harvesting/seeding program that'll guarantee nothing like this happens again." He shook his head in wonder as Nordstral's daylight side overwhelmed the stars around her with brilliant albedo. "It's too bad that it takes a disaster like this to remind us how delicately balanced everything is—and not just on Nordstral. Maybe if every planet threw off earthquakes and magnetic storms whenever things got out of whack, sentient races all over the galaxy wouldn't have messed up some of the things they did."

Kirk clapped his friend on the shoulder, breathing a little sigh. "Every planet gives its people whatever they need to do what's right. So long as we go the right direction in the end, that's all that matters."

"Let us hope," Spock said, "that Nordstral has learned everything required."

McCoy snorted before he thought better of it, and found himself facing curious glances from both his companions. "Well, I don't know about Nordstral," he grumbled, shifting his weight a little nervously, "but I've certainly learned *my* lesson just fine."

"Oh?" Kirk asked, eyebrows raised. "And what's that?"

"The next time you expect me to go swimming around some planet with millions of tons of freezing water on top of my head, I'm gonna pretend to be a Vulcan. That way, you'll leave me at home!"